'Do oth ....... und, as if you've s...... g witty?'

B53 102 886 8

## Author Note

I am drawn to the slightly unusual character—the individual with quirks. I enjoyed Rilla for her character's strength, her paranormal abilities and her love of invention. As an added bonus, I learned about many unsung female inventors.

Ada Lovelace collaborated with Charles Babbage and developed the first mechanical thinking-calculating machine. Sadly, she didn't patent her work as it was considered socially inappropriate for women to be filing patents.

Margaret Knight designed and fought to keep the patent for the flat-bottomed paper bag. She won, by the way, despite a certain gentleman who claimed that a woman could not possibly have the mechanical knowledge required for such an invention.

Other inventions created by women include windscreen wipers, disposable nappies, the dishwasher and liquid paper.

For me, Rilla's character is an acknowledgement of the contributions women have made, and still make—particularly when they step from the realms of what is considered 'appropriate'.

# NO CONVENTIONAL MISS

Eleanor Webster

Published in Great Britain 2015
by Mills & Boon, an imprint of Harlequin (UK) Limited,
Eton House, 18-24 Paradise Road, Richmond, Surrey, TW9 1SR

ISBN: 978-0-263-24811-1

**Eleanor Webster** loves high-heels and sun—which is ironic as she lives in northern Canada, the land of snow hills and unflattering footwear. Various crafting experiences, including a nasty glue gun episode, have proved that her creative soul is best expressed through the written word. Eleanor is currently pursuing a doctoral degree in psychology and holds an undergraduate degree in history. She loves to use her writing to explore her fascination with the past.

*No Conventional Miss*
**is Eleanor Webster's enchanting debut**
**for Mills & Boon Historical Romance!**

To the little girl who played with Barbie dolls,
weaving stories of romance, adventure and intrigue.

To the mother who tirelessly made minuscule frocks
and dress-up gowns, so wonderfully fostering
all things imaginative.

# Prologue

*Gibson Manor—1805*

The child had been missing for three days.

Through the nursery windowpanes, Rilla watched the faint flickering of the men's torches as they searched. Occasionally she heard their hoarse cries.

It was a wet spring. Heavy raindrops fell rhythmically off the shrubbery. A thick, obscuring mist hung low, tangling in the bare branches and turning the countryside a flat, featureless grey.

Rilla shivered and rested her head against the cool windowpane. She thought of Sophie. The little girl was new to the neighbourhood, a visitor and only five. Even at nine, Rilla would hate to be outside in this weather. And Rilla was strong and tall. She climbed trees, building perches in their upper branches and swinging from their limbs.

Oh, why did her head ache? Why did her limbs

feel heavy as though weighted with huge sacks of flour?

Even the glow of twilight hurt and she squeezed her lids tight shut, pressing her palms to her eyes to cut out any vestige of light.

And then 'it' happened.

For ever after, Rilla said she slept and dreamed. There was, could be, no other explanation.

Except Rilla did not remember lying down. There was no rest, no comfortable drifting into slumber.

Instead, it felt as though she remained standing while everything about her changed and mutated: the whitewashed walls, the books, the rocking horse with its worn paint, the brick hearth, her grandmother's ugly portrait and equally ugly embroidered sampler—gone.

Cold mist dampened her skin. Goosebumps prickled. Her breath came in harsh gulps. She stared into the fog's whiteness, trying to make out indistinct forms and shadows.

Yes, she knew the place. It was the gamekeeper's cottage, burned down years earlier and now a ruin, its blackened beams softened by ivy.

*Sophie.*

Sophie was here.

The knowledge came suddenly and completely, without doubt or question.

Sophie was trapped within the cellar, under the slate floor of the broken kitchen.

\* \* \*

Rilla blinked. She was lying on the cold nursery floor, staring upwards at the whitewashed ceiling with its singular crack which looked like a lamb's hind leg. She sat up. Tentatively she touched the cloth of her dress and twisted her fingers through the unruly tresses of her red hair.

Dry.

Her shoes were clean and dry also.

And yet…

In the distance, she heard the shouts of the men's voices.

She jumped up, suddenly urgent. She must tell them. They did not know yet. They must know. Then they would find Sophie and save her.

Thank goodness.

And everything would change.

# Chapter One

Lyngate Estate—1817

'This sounds like yet another of your ill-advised schemes,' said Paul Lindsey, Viscount Wyburn, with as much patience as he could muster.

'Piffle,' his stepmother retorted, shaking her grey ringlets. 'It would be a crime to allow such delightful girls to languish in the country.'

'But hardly incumbent upon you to rectify the situation.' Paul stood by the mantel. His gaze drifted from the china figurines to the requisite pink, dimpled Cupids depicted across the drawing-room ceiling.

'Who else will take them in hand? Their dear mother is dead, and Sir George has a predilection for horses and cards. Very sad.' Lady Wyburn bent with apparent diligence over her needlework.

Turning, Paul sat across from his relative and studied her more closely. He drummed his fingers on the low rosewood table. Lady Wyburn was the only person on God's earth he gave tuppence for, and he'd not allow some sticky-fingered squire to rob her blind.

'Stepmother.' He leaned forward on the ludicrously low sofa. 'People tend to take advantage of you. If you recall, your young nephew—'

'Not the same thing.' She fluttered her hand in front of her face as though shooing a non-existent pest. 'Rilla and her younger sister, Imogene, are charming. Imogene's looks are exceptional and Rilla is refreshing. Not beautiful exactly, but exotic and interesting.'

'Admirable attributes in a book or a flower.'

'Don't be flippant, dear.' She waved her needlepoint, a colourful object of pinks and purples with no discernible pattern. 'Anyway, Sir George hasn't a clue how to find them suitable husbands and lacks the funds—'

'And sees you as a lucrative prospect, I suppose.' Paul shifted his legs, moving them away from the fire's warmth, again drumming his fingers. He stopped. The noise irritated and revealed an emotional response he would not allow.

'Nonsense. Sir George is an academic of repute. The only prospects that interest him involve ancient Greeks or Romans.'

'Except for the occasional English racehorse. What about their dowries? Will you contribute to that charity?' he questioned.

'Dear Sir George would not agree. Besides, Rilla

would create a rumpus. She is proud and not at all keen on marriage.'

'That will be a change. Rilla? An unusual name.'

'Short for Amaryllis.'

'How unfortunate. Her mother was in a botanical mood, I presume.' But the name was unforgettable. He'd heard it before.

*Good God!*

'Not that girl who rode the pig through Lady Lockhart's garden at that party we attended before I went to the Continent?' he asked with dawning comprehension.

'A goat, actually. And she was younger then.'

'You plan to present this…um, young lady?' A smile tugged at his mouth.

'Rilla is much improved. And we all fall into scrapes in our youth.'

'I do not remember riding stray barnyard animals.'

'You were always a responsible youth. Besides, as I recall, you said it was the best part of the day.'

'That was a long time ago.' Paul stood and walked to the window, stifling a yawn.

'You're tired.' Lady Wyburn spoke sharply. 'You did not sleep well.'

Of course he had not slept well. He'd been at Wyburn, hadn't he? He never slept well at his estate. Or within a ten-mile radius of that cursed lake.

He rolled his shoulders. 'It is more likely the heat in this room and not my sleeping habits which make me yawn. Might we return to the subject of your neighbours?'

'Delightful girls.'

'Generally people you find delightful prove unscrupulous.' He turned from the window with sudden decision. 'I will pay my respects to the Gibsons this afternoon. I trust you will take note if I am dissatisfied with their character.'

'I always listen to your insights. Ride over now, dear.' Lady Wyburn waved a hand in the direction of the French window as if expecting him to leap through it on his mission.

Paul preferred a more conventional exit.

'Goodbye, Stepmother,' he said, kissing her cheek.

'Enjoy yourself.'

'As I would a visit to the tooth extractor,' he muttered, striding from the room.

Miss Amaryllis Gibson sat on the wooden swing that hung from the lowest limb of the chestnut tree. She scuffed her feet. This was her favourite spot on the estate. She liked the view of their solid redbrick house. She enjoyed the ramshackle shapes of the dairy, wash house and stable. She even appreciated the smell, a sweet mix of soap, grass and horses.

But today, none of this helped. She poked the toe of her shabby black-buttoned boot into the earth.

She'd woken with one of her *feelings*.

Rilla hated her *feelings*. No, hatred would be

a far preferable emotion. She feared them. They made goosebumps prickle her arms and her shoulders tense. She wanted to run or gallop, as though with enough speed she could escape from her own mind.

Pushing the swing higher, she breathed deeply. Her petticoats billowed as she stretched too-long legs, gaining height and speed. Loose strands of hair tickled her face and the fields blurred.

Briefly, her stomach lurched as she hung at the highest point, only to fly down in tumultuous descent. Momentum, it was called. Momentum fascinated her.

Many improper things fascinated Rilla: Roman aqueducts, force, gravity, Sir Isaac Newton's theories and her mechanised butter churn. Unfortunately, no one appreciated such items, and her water-powered churn had only succeeded in flooding the dairy.

Rilla frowned. Of course, in London she'd have little time for her inventions. Proper ladies did not develop churns.

Or flood dairies.

Or have *feelings*.

Sliding to a stop, Rilla jumped from the swing. Even thinking about London bothered her. She had no desire for the city with its meaningless social niceties and the constant pressure to find a husband, which was, of course, the one thing she *must not* do.

How she'd always loved this tree. She liked its

thick, sheltering canopy of green and the feeling of her own strength and invulnerability as she pulled herself, branch by branch, through its foliage. It was even the site of her first pulley. She could see it now, the wooden wheel and rope partially entangled within the twigs and leaves.

Could she? Just once more? After all, the rope should be removed for safety's sake. With a thrill of forbidden pleasure, she looked about the still garden and drive.

Nothing and no one.

Stepping forward, she touched the trunk. The bark was rough under her fingertips. She inhaled. The air smelled wonderful, of wood, and earth, and mushrooms.

Scooping up the loose cloth of her skirt, she tucked it into the sash around her waist and grabbed the lowest branch. With strong, quick movements, she reached the pulley and, leaning forward, untangled the rope and tossed it to the ground below.

Done. She exhaled, allowing herself a moment to relax in this world of green light and dappled sun. A late-spring breeze touched her cheeks and the leaves rustled.

She would have stayed longer if she hadn't heard the rhythmic *clip-clop* of a horse's hooves. She stiffened. They seldom had guests, unless they were of the card-playing variety, but Father had given that up two months since.

Bending, she squinted through the leaves.

A gentleman approached along their rutted

drive. He stopped his horse under her tree and dismounted with elegant, long-limbed grace. He was tall and lean with hair so dark it looked black.

Then it came.

The sensation was of loss and pain so intense her world spun. Branches and leaves joggled in a blur of green.

Rilla gulped for air.

The world turned dark, as though night had descended.

Dimly she saw a lake, ink black and spattered with raindrops. She was cold. So cold her fingers numbed and her grip loosened. She reached out, snatching a twig. She missed and, with a cry, fell through the sharp, splintering branches to the ground below.

She landed with a jarring jolt and gasped in shock and pain.

'What—? Miss, are you all right?' The voice came as from a distance.

She opened her eyes. Daylight reappeared.

A man bent over her, a man different than any she had met before. The straight dark brows, unyielding jaw and mouth gave her the confused impression of harsh strength. Briefly, his stark silhouette seemed mythical—Hades searching for Persephone.

'Are you hurt?' he asked again. 'Let me move the horse away.'

The prosaic words shattered the illusion.

'I'm fine, I think.' She sat up.

He crouched beside her, putting out his hand. 'Can you stand? Let me help.'

His grasp was strong, his fingers long and firm. Her stomach tightened and she felt a pulse of something akin to fear, yet not. Their gazes met and she felt a narrowing of focus that made the horse, the tree and the solid brick outline of their house inconsequential.

She jerked back, scrambling to stand. 'Who are you? Why are you here?'

'Lord Wyburn. I came to visit Sir George Gibson.' He stepped back, watching her closely. 'You are Miss Gibson?'

Of course, Lady Wyburn had mentioned an overprotective stepson. But Rilla hadn't imagined...

'Sorry, I thought—' She paused, inhaled, making a conscious effort to collect herself. 'It's a pleasure to meet you, Lord Wyburn.'

'And you.'

Her stomach tightened again, likely a natural reaction. The last thing she needed was for Father to get riled up or on his high horse. He'd hated the idea of accepting charity and she still worried he might gamble in some last-ditch effort to secure funds.

'Miss Gibson, are you still dazed from your fall?'

'No, not at all.' Rilla jerked her attention back to her visitor. 'I will get Thomas for your horse.'

'Your father is in?'

'Um—yes,' she said and whistled for Thomas.

The lad responded promptly, his eyes irritatingly wide at the sight of Wyburn and his mount. Bending, she picked up the remnants of her pulley and handed this also to the lad.

With the horse under Thomas's care, Rilla smoothed her dress, which she belatedly realised was still partially tucked up, and nodded towards the house.

'This way, my lord.'

Paul walked alongside Miss Gibson, covertly assessing her as they neared the residence. Her fall from the tree had dishevelled her gown and dirtied her face, yet she exhibited no embarrassment.

Indeed, had he been feeling charitable instead of irritated by his errand, he might have found her calm assurance impressive. She walked briskly, with confident strides. Everything about her tall physique spoke of energy and practicality of purpose which was good, he supposed. He had no tolerance for female moods. But he did not favour hoydens either.

The house proved a pleasant building of Tudor origin with brick walls half-hidden in wisteria and punctuated by mullioned windows. But the family's poverty could not be missed. He saw it in the overgrown shrubbery, the peeling strips of paint dangling from window frames and the haphazard appearance of loosened slates.

The girl pushed open the door and Paul blinked as he stepped into the dimness of the hall after the brightness outside. No servant greeted them, nor did the girl seem to expect one. Instead, she took his hat and then removed her bonnet.

He watched, briefly fascinated as her red hair escaped in a wild cascade of colour. Paul didn't know if it was beautiful or ugly and, strangely, it didn't matter. It had such life, such vibrancy.

The goat girl all grown up.

'I'll announce you to my father,' she said. 'He's in the study. May I bring refreshments? Tea, perhaps?'

He dragged his gaze from her hair. 'Tea would be fine.'

'I'll go to Father.'

Paul nodded, looking about the entrance. Sun shone through an octagonal window, forming a patchwork of golden squares on a threadbare runner. Floor wax, flowers and dog hair scented the air in a not-unpleasant combination. Indeed, there was something cosy, almost comfortable about the place.

*A load of codswallop!* He would do better to concentrate on Lady Wyburn's financial interests and not on the unlikely delights of floor wax.

Glancing up, he found Miss Gibson had not yet withdrawn, but studied him, her head to one side and eyebrows drawn together. She inhaled deeply. The bodice of her gown stretched tightly.

Her figure was not flat.

'Miss Gibson, was there something else?' He met her gaze. Her eyes, he noted, were an unusual grey-green and fringed with dark lashes in contrast to her fiery hair.

'I...trust you will not upset my father.' For the first time, she seemed uncertain.

'It is not my intent. Is Sir George distressed by social calls?'

Perhaps he was an eccentric academic, comfortable only with dry texts. And card games.

'No, but—' She frowned, and then squared her shoulders. 'You have come to discuss Lady Wyburn's plans for my sister and myself, and I want to make sure you are under no misapprehension about us.'

'I am not prone to misapprehensions and I believe my business is with your father.'

'Lady Wyburn mentioned that you worry about her and I want you to know that you need not. We intend to pay back—'

'Miss Gibson, this discussion is hardly proper.'

The girl needed a set-down or she'd not survive her own come-out.

Surprisingly, she laughed. 'We left propriety when I fell out of the tree. It is only that I'd prefer you did not worry my father about such matters. I can answer any questions you might have.'

She spoke earnestly, the love and worry for her father evident in her gaze.

He was not unmoved. 'I will keep that in mind.'

She nodded, twisting a fiery ringlet of hair about her finger. 'I also wanted you to know that I...we care greatly for Lady Wyburn.'

'I also care for her ladyship, Miss Gibson.'

'Then we are of perfect accord.'

Their gazes met. Hers was like an ocean with depth and movement. She spoke softly but with firmness, and he felt again that peculiar mix of irritation and admiration.

He also found he believed her.

'Good,' he said, after a moment. 'Now that we have clarified our mutual admiration for my stepmother, might we proceed, provided I agree not to unduly distress your father?'

'Of course. This way, my lord. Follow me.'

Good Lord, her tone was positively chivvying. Again Paul wanted to smile. He hadn't been chivvied since nursery days and never with success.

Miss Gibson led him down the hall and pushed open a dark, wood-panelled door. Sir George's study was small and full of books piled not only on shelves, but in haphazard stacks on the floor and desk. A fire crackled but did not draw properly and smoke hung in blue-grey wisps, scenting the air. A clock ticked, the steady, methodical beat of an old timepiece.

'Father, may I present Lord Wyburn? He is Lady Wyburn's stepson,' Miss Gibson said.

Sir George sat at a desk in the far corner. He wore a shabby, ill-fitting nankeen jacket and appeared small, although that might have been the effect of the books and papers piled about him.

'A timely interruption.' He stood, running his hand across his balding head and looking at Paul over gilt-framed half-spectacles. 'Just managed to finish a particularly difficult passage. But most edifying, most edifying. Now what can I do for you, my lord? I'd wager you want to reassure yourself that I have no evil intent, eh? Not likely to run off with the family silver?'

Paul's eyebrows rose. Sir George's sharp eyes, mobile face and the quick movements of his hands gave the impression of considerable energy coiled within his small frame.

Moreover, the Gibson family had breached, in one afternoon, more rules of etiquette than he'd experienced in years of Continental travel.

'I wouldn't be quite so blunt,' he said.

'I would. I would. No point beating about the bush, I always say. Time's too precious. And I don't blame you in the slightest. Lady Wyburn's much too generous. Much too generous. Do take a seat and I'll answer any question you care to pose. Fire away while Rilla fetches tea.'

With a wry smile, Paul sat.

Grabbing the copper kettle, Rilla hurried from the kitchen into the scullery and pumped, the handle whining as icy droplets splattered over her hands.

Bother. She was shaking. Even visits from her father's gambling gentlemen had not left her so… so…discombobulated.

Of course, it was that vision. It was the sight of that rain-spattered lake.

No, it was the man also—his dark good looks, that feeling of sadness which seemed a part of him and the way he made all else dwindle to unimportance.

Rilla picked up her mother's rosebud cup. She ran her finger across its rim. The gilt had worn off and the china was so fragile as to be translucent.

It would have been better if Imogene had met him. She had poise and would not be scrabbling up trees—

Imogene!

Rilla gulped. She'd quite forgotten her younger sister. She put down the cup, hurrying to the staircase that led to the bedchambers upstairs.

'Imogene! The viscount's here!'

Imogene flung open her door with unaccustomed haste. The scent of rose water spilled from the room as she stepped on to the hall landing. 'The viscount? Lord Wyburn? Here? What's he like?'

'Judgemental and unhappy.'

Imogene started, her blue eyes widening. 'He said so?'

Rilla wished she hadn't spoken. 'No,' she admitted after pause.

'Then why do think he is unhappy?'

Rilla hesitated. She rubbed her hands unnecessarily across the fabric of her gown. 'I—um— felt it.'

'Felt? No.' Imogene's voice was high with strain. 'It has been years almost.'

*Eleven months.*

'It was nothing. I am making too much of it, honestly,' Rilla said, hating to see her sister's worry. 'It was my imagination. And I'm quite well now.'

'You're still pale.'

'From my fall, I'm sure.'

'You fell? Are you hurt?' Imogene's voice rose again, threaded with anxiety as she noticed a pink scratch on Rilla's forearm.

Rilla followed her gaze. 'It's nothing. Look, you go and charm him. Convince him that we are not hoydens while I make tea.'

'And you'll not dwell on—on feelings?'

'I will concentrate entirely on the tea. You go. The gentlemen are in the study.'

'You couldn't lure Father out to the drawing room?' Imogene asked as they started back down the stairs.

'I didn't even try.'

Halfway down, they heard the kitchen door open. Mrs Marriot must be back. The housekeeper always visited her sister every Thursday.

'Good,' Imogene said. 'Let her make tea while you tidy yourself.'

Instinctively, Rilla touched her unmanageable hair. She'd never liked red hair. *Witch hair.* That is what the village children had called it.

She nodded, returning upstairs without comment. She cared nothing for beauty. The last thing she wanted was to attract a man.

But she must look sane. Above all else, she must look sane.

# Chapter Two

Rilla entered the study anxiously, but everyone seemed congenial. Imogene sat ensconced in the window seat. Their father had pulled his chair from behind the desk and was discussing the antiquities. The viscount, who had risen at her entrance, was smiling and not, at present, asking anyone pointed questions about the cost of a London début.

'Refreshments will be here shortly,' she said, a little breathlessly.

Her father nodded. 'Good, good. Make yourself comfy, m'dear. I was relating an anecdote from my most recent translation.'

He waved the papers in his hand and dust motes sparkled, dancing in a shaft of light.

The only vacant seat was on the sofa beside Lord Wyburn. Rilla hesitated. She caught his eye, but found his expression unreadable.

She swallowed and stared fixedly at the brocade upholstery. Her father waved the papers with an agitated motion. 'Do sit, m'dear.'

Rilla sat. The viscount sat. The cushioning creaked. She had ample room and yet she felt conscious of his nearness—his muscled thighs, his fingers splayed across the worsted cloth of his trousers, even the heat of his body.

This was irrational. Several inches separated them. It was, therefore, scientifically impossible to detect warmth, except perhaps in the event of a raging fever.

Generally, scientific analysis comforted her mind. Today it proved useless.

Gracious, his legs were long. His feet stretched almost to the hearth. And muscular. Although she'd best forget his legs and attend to the conversation unless she wanted to seem a complete ninny.

They were discussing antiquities, naturally. Her father seldom participated in conversations on any other subject.

'I travelled to Athens last year,' Lord Wyburn said.

'Aha!' Sir George pulled his chair forward with a scrape of its legs. 'And what, sir, is your opinion of Lord Elgin's decision to remove the marbles from Greece and bring them to England, eh?'

'It was wrong,' the viscount answered easily.

'But,' Rilla blurted because she could not help it, 'if he had not, the marbles would have been destroyed!'

The viscount shifted, turning towards her and, in so doing, narrowed the gap between them. 'Indeed, Miss Gibson, but was it not a crime to take them from Greece? To do business with the Turks and bring them here?'

Their gazes met. Again, Rilla had a disconcerting feeling that all else in the room had shrunk, diminishing and fading to unimportance.

She had thought his eyes a dark, opaque brown and now realised they weren't. Their colour was hazel, flecked with gold and green.

'A lesser crime than to do nothing and allow their destruction,' she said, with effort.

'So it is right to preserve beauty from the past and undermine a country's sovereignty in the present?'

'I—' She frowned because she had not thought of it like this and could see validity in his argument. 'Yes, I think so. The marbles are our heritage. They are the heritage not only of one country, but of mankind. We hold them in trust for future generations. The politics of today are transient.'

'I am not certain if the Greeks would agree. You are an individual with strong opinions.'

She flushed. 'A trait not generally admired.'

'I admire your honesty, but you may need to exercise discretion if you expect to do well in London society.'

'Oh, I don't,' she said.

The straight eyebrows rose. 'Then you are indeed unusual. To what do you aspire in London?'

'Well, to see the London Museum, the Rosetta Stone and—'

Rilla left the sentence unfinished, catching Imogene's look.

'It appears you do not share the dreams common to most young ladies,' Wyburn said.

'Not for myself,' she said, then stopped.

She had revealed more than she had intended.

Thankfully, Imogene interrupted the slight pause. 'You said London, Lord Wyburn. Does that mean you will not oppose Lady Wyburn's plan?'

'It means, Miss Imogene, that your début will afford my stepmother amusement and I seldom deny her pleasure.'

'We are much obliged.'

'Quite so.' The viscount turned his gaze to Rilla. 'It would seem, Miss Gibson, that I will have the pleasure of hearing more about your singular opinions in London.'

Rilla, Imogene and Lady Wyburn had arrived at the capital within the fortnight. They spent the first week shopping, drinking tea and allowing a bossy French maid to style their hair into any number of styles.

Actually, Heloise appeared to be the only member of Lady Wyburn's staff under the age of seventy. Her butler, Merryweather, was so bent and wizened that Rilla longed to take the tray and bid him sit. She didn't, however, fearing to insult his dignity.

As for Wyburn, they did not see him at all as he had gone to his estate.

'Which he hates,' Lady Wyburn explained. 'It always makes him dreadfully grumpy.'

The viscount's absence filled Rilla with both relief and irrational disappointment.

'He made me feel like I had a smudge on my face,' she explained to Imogene. 'I want to prove that I am not always like that, but have adequate social graces.'

'Except you usually *do* have a smudge on your face. Although I suppose it is a step forward that you actually care about your smudges.'

Rilla stiffened. Imogene was right. She usually didn't care. She frowned. She was sitting on Imogene's bedroom floor beside her churn and she ran her fingers along its smooth wood, twisting the waterwheel so that it moved with a clunk…clunk…

'But,' Imogene added with a nod towards this apparatus, 'if you *do* now care about smudges, you'd best stay away from that contraption.'

'It is a perfect reproduction of my churn made precisely to a quarter-scale. Besides you are quite right, I have never cared about dirt or oil before and I see no reason to start now.'

'I didn't mean—'

But Rilla was leaning over the churn as though in an embrace, absorbed in both altering the trough's angle and moving the wheel with a continued rhythmic clunk.

Lord Wyburn had announced his return with an invitation to the British Museum.

'Which is an odd choice for an excursion,' Lady Wyburn stated after reading the missive. 'Indeed, he is too fond of ancient things and is like to become as bad as your father.'

Despite these comments, Lady Wyburn quickly wrote back their acceptance and announced that the excursion would prove a pleasant change from drinking tea which was too often as weak as dishwater.

But even with warning of his return, Rilla found the sight of him standing within the entrance hall disconcerting. She jerked to an abrupt stop on the stairs, aware of a marked change in her equilibrium without any scientific cause, given that she was neither in a boat or on carriage.

Perhaps it was his size, seemingly huge as he stood within Lady Wyburn's hall. Or maybe he reminded her too much of her father's gambling 'friends'.

Indeed, that must be it, Rilla decided, glad of this explanation.

Certainly, he looked every inch the Corinthian in a well-tailored jacket, beige pantaloons and polished Hessians.

Yet, as she studied him unseen, she was conscious of sadness. It was not, thank goodness, a feeling, but rather she was aware of a shadowed bleakness in his expression, a tightness in his jaw and the sense that unpleasant topics occupied his mind.

Moreover, she realised, with a second start of

surprise, that she longed to change that. She wanted to see his expression lighten with wit and interest.

'Ah, there you are. Lovely to see you, dear boy.' Lady Wyburn bustled into the hall.

Wyburn turned and bowed. 'And you, my lady.'

'Although whatever made you think of the museum, I do not know. Not that I'm not delighted, of course, but I have never truly appreciated the fascination accorded to ancient things. I mean, a jug is a jug even if it is thousands of years old. Besides, we don't even know if it was part of someone's second-best set. I would hate my second-best crockery to be on display.'

'That is a novel perspective. I suggested the museum because I recalled that Miss Gibson had expressed an interest. Indeed, here she is now.'

He smiled as Rilla descended the stairs. He had a dimple, just one, set within his left cheek. Rilla hadn't noticed it previously. Briefly that dimple fascinated. Again, she had an off-kilter, slightly breathless feeling as though climbing too high or galloping fast.

'I could have waited.' Her stomach also felt odd. Perhaps she had eaten insufficient breakfast.

'But it is lovely for you to think of my sister's interests. We are both much obliged,' Imogene added, also descending the stairs.

They now stood in the hall. Wyburn seemed taller than ever. Rilla felt an irrational irritation both with his height and the crush. She wondered if perhaps London houses had dimensions smaller than that of their country counterparts and whether this might be suitable for scientific study.

The carriage ride through Bloomsbury fascinated Rilla. Thoughts of the museum crowded her mind, but she soon found the journey interesting on its own account. She loved the busy, bustling streets filled with vendors, newsboys, pedestrians and even stray dogs hunting for scraps. She loved also the interesting mix of carriages, high-sprung phaetons, carts and tradesmen's vehicles.

She actually found it far pleasanter to focus on the activities outside the carriage than its interior. She knew she did not have a shy bone in her body, but somehow Lord Wyburn's proximity or the carriage's stuffy closeness had scattered her thoughts like so much dandelion fluff.

Indeed, only by pressing her face to the window and analysing the differing designs of carriage wheels could she keep her usual composure.

When they drew to a stop at the museum, Rilla felt a moment of disappointment. The external façade looked so ordinary. It was a solid building with a slate roof and two wings jutting out for stables.

But what did she expect, statues lining the drive?

It was the inside that mattered and which had inhabited her dreams for so long. Her earliest memories were filled with stories of Greeks, Romans and Egyptians. They were her bedtime stories, her fairy tales…

After descending from the coach, the party entered the building and a short, bent gentleman ambled forward to greet the visitors. He spoke in guttural tones and nodded towards a staircase leading to the first floor.

'We have exhibits up there as well as in our newer addition, the Townley Gallery,' he said by way of greeting.

Imogene looked upward.

'Gracious.' Rilla followed her sister's gaze. Three life-size giraffes stood at the top of the stairs. 'They look so lifelike. I wonder how that effect is achieved.'

'They have been specially preserved,' Wyburn said. 'We could enquire as to the scientific method if you'd like.'

'That would be fascin—' Rilla caught Imogene's eye and stopped herself.

'I wonder if giraffes ever get neck aches,' Lady Wyburn said with one of her typical rapid-fire bursts of speech. 'I recall my great-aunt Sarah used to have dreadful aches, particularly when it rained. And a giraffe would have such a lot of neck to ache. Perhaps that is why giraffes live in sunny climes.'

'Perhaps,' said Lord Wyburn.

Rilla saw the amused tolerance in his glance and felt herself warm to him.

*I could almost like him.* The thought flickered unbidden through her mind. She pushed it away. He was a viscount and one who, no doubt, still considered her likely to waste his stepmother's money while swinging from trees or chandeliers.

Besides, he was too intelligent, too observant… the last sort of person with whom she should strike up an acquaintance. With this thought, she chose not to follow her relatives upstairs, but walked briskly towards the entrance of the new gallery which she had read contained the classical collection.

'I believe the antiquities are unlikely to change in any marked degree within the next few moments.' Lord Wyburn's amused voice sounded from behind her. 'Do you ever walk slowly or, perhaps, saunter?'

'I don't like to waste time. Besides, this is the Townley Gallery and I've heard wonderful things about it.'

The gallery was a long, rectangular room with large windows and fascinating circular roof lights providing an airy, spacious feeling. Despite her haste, Rilla paused on its threshold, surveying the statues and glass cases, instinctively savouring a delicious anticipation, an almost goosebumpy feeling of delight.

'When I stood at the Parthenon, I thought I could hear the voices of the ancients. In here, I hear their echoes,' Lord Wyburn said softly.

'You really *do* love the antiquities,' Rilla said.

She glanced at him. His chiselled features reflected his awe, wonder and curiosity. She had known no one, except her father, to understand or share such feelings.

'I have always been fascinated.'

'Have you visited Italy as well as Greece?'

'And Egypt.'

'You saw the pyramids?' she asked, breathlessly.

'Yes, they are as magnificent as ever, despite Napoleon.'

'You are fortunate.' She stepped towards the displays but jerked to a standstill. 'Is—is that the Rosetta Stone?'

'Yes, although many are disappointed...'

'Disappointed?' She stared at the pinkish stone. Tentatively she leaned towards it, pressing a gloved finger against the glass as though to feel its contours and trace the intricate inscriptions. 'Don't they understand? It is the key! The most exciting discovery. It may unlock the meaning of hieroglyphs and a whole culture from the past—'

She stopped and felt the heat rushing into her cheeks.

'Passionate.' He spoke so softly, she barely heard the word.

He stood beside her. She no longer resented his intrusion. Indeed, it felt as though they were removed from the outside world, just the two of them, and had found a kinship amid these past treasures.

She smelled the faint lingering scent of tobacco and heard the infinitesimal rustle of his linen shirt as it shifted against his skin. Even the air stilled, as though trapped like a fly in amber.

She swallowed, shifting, wanting to both hold on to this moment and, conversely, end it.

'My father wanted to translate the Rosetta Stone,' she said at last.

He straightened. She instantly felt his withdrawal as he stepped back and was conscious of her own conflicting sense of regret and relief.

'I am not surprised. It is one of the most important discoveries in modern times. Has he been to the museum since it arrived?' he asked.

'No, I—he—' London was not a good place for him, but she could not say that.

'His responsibilities have been too great at home,' the viscount said gently as though understanding that which she'd left unspoken.

'Yes.'

And then it happened—without warning—without the usual feeling of dread or oppression. The present diminished. The man, the Rosetta Stone, the display cases, even the long windows dwarfed into minutia as though viewed through the wrong end of Father's old telescope.

She felt cold, a deep internal cold that started from her core and spread into her limbs.

A child—a boy—appeared to her. She saw him so clearly that she lifted her hand as though to push aside the wet strands of hair that hung into tawny, leonine eyes. He stared at her, his gaze stricken with a dry-eyed grief.

She recognised those eyes. 'I— What's wrong?'

'Miss Gibson?' the viscount spoke.

She blinked, the boy still remaining clearer than the man or the museum.

'Miss Gibson,' the viscount said again.

'You were so young—'

'What?' He thrust the word at her, a harsh blast of sound.

'When she died.'

The boy vanished.

'Who died?' Lord Wyburn asked as the present sharpened again into crisp-edged reality.

His eyes bore into her, his jaw tight and expression harsh. She dropped her gaze from his face, focusing instead on the intricate folds of his neck cloth.

What had she said? What had she revealed?

'Has my stepmother been speaking about me?' A twitch flickered under the skin of his cheek.

'No, we didn't, I—' she said, then stopped.

'I will not be the subject of gossip and you will not do well in London if you cannot be appropriate in word and deed.'

A welcome surge of anger flashed through her. 'I am visiting a museum, that is scarcely inappropriate.'

'Discussions of a personal nature are unseemly.'

'Then I will endeavour to discuss only the weather or hair ribbons.'

'Good.'

He made no other comment and the silence lengthened, no longer easy. She wanted to speak, to cover this awkwardness but, after that momentary anger, lassitude filled her.

This often happened. Exhaustion leadened her limbs only to be replaced later by a need to run, to jump, to ride. None of which she would do here, of course.

'Wonderful! There you are!' Lady Wyburn's sing-song tones rang out.

Rilla turned gratefully as Lady Wyburn and Imogene appeared at the doorway.

'No doubt you are both entranced with these ancient objects, but I admit I am done with them,' Lady Wyburn announced.

'Indeed, let's go.' The wonders of the Rosetta Stone had dissipated and Rilla longed for her own company.

As they walked through the corridor and into the entrance way, she could feel Lord Wyburn's silent scrutiny and her sister's concerned gaze.

Only Lady Wyburn seemed impervious to any discord and happily related a discussion with Lady Alice Fainsborough. Apparently, they had met Lady Alice while admiring the giraffe on the second floor.

'A lovely girl,' Lady Wyburn said as the wizened caretaker pushed open the oak door. 'Although unfortunately she resembles her mother with her propensity for chins. Still, it is good to know a few people prior to your début and one cannot hold her chins against her.'

The door creaked closed as they exited into the dampness of the London spring. Rilla exhaled with relief as if leaving the museum made her less vulnerable.

The rain had stopped, but the cobblestones gleamed with damp and raindrops clung to twigs of grass, glittering as weak sunlight peeked through still-heavy clouds.

But the smell—it was the smell she noted.

Earlier, the courtyard had smelled of fresh grass, mixed with the less pleasant odour of horse manure or sewage from the Thames. Now it smelled of neither. Instead, it was sweet, cloying and strangely old-fashioned.

She wrinkled her nose. 'Lavender. I smell lavender.'

Lord Wyburn stopped. She felt the jerk of his body beside her.

'I hate lavender,' he said.

Even hours later, Paul could feel his bad humour as he sat astride his mount. Ironically, his own ill temper irritated. There was no sensible reason for it and he had no tolerance for moods. Rotten Row was pleasant and unusually quiet and while the clouds looked dark, it had not rained.

He rolled his shoulders. They felt tight as bands of steel. Amaryllis Gibson had unnerved him. The way she'd looked at him or through him as though seeing too much or not seeing at all. And her change from vivacious interest to unnatural stillness.

And lavender.

Why had she smelled lavender? No one smelled lavender on a London street.

His fingers tightened on the reins. Responsive to the movement, Stalwart shook his head with a metallic jangle.

Paul had hoped a pleasant ride and fresh air would calm him. It hadn't.

All this nonsense about a début. He should have put a stop to the business. Now, he could only hope that his stepmother got both girls married off expeditiously so that he would have little reason to spend time in their company.

A sudden thundering of hooves grabbed his attention. He swung about as a horse going much too fast cut obliquely across his path. Stalwart snorted, stamping his hooves and shifting in a nervous sideways dance.

Instinctively, Paul soothed his mount, even as he tracked the other horse. Some crazy pup, no doubt. Thank goodness the park was unusually empty.

Except—the rider rode side-saddle.

'Blast!'

Paul spurred Stalwart ahead, but the other animal had the advantage of several seconds and Stalwart was already winded. Hunkering close to his animal's neck, Paul pushed the horse as fast as he dared and, squinting, discerned a woman's form, her turquoise habit bright against the horse's flank. Her hair had loosened, falling over her shoulders in a brilliant red-gold mass.

Paul gripped the reins tighter still. He knew only one woman with hair like that.

Irritation and a deeper, more primitive emotion clawed at him. Sweat dampened his palms. He was gaining ground. He'd be able to grab her reins soon enough.

He must be careful not to startle her animal. For a moment he imagined her thrown, her face smashed or her body crippled.

Half-standing in the stirrups, he leaned forward, his thighs clamped hard around the horse's chest.

Then, without warning, her horse slowed.

Stalwart bolted ahead. Sitting heavily, Paul swung his animal about. Relief rushed through his body.

'Miss Gibson!' he shouted. 'Hand me the reins! What on earth happened? How did he get away on you?'

'My lord?'

The woman looked across at him. He saw no anxiety, no worry or apology. In fact, she was smiling and looked considerably happier than she'd appeared at the museum.

'Are you all right?'

She rubbed the horse's neck. Her hair fell forward, tangling in its mane. 'I'm fine.'

'Fine? Fine! You could have been killed.'

The impertinent wench laughed. 'I was perfectly safe. Grey Lady's a lamb and I've been riding for ever.'

That was true. He could see it now that the blindness of fear had lifted. He'd seldom seen a better seat, or a more foolhardy display.

'That may be so, but you are not in the country and Grey Lady is no plough horse.'

'She's beautiful. It has been ages since I rode such a creature.' Her voice softened, her hand still caressing the horse's neck.

Paul prided himself on his rational calm. He did not give way to emotion. But the hammering of his heart did not feel rational.

Or calm.

'Where are her ladyship and your sister? Why are you riding alone and at such a pace?' he asked abruptly.

His question seemed to confuse her. She glanced over her shoulder. 'Lady Wyburn said I might ride ahead.'

'I assure you she did not mean for you to dash off to Rotten Row. Ladies do not gallop on Rotten Row. Nobody gallops here even on quiet days.'

'Really? I made certain I did not collide with anyone and a good ride is such fun.'

'As is climbing a tree and riding livestock.'

'Livestock?' She stopped, head cocked, as though confused. Then her countenance cleared. 'Why, I remember now where we met. Lady Lockhart's garden party years ago.'

'I hope you will not repeat that particular performance.'

'No, that goat was too uncomfortable. I couldn't walk for weeks. Besides, there seems a sad dearth of goats in London salons.'

Oddly, Paul wanted to smile. More than smile,

he wanted to laugh. The girl's wit, her zest for life was contagious and blotted out her odd behaviour that morning.

He felt absurdly relieved for this.

Although why he should care, he did not know. 'You must curb your enthusiasms, Miss Gibson. Your manners are too forward,' he said sharply.

Her face fell, the laughter leaving her gaze and two spots of anger flushing her cheeks. 'I apologise for my rudeness and any lack of propriety, my lord.'

He nodded. 'I do not wish my stepmother to become the subject of gossip.'

'I would never dishonour her ladyship. I will return to her now before she becomes anxious. Goodbye, my lord.'

She spoke quietly, but he saw her anger in the toss of her head and that wild, wonderful hair. Then, to his surprise, she pulled her animal short. He wondered what insult she had forgotten.

'About cutting so close to you,' she said, speaking the words he least expected. 'I should…will apologise for that. You were hidden from my view, but that is no excuse. I had my mind on other matters and could have spooked your horse.'

The fire fizzled from him. 'It is of no consequence.'

She nodded, urging her horse ahead.

'And, Miss Gibson?'

'My lord?'

'You have an excellent seat and are a fine horsewoman.' Which, he guessed, were the words she least expected.

She nodded and turned away, urging her mare to a trot. Paul watched with reluctant admiration. He liked her wide generous smile which somehow transformed her face. More than that, he liked her vibrancy, the love of life, which seemed to exude from her.

*Damn.*

The realisation jolted through him. He stiffened and Stalwart stepped sideways with a nervous whinny.

He was, Paul realised, physically attracted to Miss Amaryllis Gibson.

No, it was more than that. It was more than just the physical desire he might feel for an actress or light skirt. He liked her. He liked her intelligence, her wit, her peculiar interests, even her opinions.

What other woman would be so enchanted with the Elgin Marbles?

But he would not, must not, allow it.

Miss Amaryllis was the last person for whom he should form an attachment. She was impulsive, immature and unpredictable.

Paul did not like the unpredictable.

His childhood had been a steeplechase of unpredictable, ruled by his mother's moods. One day there would be laughter and the next...

On the next, her mood would overwhelm all else so that even the servants stooped under its weight.

And as for his father...

## Chapter Three

'At last!' Imogene said. 'Our first grand ball!'

The sisters stood before the looking glass in Rilla's bedchamber, under strict instructions from Heloise to touch nothing.

Rilla stared at her reflection with a peculiar feeling of disbelief.

It was her, of course. Yet she looked so different.

Tentatively, Rilla rubbed her hand across the expanse of skin exposed by the low neckline and watched the image do so too. The neckline, the lightness of the muslin, the way if fell loosely about her waist and hips gave her a feeling of nakedness which was both disconcerting and exciting all at once.

Of course, Rilla knew she was too tall and her movements too brisk but, despite this, she looked… good.

Well, better than she would have supposed and quite different from a girl who habitually fell out of trees.

Indeed, it would be satisfying to have Wyburn see that she did not always gallop or do outlandish things.

Not that she particularly cared what Wyburn thought.

Abruptly, Rilla shifted her gaze to her sister. Now Imogene was truly beautiful—exquisite in a light blue gown with pearls encircling her throat.

And so like their mother.

Rilla had forgotten how beautiful her mother had looked before her last illness. She remembered her now—taller than Imogene, but with that delicate pale beauty. She remembered also how her father would even abandon his Greeks and Romans to escort her. He would complain, of course, saying he was trussed up like a Christmas goose, but his gaze would fix on their mother, the love evident.

What would it be like to be loved like that?

For a fleeting, disturbing second, the image of the Viscount Wyburn flickered before her inner eye.

Rilla pushed this aside. She would do better to focus on her sister who, Rilla realised, was looking a bit *too* ethereal.

'Are you all right?'

'Nervous,' Imogene admitted. 'I fear I will forget all Mr Arnold's instructions and fall over my feet.'

Mr Arnold was their dance instructor, a portly gentleman with plump puce-coloured cheeks.

'You have never fallen over your feet in your life,' Rilla said.

'I have never gone to a dance of this size and I have never felt so nervous. Besides, Mr Arnold said it was so important that a débutante is proficient in all the steps.'

'Mr Arnold can't even see his feet and I am certain he wears a corset so I refuse to take his word as law.'

'A lady is not supposed to discuss a gentleman's undergarments.'

'Then I will resist the temptation to discuss undergarments tonight,' Rilla said, putting an arm about her sister's shoulders.

Imogene smiled wanly. She looked so young and vulnerable, her eyes large within her heart-shaped face. It reminded Rilla of their childhood when the two years between them had been a lifetime.

'Everyone will be enchanted by you,' Rilla said gently. 'Why wouldn't they be? You're beautiful and witty.'

'I feel like I did at Lady Lockhart's piano recital when I was ten.'

'You played perfectly. I was the one who ruined everything by dropping a spider down Jack St John's collar. You were meant for this night.'

'You are good for me,' Imogene said. 'Mother always knew what to say at times like this.'

Rilla nodded, touching the gold locket about her neck. It was smooth and warmed by her skin. 'I miss her, too.'

'This was her dream for us.'

'For you. She wanted you to have a choice and to find someone you could love.'

'She met Father during her first Season.' Imogene carefully rearranged one of the blonde curls framing her face. 'Rilla?'

'Hmm?'

'When…when you have your feelings, do you ever see her?'

Rilla stilled, except for her fingers, which continued to twist the thin gold chain at her neck. Imogene seldom spoke of her 'moments' and never without fear or loathing. 'No.'

Imogene nodded, turning to pick up her reticule.

'But,' Rilla added softly, 'I think that is good. I think it means she is at peace.'

Imogene shivered. 'I wish you had grown out of your moments like we all hoped. Then you could fall in love and marry. '

'I am much too ornery to marry, even if I did not fear that any husband might commit me to Bedlam. Besides,' Rilla added, determined to lighten the mood. 'I have my Greeks and butter churn for company.'

'Do not discuss Greeks or your churn tonight.'

'No Greeks, churns or undergarments. I will discuss only Romans and my automated cake mixer. Come on.' Rilla swung her arm around her sister's waist. 'Enough serious talk. Your dream awaits. And you are going to be fabulous.'

\* \* \*

Three hours later, Rilla stood in the Thorntons' ballroom. Dancing required more stamina than tree climbing. Her feet hurt, her head pounded and her face ached from smiling.

Although she was enjoying the dance. It was rather wonderful, like entering a separate world of golden light, music and magic—Oberon's palace, peopled with fairies.

And there she had no shortage of partners. Indeed, she had only sat out two dances and had not yet chatted with any of her new London acquaintances or, more importantly, her neighbour and best friend Julie St John, freshly arrived from the country.

Perhaps she could find her now. Rilla scanned the ballroom. A familiar face would be so reassuring. Plus Julie had been out for three Seasons and would doubtless have all manner of suggestions. Hopefully, one of which might include a cure for blisters.

And then she saw him.

Wyburn.

All thoughts of Julie scattered from her mind.

Wyburn stood a few feet from the entrance. Her body stiffened and she knew, in that second, she had been unconsciously waiting for him. She felt a peculiar mix of hot and cold, and heard the quickened thump of her heart.

His very darkness made him different.

He stood tall, surveying the ballroom with an

indolent gaze. Dark hair, dark straight brows and dark jacket made the others seem overdressed like brightly costumed actors.

She touched her hair. Then dropped her hand. She refused to primp. She would not even acknowledge that peculiar bubble of pleasure that he would see her here and in this dress.

But gracious, it was hot. She fanned herself. He had moved from the step and was now chatting with several gentlemen. Lady Wyburn had stated that he would ask both herself and Imogene to dance, as they were her protégées.

Except Rilla didn't want to dance with him. She hadn't seen him since Rotten Row and, as always, he made her feel like she had two left feet.

And yet to not dance with him would also be peculiarly dampening to the spirits.

She frowned. Since when had she become such a ninnyhammer? A person able to understand the laws of physics should certainly be capable of deciding with whom she wanted to dance.

Perhaps she should consider a suitable design for an automated fan which might be suspended from the ceiling—a much better use of brain power than the tracking of Lord Wyburn's movements.

Not that he seemed in any great hurry to perform his duty towards his stepmother's protégées. He was now escorting a large young lady in pink silk to the dance floor.

He'd likely regret that choice. The lady in pink did not appear light on her feet.

And then, in that split second of amused derision, it came.

The horrid, familiar, unwanted cold struck. It spread from the centre of her body down into her limbs. The candelabra and brightly coloured dancers dimmed. The purple-and-pink bouquets swirled and the music muted, as though coming from some great distance.

In its stead she heard a soft, sad whisper.

*'Help him.'*

Rilla twisted left and right, but saw only the rubber plant and the blank wall behind it. Goosebumps prickled. Her hand tightened on her fan so that its hard edges pressed almost painfully against her palm.

*I will not faint. Or cause a scene. Not here. Not now.*

The words repeated in her mind like a mantra or the thumping of indigenous drums. *I will not faint. I will not faint.*

'Rilla! Are you all right?'

A tall figure in ruffled green stood before her.

'Julie,' Rilla said, her voice oddly distant to her own ears.

'Are you ill?'

The sweet cloying scent of lavender filled her nostrils.

'Lavender. I smell— Are you—wearing—lavender?' she asked, the simple question difficult to phrase.

'No, I don't like the smell. But, Rilla, what is it? You look awful.'

'Fine. Really.'

Rilla had fought this before. She knew how to do it. She knew she must root herself in this hot, overcrowded room. She must focus on Julie and her frilly green dress. She must press her palm hard against the edge of her fan. She must escape the scent of lavender and immerse herself in the smell of flowers and sweat and food from the buffet.

She must ignore the man on the dance floor who was so impossible to ignore.

She exhaled in a slow whoosh.

'It is the heat,' Julie said.

'Yes,' Rilla said, disregarding the goosebumps still prickling her arms.

'You will get used to it. I have. This is my fourth Season.'

'When did you get into town?' Rilla managed to ask, ludicrously proud to have said the simple sentence without pause or stammer.

'Only two days ago. Mother wants to keep our costs to the minimum, you know.'

'And how is she? Your mother, I mean?'

Julie shrugged with a rustle of fabric. 'Dragging every unmarried man under a hundred to meet me. I'm a disappointment, although I'd likely do better if I did not resemble a wilted lettuce.'

'You look lovely.'

'For a lettuce.'

'But never a wilted one,' Rilla said and even smiled.

She took her friend's hands, glad of the human contact, the reassuring pressure of Julie's finger and the clean, wholesome talcum scent of her. 'I am so happy you are here.'

'And I you.' Julie paused, looking towards the wide sweeping staircase which descended into the ballroom. 'Gracious, he's here too. We could have a schoolroom reunion.'

'Pardon?'

'Jack.'

Dislike knotted her stomach as Rilla saw a familiar young blond gentleman descend the staircase, his expression one of cynical indolence.

'Roving for an heiress, I would guess. He needs one. Is he deigning to acknowledge us?' Julie asked.

'Apparently.' Rilla watched the man's approach. Jack St John, Earl of Lockhart, looked well enough. His clothes were well cut, his movements easy. Yet she felt herself cringe, edging towards the rubber plant.

'My dear sister and Miss Gibson.' He made his bow.

'Lord Lockhart.'

'Miss Gibson, I did not know you and your sister were coming for the Season. I hope you are enjoying the evening and that it has been convivial.'

The earl gave the last word peculiar emphasis, rolling it in his mouth.

An emotion, close to fear, twisted through Rilla's body, although his words were innocuous enough. 'Everyone is very pleasant,' she said.

'Ah, yes, the *ton* can be delightful, but then the mere whisper of a rumour can make it cruel.' He smiled. His face was pale and, in stark contrast, his lips looked too red for a man.

Rilla swallowed. The fear grew. Her palms felt clammy within her gloves.

'Jack, don't say you've done something scandalous?' Julie asked, worry lacing her tone.

'Not at all.' His smile widened. 'And Miss Gibson is fortunate that she has such an admirable character she need never fear rumours or odd tales.'

Did he linger on that word 'odd' like a man tasting brandy or was it her imagination?

But before Rilla could formulate a response, the earl made his bow and left. Rilla swallowed. The heat, the dancers, the music pressed in on her.

Julie touched her arm. 'You've gone quite pale again. Don't worry about Jack. He probably remembers the goat.'

'The goat?' Rilla said blankly.

'The one you rode?'

But, of course, the goat. The relief was so great she almost laughed out loud. Her smile grew wide. She had quite forgotten the goat. Good lord, he could talk about the goat ad infinitum, if he chose.

'Julie!' Lady Lockhart's strident voice startled both girls. Julie turned so quickly she nearly tumbled into the rubber plant.

Her mother approached, bearing down on them in a well-corseted purple dress. 'There you are. Whatever are you doing, hiding in the shadows? People want to dance with you! You'll never make a match indulging in idle chatter.'

'No, Mama.'

'Good evening, Amaryllis.' Her ladyship cast an appraising glance over Rilla's gown and coiffure. 'You'd best be standing straight. Giggling is never attractive in girls. They appear vapid. Indeed, you'd best make yourself presentable if you hope to find a husband.'

'Yes, my lady.' Rilla dropped a curtsy.

'Come along!' Lady Lockhart propelled her daughter away. Rilla watched. Julie looked smaller, as though only propped up by the abundant cloth of her gown.

Alone once more, Rilla glanced back to Jack as he crossed the room. He had all the swaggered arrogance she remembered from the schoolroom and, more recently, when he'd visited Father. If only they hadn't gambled—

To be beholden to such a man.

An unladylike swear word flashed through her mind and she had to bite her lip to keep from saying it aloud. The obnoxious man had gone to Imogene.

The earl was asking her to dance.

For a brief unreasonable instant Rilla wanted to sprint across the floor and physically pull him from her sister. An impotent anger vibrated through her and she felt her fists tighten.

'Goodness, why so fierce, Miss Gibson?'

Rilla jumped at the low male voice. Turning, she found herself staring at a broad masculine chest encased in a white-satin waistcoat and black jacket.

The girl looked more like a golden statue than a human form. The cream muslin dress was shot with gold and shimmered with her every move. Her hair was a crown of ruddy gold, piled high with soft tendrils curling at her neck.

Miss Gibson was definitely not pretty, that would be too insipid. Nor beautiful, her face was not cast in classic lines. No, she was striking, inspiring almost.

Good Lord, and he was staring at her like a goggle-eyed fool.

'Miss Gibson.' He made his bow.

She turned and frowned as though disorientated. 'Lord Wyburn, you startled me.'

'My apologies, Miss Gibson. You were engrossed,' he said.

'Yes, I was watching—'

'Your sister's success. Without much pleasure, it would appear.'

Colour rushed into her cheeks, but she caught his meaning quick enough.

'I'm not jealous of my sister, if that is what you mean,' she said.

'Blunt again. Jealousy is a natural feeling.'

'Natural to some—not me. I'm happy for my sister.'

'If not envy, then why the angry countenance?' Paul asked more gently.

'I disapprove of my sister's partner.'

Good Lord, the girl really did have a penchant for direct speech—a rarity in the female sex.

'I agree, although your bluntness will cause you no end of grief.'

'I might insult someone?'

Paul smiled despite himself. 'Even in secluded corners, one may be overheard.'

She made a face, seemingly unimpressed with the suggestion. 'I am not afraid of Lockhart. Straight talk might do him good.'

'But it might do the speaker harm, particularly if the object of her speech chooses to use his influence to discredit her.'

He saw a flicker of apprehension, quickly squashed.

'So,' he asked lightly, wanting to relieve the very anxiety he had caused, 'are you enjoying it?'

'The dance?' she said, with uncharacteristic vagueness.

'That is the event we are currently attending.'

'Yes.' She looked about her with genuine admiration and smiled. 'Yes, it is beautiful, magical almost.'

Paul followed her gaze and watched the expressions flicker across her mobile features. For a moment, he forgot that he had been to hundreds of balls and that their allure had long since tarnished.

Instead, he saw the room as she did, a fairyland of flickering light, mirrors, music and perfumed air.

'Dance with me,' he said.

'I beg your pardon?'

'Your card is not full and I fear the current situation is not appropriate.'

'In what way?' Her brows drew together.

'We have not yet danced. May I have the honour, Miss Gibson?'

Her face registered an interesting mix of emotion: surprise, confusion, reluctance. She shifted back towards the rubber plant. Good lord, the chit actually wanted to refuse. No one had turned him down since he was a callow youth. He did not know whether to be angered or amused.

'I believe that hiding is not acting with the utmost propriety,' he added.

'I am not hiding!'

'And refusing to dance with the stepson of one's benefactress might not be entirely appropriate.'

'Then, pray tell, what would you have me do?'

'Accompany me to the dance floor,' he said, inclining his head towards the orchestra.

'Very well,' she said. 'I wouldn't wish to be improper. Lady Wyburn said you would feel obligated to ask.'

He frowned, perversely irritated. 'She exaggerates my sense of social obligation, I assure you.'

'I am certain she meant it as a compliment.'

'No doubt. But now you are looking much too serious. Smile as though I've said something particularly witty.'

'Is that what all the other women do?' she asked.

She smelled of soap and lemons, he thought, as he led her to the dance floor. He liked the smell, tangy and fresh, so different from the perfumed scents of other women.

'My lord?'

'I beg your pardon?' He jerked his attention back to the conversation.

'Do other women look spellbound as if you've said something witty?'

'Naturally.'

He took her gloved hand and felt it tremble within his palm. The dance started and they broke apart in time to the music.

'Even when you haven't said anything either inspiring or witty?' she asked as they came together again.

'Especially then.'

'How tiresome for you.'

'Why so?'

'Well, it must make you feel as though you're not a real person, but just a viscount.'

He laughed. 'That's the first time I've been called "just a viscount".'

'I meant no offence.'

'I know.' And it was true, he thought, surprised by her perception. Few people saw him as a person and women never did. He was a good catch, with a title, estate and ample income.

'Now you're much too serious,' she said. 'Aren't you supposed to look as though I've also said something remarkably entertaining?' She stepped under his raised arm. 'Or does it not work both ways?'

'It does and can be tedious, I assure you.'

'Indeed, I find discussions about the weather highly overrated.'

'Try looking fascinated by a spaniel's earwax,' he said, remembering a conversation with a certain Miss Twinning.

Miss Gibson laughed, a rich spontaneous sound. No, she was no statue. She was too vibrant—more like a flame caught in human form.

'I take it you do not discuss earwax?' he asked.

'I steer clear of that subject. In fact, I say remarkably little and endeavour to stick to Imogene's list of suitable topics.' She spoke with mock solemnity, the amusement in her eyes belying her tone. She had remarkable eyes.

'Which include?'

'Fashion and the weather.'

'Really.' They were dancing side by side. He caught another whiff of lemon. 'And what,' he murmured, bending so close that her hair tickled his cheek, 'would you discuss if left to your own devices?'

'My waterwheel and butter churn.'

'Your what?' His fashionable ennui deserted

him and he almost missed a step, narrowly avoiding the Earl of Pembroke's solid form.

'My butter churn,' she said more slowly.

'And what makes this churn so worthy of conversation?'

'Nothing really. I should not have mentioned it.' She looked regretful, glancing downward so that her lashes cast lacy shadows against her cheeks.

'Oh, but you should. I'm fascinated.' This was, surprisingly, true. He wanted to lean into her and catch again that delightful whiff of lemon. He wanted to see the intelligence sparkle in her eyes and feel her hand tremble, belying her external calm.

'The churn is automated by a waterwheel, you see, and I believe it would save our dairy maid so much hard labour.' She spoke quickly, her cheeks delightfully flushed with either enthusiasm or embarrassment.

'And have you had the opportunity to test its efficiency?'

'Once,' she said.

'Successfully, I trust.'

Her lips twitched and she looked up, merriment twinkling. 'The water succeeded in flooding the dairy. After that my device was banished.'

'Unfortunate.'

'However, I have constructed a small model so that I can perfect the design during my baths.'

'Your baths?' He choked on the word.

His mind conjured a vision of long, wet hair,

full breasts and alabaster limbs. He caught his breath.

Her cheeks reddened. 'One of those forbidden subjects like undergarments. I mean—I only mentioned baths because my churn is run by a waterwheel. Hence I need a source of water to move the wheel.'

He laughed. He could not help himself. Her conversational style might be unusual, but it was certainly more edifying than the weather.

Or earwax, for that matter.

She was, Paul realised, a good dancer. This surprised him. He'd always thought of her as moving with unladylike speed, charging full tilt into the museum or galloping on Rotten Row.

Now she kept perfect time, her body graceful and her movements fluid and rhythmic.

'You love music,' he said.

'I do. And you?'

For a second he could not recall her question.

'Like music?' she prompted. 'My lord, if I recall, you are supposed to at least pretend to pay attention.'

'I must take you to the opera.'

She missed a step.

*Blast.* And curse his operatic suggestion. In fact, he should not spend another second in the girl's company. Already, he was behaving out of character. He'd chortled at her impudence, enjoyed an entirely inappropriate conversation about churns, baths and undergarments, and was inordinately interested in eyes of an indeterminate grey-green and a pair of quite ordinary lips. No, not really ordinary. Their shape was too fine… And she licked them delightfully when discussing a scientific principle.

He frowned.

'You are under no duress to entertain me—or take us to the opera,' she said with sudden stiffness, her jaw lifting and her movements turning mechanical. 'I understand from Lady Wyburn that our evenings are extremely full.'

'If I choose to invite you to the opera, you will go,' he retorted, unreasonably irritated.

'If you choose to invite me in a civil manner, I will consider your invitation.'

'I…' He paused.

'You must learn to school your features, my lord. I'm sure scowling at your partner is scarcely appropriate.'

'And you must learn the art of polite conversation.' He glowered with greater ferocity.

'You suggested I discuss my churn.'

'Before I knew there were baths involved.'

She arched an eyebrow. 'Only as a source of water. Much like a puddle. There can be nothing inappropriate about a puddle.'

And now he wanted to laugh. 'I believe you might be advised to heed your sister,' he said instead.

'And I believe that the music has stopped, my lord.'

'What?'

'The music has ended,' she repeated.

This was true and the gentlemen were already making their bows and leaving the floor with their partners.

'Moreover, standing stock still in the middle of the dance floor might cause comment which would not, I know, be appropriate.'

# *Chapter Four*

'I'm glad someone hung out a moon for our special night,' Rilla whispered hours later as she stared from the window of her sister's bedchamber. She traced the white disc with her fingernail, the pane cool against her skin.

They had returned from the Thorntons' ball a half hour since and Imogene lay reclining amongst the lace cushions on her bed, stretched like a contented cat.

'Rilla, how can you talk about the moon? Did you not notice Lady Alice's dress and her mother's tiara? The diamonds lit up the room. Can you imagine owning such jewels? Those are the things I dream about—not moons.'

'And I will dream of them for you. But the moon will do for me.'

'And the gentlemen! They were most kind and made such pretty speeches. I cannot believe I was nervous earlier. Indeed, I cannot decide which I enjoyed more, the dancing or the conversation. And all the gentlemen thought me witty.'

'With good reason, but…' Rilla paused, turning from the window and picking up a hairbrush from the dressing table. She pushed her palm against it so that the bristles prickled her skin. 'Do be careful. Not everyone is as nice as you suppose.'

This got Imogene's attention. Her eyes widened and she propped herself upright. 'Are you referring to someone in particular?'

'Not really. Most of your partners were delight-ful—'

'But?' Imogene interrupted impatiently. 'What is it, what do you want to say?' Her voice took on a childish tone.

'Well…' Rilla tugged the brush through her hair.

'You have some big-sisterly criticism. You disliked someone with whom I danced?'

Rilla paused. 'Jack St John, if you must know. He was obnoxious as a child and has not improved since. Julie says he gambles and drinks.'

'Lud, every gentleman gambles and drinks. Even Father—'

'I know. That's why—' Rilla stopped, gulping back her words. Imogene knew nothing of Father's debts. Or Lockhart's involvement. 'I mean, I just think you should be wary. Be polite, but—keep him at arm's length.'

'Goodness, I only danced with him.'

'And joined him for lemonade.'

'Lud, how dreadful. What should be my punishment?' Imogene had now abandoned all lassitude and sat bolt upright, her fingers working at the lace trim of the pillowcase.

'Don't be foolish. I am only worried for you.'

'Foolish? May I remind you that I have been reading the *Tatler* for years? It is perhaps you who are foolish with your Greeks and…and butter churn.'

'My churn? My churn has nothing to do with this. I just wanted to warn you.'

'I don't need your warnings.'

'Obviously.' Rilla pushed her hair back from her forehead and dropped the brush with a clatter on to the dressing table.

What a mess. She should have known not to mention the matter while Imogene was both tired and excited from the ball. Likely she was still raw from that moment of nerves earlier. Besides, who was she worried for—Imogene or herself?

Imogene had not been the subject of Lockhart's insidious comment about 'odd tales'.

Imogene had not heard voices in the middle of a dance.

Imogene had not talked about baths or felt that peculiar, prickly, apprehensive, excited attraction to Lord Wyburn.

The silence stretched, broken only by the clock ticking and a branch tapping intermittently against the window.

'I'm sorry,' Rilla said at last. She was always the first to make peace. Her anger both came and went swiftly. 'I'm fussing, as Mrs Marriott would say. After all, you could hardly refuse to dance with a neighbour.'

'Thank you,' Imogene said, still stiff, her gaze focused on the wallpaper as though much fascinated by the painted roses. 'I certainly did not wish to give the earl any special favours. Besides you danced with Lord Alfred Thompson twice.'

'I did,' Rilla acknowledged, although the foppish Lord Alfred was a vastly different man than Lockhart. 'Anyway we shouldn't quarrel. It would be a sad way to end such a special night.'

'True,' Imogene smiled, looking away from the wallpaper. 'Besides, the earl will be too busy with his own set. We will not see him much.'

'You're right, of course.' Rilla stood and, blowing her sister a kiss, left for her own chamber.

But once alone, Rilla felt her body wilt with exhaustion and her spirits drop to an oppressive low.

She would feel better after a night's rest, she thought, as she kicked off her slippers. Yet, despite exhaustion, sleep did not come. Her thoughts jumped and flitted.

There was Lockhart with his silky tones and innuendos.

And the viscount.

And her reaction to the viscount.

Worse yet, there was that soft, desperate voice and her own growing conviction that Lord Wyburn was connected to that voice.

All of which meant, she should avoid him. She

should not dance with him or chat about Romans, Greeks, butter churns or any other topic for that matter.

And yet she could not stop seeing him. He was Lady Wyburn's stepson.

Even worse, she did not think she even wanted to…

Apparently a Wyburn soirée took as much preparation as Hannibal's invasion, minus the elephants. Shortly after the ball, Lady Wyburn had decided to follow on this success with a dinner in the girls' honour.

'It would be just the thing. We will invite anyone who is anyone, which is an extremely confusing phrase because really everyone is someone, at least in their own mind. Besides, we don't want people to forget you.'

'Highly unlikely. We drink tea with the same people every afternoon,' Rilla said.

'I meant the gentlemen, my dears.'

On the day of the event, the girls watched the bustling of all manner of servants and trades people. Florists trooped in, housemaids swept and polished so that lemon wax perfumed the air and Lady Wyburn rushed about, her grey ringlets dishevelled and her forehead shining with perspiration.

'I thought the house already immaculate,' Rilla whispered to Imogene as they looked over the banisters into the front hall.

'Indeed, and Lady Wyburn describes this as an intimate dinner,' Imogene added.

Heloise, the diminutive French maid in charge of their appearance, hurried up the stairway, her feet tapping against the wood with businesslike efficiency. 'There you are. I had been looking for you, *oui*. Miss Imogene, I need you to try on your gown. Miss Amaryllis, perhaps you should go to your chamber. You cannot be draping yourself over banisters all day.'

'Yes,' said Rilla, not unwilling to leave. With any luck she might even manage a few minutes with her churn. She had asked Heloise to save her bathwater and hoped to try out a modification in the design of her trough.

Despite her evident disapproval, Heloise had followed instructions and the bathwater remained. Although, Rilla noted, grinning, Heloise had relegated the churn to a far corner, half-hidden by the curtains.

The contraption consisted of a trough which channelled water on to a waterwheel which powered the churn. She had recently altered the design of the trough, hoping that if she carved a deeper channel, the force would increase, but less volume would be required.

Taking a small knife, Rilla scraped the wood with regular, methodical motions, enjoying the rasp of metal against wood, the roughness of the grain and even its smell. She liked this tangible link with home and the concrete practicality of the task.

Both the viscount and odious Jack St John were coming tonight. Of course, she'd seen the earl every day that week—that man was an all-too-frequent visitor, lingering like the smell of fish on Fridays. Moreover, Imogene apparently found him wildly humorous, although in Rilla's opinion he had a stolid, humourless personality.

She dug energetically into the wood.

Still, there were other gentlemen who viewed Imogene with approbation. Lord Alfred Thompson visited most days and was more intelligent and less foppish on closer acquaintance.

Yes, he might do, although Imogene didn't seem entirely smitten.

Wyburn hadn't visited. Indeed, Rilla had not seen him since the ball.

This was a great relief, of course, Rilla decided, digging with sudden ferocity until her knife skidded, narrowly missing her hand.

Must the man even jinx her from afar? Not that she missed him. He made her too confused and her usually prosaic nature and logical mind became impaired by his presence.

There. She gave a final cut and put down the knife.

That should work. She would test it now. She always found concentrating on her inventions a calming occupation. Balancing the trough over the waterwheel, she used the jug from her dresser to scoop up the chilled bathwater.

She watched carefully as it splashed into the

trough and on to the waterwheel, which then moved slowly, causing the two paddles in the churn to also shift.

'*Mademoiselle*, whatever are you doing?' Heloise hurried into the room.

Startled, Rilla almost toppled into the bath. 'Bother,' she said.

'You're getting yourself wet.'

'I'll dry.'

Rilla poured a second jug of water on to the trough, angling her body so that she could see the liquid's progress and its speed of descent.

'I meant you should rest or do something lady-like,' Heloise said, making a clicking sound with her tongue.

'I find this very calming. Besides, I think it is working better.'

'Umff. Me, I will feel calm when we have done something with that hair. We should start now. Doing your hair is a time-consuming process and it will be evening soon enough, *oui*?'

'But it is early still.'

'We need all the hours God sends. Besides, her ladyship said that the viscount, you know, Lord Wyburn, remarked that you had cleaned up re-markably well.'

'He did?' Rilla dropped the trough.

'Now look at the mess. I will clean it and then no more science.'

Rilla entered Lady Wyburn's drawing room some hours later in a low-cut emerald gown, every aspect of her appearance primped and polished by Heloise.

A fire burned in the hearth, its marble mantel smaller than anything in the Gibson household, but vastly more sophisticated.

In fact, Lady Wyburn's entire decor was one of understated elegance. Gilt trim glittered about the ceiling, reflected in the long mirrors which lined the walls. White-and-gold sofas and chairs furnished the room, and a red Indian carpet dominated the centre.

Imogene had come down already and sat on the sofa, resplendent in a pink dress and long white gloves.

'You look beautiful,' Rilla said.

It was true. Since arriving in London, Imogene had matured, transforming from a beautiful girl into the elegant woman she had always wanted to be.

'You too.'

'Thank you. Heloise worked hard and assured me I would not disgrace her which is high praise, but...' Rilla paused, adding, 'I am nervous.'

'I am sure you need not be. You have been a success to date.'

'But at other events, there has been dancing. Here we will do little but converse and I have no idea what to talk about. I'm doomed to stand mute like a pea-goose.'

'You'll be fine as long as you do not mention your inventions.'

'They'd be more interesting than the weather.'

'Ladies do not aspire to be interesting.'

Rilla giggled. 'I aspire only to survive the Season without tripping.'

'Rilla—'

'I hear something.'

Careless of her dress and hair, Rilla knelt on the sofa, pushing her head through the curtains. 'They're already come!'

Indeed, the first carriages had stopped in front of the house. Rilla could see their dark outlines within the puddles of yellow light cast by the street lamps.

Rain fell heavily, bouncing off both the cobbled streets and the black-lacquered roofs of crested coaches. Several of Lady Wyburn's liveried servants carried torches and black umbrellas as they escorted the guests towards the house.

Then, something happened. The scene warped, changing and transforming.

Her breath caught. Instinctively, she clutched at the thick velvet curtain. She swallowed. Before her eyes, the street disappeared into a black lake pitted with rain. Men waded into the water. They held flickering torches, their light reflecting on the water's ink-like surface. She could see their cloaks. She could see the thick trunks of their legs and hear the splash of water as they trudged forward.

Fear, worry and, deep in her stomach, the coldness of despair.

And lavender.

She smelled lavender.

'Rilla?' Strain tightened Imogene's distant voice.

The men stooped, lifting something from the lake and Rilla felt her gaze inexorably drawn to it. 'Please...' she whispered, half in prayer.

Then, as if it had never been, the lake diminished and Rilla was back, once more, within the pleasant room.

Her breath escaped in whistled relief.

'Come, girls!' Lady Wyburn swept into the room. 'Gracious, Rilla, whatever are you doing poking your head through the curtains? You'll wreck your hair. It is time to greet your guests.'

'Yes.' Rilla stood and forced a smile.

She cast one final look through the window, but the scene presented nothing more alarming than a cobbled street on a wet night. The horses stood, stamping their hooves, steam rising from their sleek backs. Coachmen opened carriage doors, muffled under greatcoats dark with wet.

'Rilla?' Imogene questioned, her voice low with worry.

'It was nothing,' Rilla said.

These moments could not—must not—happen here in London.

Paul noted Miss Gibson's absence almost immediately upon rejoining the ladies following dinner and port.

It wasn't that he looked for her. In fact, he'd been trying to ignore her for the better part of the evening. Rather he appreciated something lacking, like a room without a fire or a flowerbed out of bloom.

At first he surmised she'd gone to the ladies' retiring room, but as her absence lengthened, he wondered whether she was ill. She'd looked pale earlier. Indeed, even through dinner she'd been lacklustre and distracted, very different from the girl with the flushed cheeks that he'd seen after that wild gallop.

Lord Alfred's absence took Paul longer to appreciate. The man was not particularly noticeable, more cravat than person. However, after a while, Paul realised he'd not seen that gentleman either for a good hour. He also recalled that Lord Alfred had hovered about both the Misses Gibson at the Thorntons' ball and had visited Lady Wyburn's establishment on several occasions.

Paul's jaw tightened. A headache spread across his temples. Easing himself from his chair, he strolled from the room with forced indolence. Once in the corridor, his spine straightened and his thoughts turned bleak.

The girl was under Lady Wyburn's protection and he refused to let her act inappropriately with Lord Alfred, or anyone else for that matter. He looked in both the morning and music rooms.

He found no one.

'Where is Miss Gibson?' Paul asked Merryweather as the butler entered the hall, his tray heavy with refreshments.

The man started, causing the crystal to rattle. 'Haven't seen her, my lord. Perhaps check the library. She likes it there.'

'The library?' Paul frowned.

His father had liked the library rather well, although he'd spent more time consuming alcohol than literature.

The door creaked in opening. The light was dim, broken only by a small fire and two sconces. It was only as he neared the hearth that he saw the emerald figure curled within the depths of the leather armchair.

He stopped. She must be sleeping. He softened his tread so as not to startle her. Peculiarly, she clasped a miniature in her hand and her posture seemed unnaturally rigid for one in sleep.

'Miss Gibson?' He touched her shoulder.

She made no response.

'Miss Gibson?' he said again, more loudly. Still she seemed not to hear him although her eyes were open.

He shook her shoulders, almost roughly, conscious of an unfamiliar start of fear.

She stirred.

'Are you all right?' he asked.

She blinked, staring at him as though not comprehending his words.

'You were asleep,' he explained.

She shifted. The miniature dropped from her hand, clattering to the floor. Bending, he picked it up. His stomach tightened as he saw the painted face. His fingers clenched against the frame.

'What are you doing with this?' he asked.

# Chapter Five

The lake lapped at her feet. Rain stung her cheeks. She shivered, her clothing wet and clammy against her skin. Water dripped from the men's clothes and boots as they waded to shore. A few held torches, the yellow light flickered, illuminating their grim faces, their sodden clothes and the thick trunks of their legs.

'Miss Gibson.'

The voice came as from a great distance. She heard it but was still trapped, caught in this wet blackness broken only by the torches' weak light.

'Are you all right?' She felt a touch on her shoulder.

And then the black lake disappeared and she was again in Lady Wyburn's library, thank goodness.

'Are you ill?'

Wyburn. She recognised the voice.

Panicked fear ballooned in her gut. Wyburn was here. He had seen her like this. He must not suspect.

'I—am—fine,' she said, slowly and carefully.

'You look white. What happened?' Worry clouded his face and a lock of hair fell across his forehead, making him appear younger and more vulnerable.

'I—'

*She'd touched the portrait.*

She'd touched the miniature that he now held. She looked away. 'I had a headache.'

'You have been gone an hour.'

'An hour? That is not possible—' Her gaze went to the mantel clock. It had been five after eleven and now read midnight. 'I must have dropped off.'

Except she hadn't slept. Where had the last hour gone? Where had she gone? She shivered.

'You're cold.'

She watched as he took the shawl she had discarded, putting it about her shoulders. His fingers grazed her arm. They felt warm with a tingling roughness at the tips.

For a foolish, impulsive moment she wanted to touch them, to hold on to them.

'I hope you're not sickening for something?' he said. 'You did not look entirely well at dinner.'

'Is that why you came looking for me?'

'I feared your absence would cause comment.'

She nodded, her mind working again, but with pedestrian movement. 'I suppose I should thank you.'

'That would set a precedent.' His lips curved just a little.

'Absent at my own party. Hardly a forgivable offence.'

'Particularly as not everyone may have assumed any indisposition.' His tone hardened.

'Pardon?'

He shrugged. 'Lord Alfred was also absent from the room.'

'And that is not permitted?'

'Not if it could be presumed that you were "unwell" together.'

Rilla blinked. Anger pushed past her distress, a welcome revitalising heat. 'And did you think that, my lord?'

'It seemed a logical conclusion.'

The man could say the most obnoxious things without batting so much as a hooded lid. 'Logical?'

'I know Lord Alfred admires you. I thought his feelings might be reciprocated.'

The rage grew, pushing past the heavy-limbed lethargy, speeding her thoughts and pumping her blood. The anger was not just at Wyburn, but at herself. At this unnatural aspect of her being that came from God or the devil. She balled her hands, digging her nails into her palm with almost welcome pain.

'I sought solitude, but not with Lord Alfred. I am no fool.' The words came easier now.

'I did not think you were. But I know you to be impetuous.'

'Impetuous, not immoral.'

His face remained impassive. 'Women do strange things for love.'

'I do not love Lord Alfred, or anyone else for that matter.'

'For your sake, I hope it will remain so.' His gaze fell on the miniature. She noted shadows under his eyes and a weariness in his demeanour.

'You do not believe in the sentiment?'

'No.'

'Why?' Even as she spoke, she knew she shouldn't, that she was stepping over a boundary.

'Love destroys.' He spoke flatly and sat heavily in the chair opposite, without his usual elegance.

The clock above the mantel ticked and the fire gave a sudden crackle. She twisted the fabric of her shawl about her fingers.

'Not always,' she said softly. 'Our most noble deeds are done for love. It gives us the capacity for good as well as evil. One must believe that. Otherwise the world becomes hopeless…' She stopped, biting her lip.

A thread had pulled loose and she wound it around her finger, so tight it left fine white lines across her skin.

He flashed a cynical smile. 'I doubt the Trojan warriors would share that view.'

'Shakespeare might. "Love is not love which alters when it alteration finds, Or bends with the remover to remove".'

'He also wrote *Romeo and Juliet.*'

'Which was a tragedy because of the impediments to love, not because of love itself.'

He smiled, his expression more sad than cynical. 'You are a romantic. But do you base these beliefs purely on the work of poets or have you real-life experience?'

The room felt still, a stillness that was tangible. Self-preservation urged her to laugh, to mock, to say something careless and witty or even foolish. Yet she could not. It was suddenly important to her that he regain hope.

'I base them on my parents, because they were truthful and loving,' she said at last.

'Mine weren't.'

The words sounded unwilling, as though drawn from him.

'I'm sorry,' she said, at once hating the triteness of the phrase.

She glanced at him. Candlelight flickered across the harsh planes of his face. He looked so sad that she reached to touch his cheek, the movement involuntary.

He jerked at her caress. She dropped her hand.

'I'm sorry,' she said again.

'Don't be.' He spoke so softly that she wondered if she'd dreamed the words.

As though handling fine porcelain, he took her hand. Her skin tingled. All thoughts, all feelings seemed centred on their two hands as he rubbed his thumb against her open palm, a feathered touch. 'You have a quality, Miss Gibson, which makes me want to believe the impossible. That water can churn butter.'

Slowly, he lifted her hand and kissed it.

Her heart thundered and her breath quickened.

Letting go of her hand, he raised his forefinger and touched the tip of her chin, tracing the smooth line of her cheek up to her temple.

She felt the touch into the very core of her being. His fingers slid down to her throat, tracing her collarbone and touching the sleeve of her dress. The fabric shifted. His fingers pushed under it, edging it from her shoulder.

'Paul.' It was a whisper.

She was filled with sensations different from anything she had experienced—a warmth, a need, an exhilarating recklessness. She met his gaze. His eyes were no longer cold but smouldering as his gaze roamed over her face, her neck, her shoulders and the *décolleté* of her gown.

A log crackled.

With the sound, his mood shifted. He dropped his hand, jerking it away as though stung. 'I don't know what I was thinking. I'm sorry.'

'I wanted—'

'I know.' He stood abruptly. The chair grated on the hardwood. He walked to the fireplace, his back rigid. 'You must go back.'

'Yes,' she said, still dazed.

'Miss Gibson,' he spoke with sudden force. 'I apologise for my behaviour. It was unpardonable.'

'It's no matter.'

'Miss Gibson?' He turned to her.

'Yes.'

'This will not happen again, you have my word.'

He left the room swiftly, closing the door behind him with a muted click.

Slowly, as though needing to orchestrate the movement of her limbs, Rilla rose and walked to the hearth. She felt the warmth of the fire on her legs. She gripped the mantel, glad of the feel of solid wood against her hands. In front of her, she could see her own reflection in the huge mirror which hung over the hearth.

How could she look so outwardly unchanged? And yet she was immeasurably altered. She'd wanted to kiss the viscount. She'd never wanted to kiss anyone before…ever…

Now she did.

And her body was a stranger to her, demanding things she didn't understand and knew she could not…*must not*…have.

She'd known since she was a child that she should not love or marry.

This was truer now than ever, particularly with this man. Despite herself, her gaze slid to the miniature as it lay face down on the side table.

But for the first time, she had an inkling of what she must forgo.

And if she couldn't?

If this heat…this feeling…proved too strong.

With a jerk of sudden energy, she pushed herself away from the mantel. She had to get away from here; from the miniature and from her own scared, wide-eyed reflection.

Almost violently, she pushed open the door, half running into the corridor.

'Evening.'

The voice was cool. She jerked about, half stumbling. Jack St John lolled against a wall adjacent, smiling.

'What are you doing here?' she questioned.

'I am,' he said, taking out both handkerchief and silver snuffbox, 'on my way to the card game.'

'Oh—I...I wish you luck.'

'Indeed.' He smiled. 'I am feeling lucky tonight.'

She watched as he took a pinch of snuff and sniffed, before carefully dabbing his nostrils with his handkerchief. 'Prodigiously lucky, in fact.'

Rilla flung herself down beside her churn. She kicked off her slippers and pulled out the ribbons Heloise had so painstakingly twisted into her unruly hair.

The whole evening had been a nightmare from start to finish. Instinctively, she reached for the solid wood of her churn like a sailor for a life ring. She rubbed her fingers along the grain, moving the wheel so that it made a comforting *thump... thump...thump*.

Surely if she stayed focused on force and momentum and mathematical calculations she would be safe. Such activities had helped her in the days after Sophie's disappearance and rescue, during her mother's illness and her father's gambling.

Yes, if she occupied her mind with force, gravity and momentum, her skin would no longer tingle from his touch.

Besides, she was being highly illogical to still feel that tingle. The touch had occurred hours past. It was scientifically impossible that she could retain any sensation of his fingers brushing her palm, trailing across her cheek or pushing the cloth down from her shoulder—

'Rilla!' Imogene's voice came from outside of the bedchamber.

Rilla lowered the trough with a clunk.

'Gracious! It is three a.m. Whatever are you doing—?' Imogene stopped on the threshold.

'Adjusting the angle of my trough.'

'Well, stop. I have news. Did you hear that Myra Kelly and Anthony Soames are engaged?'

'Do we know Myra Kelly or Anthony Soames?'

'No, but—'

'Then why would I care?'

'Because there were rumours that Lord Alfred was dangling after her and now she is off the market.' Stepping into the room, Imogene sat elegantly on Rilla's white-ruffled bed.

'Oh…' Rilla paused, frowning at her churn. She had not known that Imogene had so much interest in Lord Alfred although he visited frequently. 'Then that is well, I suppose.'

'Indeed, and he said he would call tomorrow and we could all go to the park if the weather improves.'

Perhaps if he asked for Imogene's hand, they could leave London. Yes, that would be best, although the idea left her strangely flat.

'Rilla? Are you listening?'

'Yes, what did you say?'

'Only that you are near the window and I was wondering if it was raining or just cloudy because it would be lovely to go to the park tomorrow and disappointing if we could not.'

'Today, you mean.' Rilla stood, pushing aside the curtaining. She might as well forget her churn for the moment.

Outside, everything was dark, illuminated only by a moon, half-obscured with clouds. Moisture from the evening's rain still clung to the undersides of leaves and the cobbles shone wet.

And then it came.

It came with her churn spread about her like the pathetic good-luck charm it was.

One moment Rilla watched clouds scud across the sky and, in the next, that awful coldness washed through her.

Rilla stiffened. Her fingers gripped the window ledge, the wood biting at her flesh. The cold was awful, worse than ever before. It came from inside, seeping outward through her torso and down the length of her limbs. Goosebumps prickled. Her palms slickened with sweat.

'Rilla?'

She heard her sister speak. She even turned to Imogene, but the distance was unbridgeable. It was as though she'd been swept within a tunnel. The room, her sister, and the white-ruffled bed and rose-print rug hovered distant and inconsequential.

Then her gaze returned to the window. At first, she saw a wash of light, a blurry rainbow super-imposed against the shrubbery. Then a woman's face and figure formed.

The apparition stood beside the rose bed, her arms outstretched as though in supplication. Rilla could see her clearly: her face, her hands, the folds of her sleeves. And yet she had a translucent quality and seemed to generate light from within.

'Who are you?' Rilla said, or thought she said, except she did not need to ask.

'Rilla? Rilla? What…what is it?'

Rilla blinked and turned to her sister. 'Can't you see her?'

'Who?'

'There. His mother.'

Rilla turned back, but the woman had disap-peared, leaving nothing but the darkness of night. The cold receded.

'Rilla, stop! You have to stop this.' Imogene gripped Rilla's arm, her fingers tight on her flesh.

Rilla jerked away, banging her hip against the sill. 'It came again.' Her mouth felt funny, her tongue dry and bulky.

'A feeling?' Imogene whispered. 'Again. And

in London?' As though the city should preclude such things.

'Yes.'

'It's the heat from the fire. Lady Wyburn keeps things too hot. Sit on the bed.'

Rilla sat. Bile pushed into her throat. She swallowed. Her hand lay against the loose folds of her dress. She clenched the cloth in her fingers. 'It wasn't hot in the museum or in the library.'

'The museum and library?'

'Yes,' Rilla said. It was a flat, dead word. They looked at each other. 'Imogene, it's getting worse and this time I recog—'

'Nonsense, like I said, you're tired and unused to the city's pace. I mean it is past three a.m. We are both exhausted and half-asleep on our feet.' Imogene spoke quickly, the words spilling out as though by sheer quantity they could mask the truth.

'No.' Rilla caught her sister's hand. 'It's more. We both know it.'

Imogene's grip tightened, her fingers almost painful against Rilla's palm. 'Then you must fight it. If people were to know—'

*They'd think me mad. They'd think me mad and they'd think Imogene sister to a madwoman.*

The words hammered through Rilla's mind. It had been their mother's greatest fear. The silence lengthened. The clock ticked. The fire crackled.

'I'll fight it,' she said at last.

'Good.' Imogene exhaled, her relief palpable. 'Good. Now go to bed and rest. Sleep as long as you want, if there are morning callers I will say you are indisposed.'

Rilla nodded, trying to make her voice hearty. 'I will feel better after a good night's sleep.'

'Yes, yes, I know you will.'

Imogene left. Rilla listened to the tap of her footsteps receding down the hall as she sat on the bed, her arms and legs limp.

Tomorrow, she would smile. She would push the fear away and nod and curtsy.

This must not spoil her sister's Season.

But for now, Rilla sat unnaturally still in a city filled with people and felt unbearably alone.


Paul stretched his long legs close to the crackling warmth of the fire at White's. He nursed his cognac within its fragile glass balloon and watched the embers chase into the chimney.

Unaccountably, he was reminded of Titian hair.

*Damn.* He swallowed the cognac in a fiery gulp. He had decided after the library incident to studiously ignore the elder Miss Gibson.

But the wretched woman was proving hard to ignore.

Absently, Paul opened his snuffbox, a gift from an Italian opera singer. He took a pinch of snuff, hoping it might clear his head.

Strident male laughter intruded on his thoughts. Frowning, he glanced behind him. The club was almost empty except for two gentlemen playing cards at the small round table nestled in a far corner of the room.

Paul recognised one as Jack St John. The Earl of Lockhart was from a good family, but had a loose screw, he thought, as he watched the man loll in his chair as though already inebriated.

'The bet's in the hat so to speak,' the earl said, his voice loud but with a slight slur.

'Don't count on it.' The other man spoke in a quieter voice. Paul now recognised him, a Mr Robert Conway. Another loose screw, but younger.

''Course it is. Girl's besotted,' Lockhart replied.

'She's got that red-haired sister who isn't. If looks could kill—'

'Good God, man, I do not worry about Miss Gibson's glares. Besides, my own lady is disinclined to heed her sister.' Lockhart laughed as though well pleased with his wit.

Paul's hand tightened against the leather arm of the chair, but he gave no other hint of his emotions. Languidly he rose. With care he flicked a minute piece of lint from his pantaloons before strolling towards the card table.

'Evening, gentlemen,' he drawled.

Conway stood, jarring the tabletop. His brandy spilled. He took out his handkerchief and dabbed at the amber puddle.

'Wyburn, didn't see you there.' Lockhart pushed his legs further under the table and smiled.

'So I gathered.'

'Ah, Wyburn. Well met, eh,' Conway blustered, tossing his sodden kerchief away.

'Do I understand, Lockhart, that you have bet on a lady's honour?' Paul's voice was level, congenial almost. He smiled.

'Not—not her honour, Wyburn,' Conway replied, his voice unnaturally high. 'Wouldn't actually do anything. Wouldn't go through with it. Just…whether…she would agree, you know.'

'I take it, you are the mastermind?' Paul eyed Lockhart. The man moved uneasily.

'Stop playing the high and mighty,' the earl said. 'You've been involved in questionable bets yourself, and your father—'

'Is dead and buried.' Paul narrowed his eyes. 'You are betting on a lady's honour. Moreover, both Miss Imogene and Miss Amaryllis Gibson are under my protection.' He stared at each man in turn until they looked away, their gazes dropping to the green felt of the tabletop. Conway fingered his sleeve, the *scritch-scratch* audible within the silence.

Satisfied, Paul nodded to both and strolled from the room.

# Chapter Six

'I wonder,' Imogene said, 'if I should wear my new turquoise gown, the one with the silver spangles, for the Swintons' ball tonight.'

'I cannot see why not.' Rilla squatted inelegantly on the grass beside her model butter churn. It was a fine morning and both Imogene and Rilla were in the patchwork square of garden behind Lady Wyburn's town house.

'The decor is to be blue to resemble an underwater palace, and I fear I might resemble a wall.'

'Highly unlikely.' Rilla grinned, glancing up at her pretty sister.

'Then I will wear it. I have been longing to!' Imogene pirouetted on the lawn.

Rilla's smile widened. Sometimes it seemed Imogene was not so very different from the girl she'd looked after during their mother's illness.

'What will you wear?' Imogene stopped her dance.

'I haven't thought.'

'Good gracious, then what have you been thinking about these last ten minutes?'

'This.' She fingered the wood, listening to the movement of its cogs. 'But I'll need the original here soon. There is only so much I can do with the replica.'

'Time enough for that when we return home,' Imogene said. 'Although I am almost glad to hear you talk about your inventions.'

'Gracious, that is a first.' Rilla spoke lightly but did not mistake the worry hidden behind her sister's comment.

'You know what I mean.'

'Yes, but I am absolutely well. Indeed, I am almost looking forward to the Swintons' ball and the underwater decor.'

'Lord Alfred Thompson will be there,' Imogene added, her tone tentative.

'So you *do* like him? I had wondered. I suppose he would make a good enough match.'

'Lord Alfred? For me?'

'Yes, I first suspected it when you were so happy that—who was it? Myra somebody had got engaged to a Soames something.'

'Myra *Kelly* and *Anthony* Soames,' Imogene corrected. 'And, no, I want at least a duke with a good income. Lord Alfred is only comfortably off, but Lady Wyburn thought that you and he might make a match.'

'You know I can't.'

'Maybe you will grow out of—'

'And maybe I won't. Maybe they'll get worse and I'll end up in an asylum like our great-aunt.'

'Rilla—' Imogene looked stricken.

'Besides, he takes his cravat entirely too seriously,' Rilla added lightly, eager to reassure. 'No, I'll stick to being an old maid.'

An hour later, Rilla gave up on her churn for the day. She could not get the angle of the trough right and squinting at the sun had given her a headache.

She stood, rolling her shoulders as she re-entered the house, blinking in the sudden dimness.

Merryweather was limping up the stairs, holding a bouquet of pink blossoms close to his chest and breathing heavily.

Dignity fiddlesticks.

'Here! Let me help. Are those for Miss Imogene?' she asked, hurrying behind him.

'Yourself, miss.'

'Really? I'll take them, then. No point you going upstairs while I am going up anyway.'

'Yes, miss.' He turned and handed her the bouquet, before shuffling back down into the hall.

Rilla read the card. They were from Mr Haigh, a portly gentleman from Yorkshire. She smiled, enjoying their scent. It was nice to get flowers if only from the portly Mr Haigh.

Then, with that instinctive knowledge of one who is no longer alone in a room, her muscles tensed. Awareness flickered through her limbs.

Her cheeks warmed. She swallowed and, even as she lifted her gaze, she knew who she would see.

Wyburn dominated the hall. He stood tall in a tailored blue jacket of superfine and tan pantaloons. The very air around him quivered.

Her fingers tightened against the flower stems. She hadn't seen him since, well, since the library.

'Good morning, Miss Gibson.'

'How did you get in? I didn't hear the bell,' she said, descending quickly and pausing on the bottom stair, suddenly hesitant.

'Through the conservatory. Merryweather's getting too old to be answering doors.'

'That was kind.'

'I have my moments.'

At this point the conversation halted and, looking for distraction, Rilla sniffed the bouquet and promptly sneezed.

'Bless you.' Wyburn pulled out his handkerchief and, stepping forward, handed it to her.

'Thank you.' Their fingers touched and, simultaneously, they pulled away.

A heavy, cloaking silence fell, magnifying each whispered sound. From her position, raised upon the first stair, Rilla stared directly into those disconcerting eyes. She stood so close to that dark lock of hair that she need only raise her hand to push it back. Or reach to run her fingertips across his lean cheek and touch the single dimple—

'Paul!' Lady Wyburn's high tones shattered the moment.

Rilla stepped back, half stumbling. Paul steadied her, his hand at her elbow.

'Lovely to see you, Paul dear. Gracious, Rilla, do be careful. Is that a handkerchief? Have you a nosebleed? I had a cousin who always got nosebleeds at inconvenient moments. I believe she got one when she was being presented at court which was most inconvenient particularly as one must wear white. And I do not know if she thought to remember a handkerchief. She never was a thoughtful creature. Although her maid might have remembered—'

'Stepmother, I require a moment of your time,' the viscount said, interrupting the narrative.

'Naturally, my dear, but first will you do me a teeny-tiny favour? Dear Imogene and Rilla require to practise dancing. The waltz. 'Tis all the rage, you know, but dear Mr Arnold is unavailable. You will help in his place?'

'Help?' One dark eyebrow rose.

'I'll lead Imogene and you can partner Rilla.' Lady Wyburn smiled, her cheeks bunching like rosy balls of wrinkled netting. 'Now, go into the drawing room, my dears. Do not dally!'

With those words, Lady Wyburn surged ahead of them, her heels rapping against the hardwood and her jewellery jangling.

'Stepmama, it is important that I talk to you.'

'Of course, dear, and I know I will concentrate so much better once I am assured that the girls are ready for tonight's ball. All of London will be there, you know—'

'Goodness, ma'am, if it is that important I will dance, but I insist on talking to you later and without interruption or delay.'

'Yes, dear,' Lady Wyburn said, quite meekly.

The drawing room was brighter than the hall. Morning sunlight poured through the window, reflecting off the chandelier and splashing rainbow colours on to the mirrors and walls.

'Roll up the rug.' Lady Wyburn waved imperiously to the footmen. 'And push the furniture against the wall. Oh, and relieve Miss Gibson of those blooms. She's brandishing them about like a medieval knight. I mean, not as she would brandish a knight, but as a knight might brandish a sword or scabbard, if that's the right word?'

'We have no music,' Rilla said a trifle flatly, as she handed over the flowers.

'No matter, I will keep the beat. Ah, here's Imogene.'

Lady Wyburn beamed as Imogene walked into the room flushed from the sun outside, but otherwise cool and calm. Rilla rubbed her hand across her forehead. It felt hot and sticky. Several tendrils had loosened from her hairpins and dangled into her eyes.

Nor did it help that Wyburn appeared doubled and trebled within the huge gilt-framed mirrors. She was surrounded by the man—each image tall and muscled and with a solitary dimple.

'Imogene, dear, we're practising the waltz. Now—one-two-three.' Lady Wyburn grasped

Imogene's hand and led her about the room with surprising energy, grey ringlets bobbing.

'I believe that is our cue.' Again Paul smiled, half-cynical yet softened by gentler humour.

He must be very fond of his stepmother, Rilla thought, or he would not let her get away with such nonsense. His affection for her was endearing.

'One-two-three.' Lady Wyburn and Imogene narrowly missed the sofa.

Rilla wanted to giggle but, as Paul placed his hand at her waist, the giggle turned to muted gasp. The touch was light, yet through the cloth the imprint scorched. Her skin tingled. She knew the exact inches his fingers touched.

'Shall we?'

Rilla had never waltzed with anyone save Imogene and the dancing instructor. But dancing with Paul seemed entirely different from either experience. Indeed, the proximity of this male creature seemed indecent. His legs brushed her thighs. She felt their hardness and rhythmic movement. Everything about him was big and warm and near.

Her emotions veered from that of extreme discomfort to a wonderful, joyful vitality. She knew she should find some excuse, any excuse, to leave. Instead she felt only a tantalising longing to pull him closer, to feel the hard, lean length of him and touch the muscled width of his shoulders with her fingers.

Every sensation intensified. The room brightened, lit by sunlight and rainbows. She heard each sound—the swish of her skirts, the shuffle of shoes, the exhalation of mingled breaths.

And all the while she felt the friction of her inner thighs, a throbbing, rippling, growing warmth.

And her breasts… She flushed. Good lord, she should not be thinking about her breasts.

Nor should her breasts feel like this, prickly like pins and needles, only nicer. Paul's gaze caught hers. Blood heated her cheeks and roared into her ears.

She licked her lips.

'One-two-three and one-two-three,' Lady Wyburn warbled.

Rilla swallowed. She must not think about Paul. She must not allow herself to feel these…sensations….

Instead, she would focus on the movement of her feet, Lady Wyburn's rhythmic counting, or even Latin declensions. Yes, Latin declensions…*Puella, puella, puellis, puellam, puellae…*

Latin declensions did not help.

'Pray, Miss Gibson, are you seeking divine intervention?' Paul asked, breaking the tension that stretched between them like a violin string pulled taut.

'I was reviewing my Latin.'

'I had hoped my dancing more pleasant than studying.'

'It is. I mean—' She was sure his leg shifted.

'Perhaps my stepmother now includes Latin

review among the necessary preparations for the Season?'

'No, but it calms my mind,' Rilla blurted and then bit her lip.

'Is your mind in need of calming?'

'No, it is only that this is a new dance and I've had little practice.'

'It is often best not to analyse each step. We can talk about something. Your inventions, perhaps?'

'My inventions?' Did her voice squeak?

'I recall you mentioned that you would enjoy discussing them while dancing, if allowed to abandon the weather.'

'And earwax.'

Then Wyburn laughed, a real laugh. It had a full, rich sound. His face lit up and his eyes brightened. In that moment, she found the laughter and the impudence of his one dimple more seductive than all the rest.

Rilla heard the quick exhalation of her own breath and felt at once both incredibly safe and infinitely vulnerable.

'I believe we have practised sufficiently,' Paul said, abruptly interrupting Lady Wyburn's rhythmic count.

Enough was enough. The waltz was affecting him too much.

Much more than was sensible. He did not usually have any problem in controlling either his thoughts or his physical desires.

'Yes, yes, indeed, I really must go,' Rilla said and the chit stepped from his arms as though chased by the hounds of hell.

Perversely this irritated although he had been wanting rid of her a split second earlier.

'Go? Go where, dear?' Lady Wyburn cocked her head. 'Perhaps a walk? Paul would love a walk.'

'No, I would not love a walk,' he ground out. 'I need to talk to you, my lady, and I will do so now and without delay.'

'If you must, dear boy,' Lady Wyburn said, apparently recognising his determination.

'I will go and write to our father,' Rilla said, positively bolting from the room, followed more slowly by her sister.

Lady Wyburn made herself comfortable on the low sofa and studied Paul with apparent concern. 'I do hope that you are eating your vegetables, dear.'

'Pardon?'

'You look of an irritable disposition. I always tell my solicitor, Mr Begby, that he should eat additional vegetables when he gets a dyspeptic countenance.'

'I do not need vegetables and I am not dyspeptic. I would be in infinitely better humour if you could concentrate for a few moments, ma'am.'

'I am listening with rapt attention,' she said, reaching for her needlepoint.

'Good.' Paul paced to the fireplace and back. 'It has come to my attention that Jack St John has been spending considerable time with both the Misses Gibson, particularly Imogene.'

'He has visited, among other suitors.'

'I want such contact to lessen forthwith. I do not like the man.' Paul sat heavily in a chair opposite his stepmother. His foot tapped an irritable tattoo.

'Gracious, you sound like Rilla.'

'In this instance, she might be right.'

'But what can I do?' Lady Wyburn's plump face creased with worry. 'We cannot possibly give him the cut direct.'

'Drop a word in the girl's ear. Encourage her to be less available. She has sufficient other beaus.'

'Such action might make him the more determined. Or her. Imogene is not without a stubborn streak.'

'They are your protégées, ma'am, surely you can manage them?' His foot tapped again with greater velocity.

'Sometimes there is management in doing little. Besides, his attentions benefit. Without them, the girls might have been overlooked as so many débutantes are. Why, I recall at my own come-out poor Miss Marr was never given a second glance although her looks were quite remarkable.'

'If we could remain in this century.'

'Yes, yes. I just meant that we are fortunate Rilla and Imogene have so many admirers. I believe that Lord Alfred is taken with Amaryllis. Such a lovely boy. A bit foppish, of course, but he'd make a kind, considerate husband—'

'Husband?' Paul straightened. 'He'd get too tangled in his neckties to notice a wife. Besides, he would be quite wrong for Rilla. She'd ride roughshod over him.'

'I didn't know you'd given Rilla's matrimonial chances or—um—needs such consideration.'

'I have not. But it's obvious they're ill suited.'

'Quite possibly, dear,' his stepmother agreed equitably.

Paul stood. As usual, the room was too hot. 'Anyway, I am not here to discuss their matrimonial prospects, but rather their honour, without which your dear Lord Alfred and everyone else will disappear into the woodwork.'

'You think Lockhart would act dishonourably?' Lady Wyburn looked more worried now, her face falling into serious lines.

'Yes, and I am determined not to give him the opportunity.'

'What would you have me do?'

'I will keep Lockhart in my sights, and I suggest you do likewise with Imogene. Starting tonight.'

'Tonight? You mean at the Swintons' ball. You think he would try something there?'

'Yes,' Paul said.

Paul returned from his stepmother's home in bad humour and retired to his study. He wished he did not have to go out tonight.

But he would not shirk his duty. He needed to keep an eye on Lockhart. He did not trust the man.

Moreover, he'd committed to the Swintons' weeks previous and Lord Swinton was not without influence in Parliament. Paul required all the help he could get if he were to convince the landed gentry to repeal the Corn Laws. An uphill battle if ever there was one.

Paul lifted the fragile glass bubble of his brandy snifter, swirling the amber liquid. He swallowed, the liquor fiery in his throat.

It appeared he would have to attend a number of such events this Season. He frowned. He would prefer to steer clear of them until ready for marriage. Eventually he would have to marry, he knew, for duty if nothing else.

Of course, he could kill two birds with one stone. Why not keep an eye open for someone suitable—sensible, with decent lineage and adequate looks?

Yes, Paul decided, standing with sudden energy. Yes, it would serve him well to have a more practical purpose if he must waste his time at débutante balls.

He went to the window, pushed open the curtaining and stared into the dull grey of late afternoon.

A wife he could honour but not love because that, of course, was the sticking point.

He would respect his wife, provide for her and even have a fondness for her, but he must never love her. Love destroyed.

It had killed his mother and crippled his father.

The image of his mother's body flickered before his mind's eye.

'Blast!'

The snifter's fragile glass had shattered. Brandy splashed on to his trousers. Blood trickled from his palm, forming a dark line, black in the half-light.

He would never love a woman.

Rilla stood in the Swintons' entrance hall. The decor was, indeed, exquisite. Turquoise-and-blue curtains decorated the walls, undulating gently as guests passed. Silver banners sparkled and huge banks of candles bathed the hall and staircase in twinkling light.

The Mediterranean would look thus.

'Dear ladies.'

Rilla turned sharply, startled by the silky smooth tones.

She took an involuntary step back from Lockhart's bulky torso and flamboyant cravat. He wore cologne so strong and cloying that the scent seemed to coat her tongue.

'How fortunate.' The earl surged forward, bending low over Lady Wyburn's hand. 'It is wonderful to be in proximity of three ladies of such beauty.'

Rilla suppressed an unladylike snort. Her fingers tightened on her fan and her back molars clamped uncomfortably tight.

'My lord, you put us to blush.' Imogene fluttered long lashes.

Rilla concentrated on removing her cloak, with its intricate silver clasp.

'Pray, may I have the honour of escorting your party to the ballroom?' Lockhart questioned. 'I hear it is spectacular. Apparently, a ten-foot ice sculpture has been created. Poseidon, I believe. It is said to surpass even the one created for Lord and Lady Samuel last Season. Were you able to see it, Lady Wyburn?'

'Pardon? Yes, lovely,' Lady Wyburn said with both unusual brevity and abstraction.

Rilla frowned, pausing as she fiddled with the difficult clasp. Lady Wyburn looked unhappy. Her mouth drooped and creases bracketed her mouth.

Still, Rilla had no time to contemplate Lady Wyburn's emotions. Already Imogene had placed a gloved hand on Jack's arm, and smiled at him as though he were a man of either charm or intellect.

'Are you ready, Miss Gibson?' He turned to Rilla, pulling his lips into a smile. 'I have every hope and expectation that this will be an unforgettable evening.'

Rilla shivered, although the hall was warm and muggy. Was it her imagination or did he layer 'unforgettable' with meaning?

She followed as Jack escorted Imogene and Lady Wyburn up the huge curved staircase to the first floor where Rilla could already hear laughter and music spilling from the ballroom.

Her sister's sharp cry jerked Rilla back to reality.

'Imogene!'

A few steps forward, her sister had stumbled and now sat inelegantly on the step.

'Are you all right? Did you break something? Or twist your ankle?' Rilla asked, rushing forward.

'I don't think so.'

'I might have some smelling salts,' Lady Wyburn offered, rummaging enthusiastically in her reticule. 'I never get the opportunity to use them and it would be so satisfying if they were put to good purpose.'

'My fault entirely,' Jack said, hovering close. 'I fear Miss Imogene may have tripped on my walking stick.' He held up the offending cane.

'You don't use a stick. Why do you have one now?' Rilla questioned sharply.

'What does it matter?' Imogene said. 'I am not hurt, merely careless. Please help me up before too many people notice.'

'Of course,' the earl said, offering his arm.

'The problem is the heat,' Lady Wyburn said. 'I believe Lady Swinton aims to remind us too closely of the tropics. And I cannot find my salts. No doubt I will find them at a time when they are of no earthly use. But let us continue to the ballroom and find Imogene a chair. Lord Lockhart, perhaps you could procure refreshments.'

'Of course, I will find seats and drinks with all speed.'

Rilla was about to follow Lady Wyburn and her sister when she noticed an envelope, a white rectangle starkly outlined against the step's crimson carpet. Curious, she looked around to find a potential owner, but saw no one in the immediate vicinity.

She snatched up the envelope. With an unpleasant lurch, she saw that Imogene's name was written on it in a bold, black scrawl. She stared after her sister and Lockhart, suspicion rising.

The seal had been broken.

Dazed, she followed an elderly dowager with wilting purple ostrich feathers up the stairs and into the ballroom.

Once inside, she stood against a side wall, glancing about warily, but thankfully no one paid her any mind. Everyone appeared engrossed, dancing in swirling, multicoloured patterns, doubled and trebled within long mirrors.

Rilla held the crisp, thick vellum between tight fingers. She shouldn't...

She opened the envelope. It crackled inordinately loud, audible above the music. For a stunned second, she stared at the simple sentence, starkly written. Then she stuffed the paper away and pulled tight the ribbons of her reticule as though the note might escape if not well secured.

This could not, must not be. She would not allow it. She would prevent it at any cost.

# Chapter Seven

Paul arrived late. After relieving himself of his outer garments, he headed to the ballroom. Lady Swinton, he noted, had outdone previous decorating endeavours. Indeed, the effect was so marine as to induce a bilious stomach.

Glancing past the billowing blue, he saw Rilla dancing with Lord Alfred. She looked well enough, except…Paul studied her, eyes narrowing.

Her smile appeared too bright, her mouth stretched too wide and she looked flushed. He could almost feel the tension crackling through her tall, lithe body.

None of which mattered to him one whit. He was here to keep an eye on Lockhart, not monitor Miss Amaryllis Gibson's mercurial moods. His fascination with the woman was bordering on the absurd.

With determination, Paul strode in the direction of the card room. It had been set up in the library, a snug space with a roaring fire and the low rumble of male conversation.

Groups of men sat around card tables or in comfortable couches set about the room's perimeter. The fire crackled and a blue haze of cigar smoke perfumed the atmosphere.

Lockhart was not there.

'Greetings, Wyburn, old chap. Do sit down, eh. Do sit down.' The Earl of Coventry sat at a nearby table. He was deaf, and consequently spoke too loudly, his voice a booming bellow.

'Certainly.' Paul lowered himself between Coventry and his friend, Mr Elliot.

The former was so fat and the latter so thin that they made a comical pair like the children's nursery rhyme.

'Join us for a hand, eh? Join us for a hand?' Coventry asked.

'Of course,' Paul said. Lockhart would come here eventually, like a fox to its lair.

Coventry shuffled the cards and began to deal.

As though on cue, the door opened. A breeze wafted through the muggy heat as Jack strolled into the chamber.

'Here's Lockhart,' Coventry announced unnecessarily. 'Shall I deal you in, Lockhart, what? Shall I deal you in?'

'I must decline.'

Paul quirked his eyebrows. Jack loved cards and seldom refused a game. Indeed, he loved any form of gambling and had once bet on the speed of two snails crossing a paving stone.

'You sure, old fellow, what?' Coventry asked.

'I have another engagement.'

Paul did not let his tension show, not even by the flicker of an eyelash. It was entirely possible and probable that Jack might have an appointment with any number of gentlemen.

Or ladies not under Paul's protection.

With lazy indolence, Paul lounged back in his chair, watching Jack above the rounded edge of his queen.

The game continued, punctuated by Coventry's verbal byplay and the steady ticking of the clock. To Paul, it seemed that a peculiar feeling of waiting enveloped the room, as though everyone held their breath in collective accord.

He shuffled. It was getting hot. Perspiration prickled beneath his shirt. He was about to deal when he saw that Lockhart had risen. The man moved slowly but, Paul thought, with a casualness that seemed forced. He sauntered from the room, the door closing with a second whistle of wind.

Paul followed Lockhart the second he was able to do so without attracting undue attention. Even so, he saw no sign of the man either in the corridor or within the ballroom.

But across the room, the undulating movement of the turquoise curtains caught his attention. They moved as by a breeze and he noted that the French doors were open behind them.

Which meant the terrace beyond lay beyond.

'I wonder…' Paul muttered.

Rilla had slipped outside. Jack Lockhart would not spoil her sister's life, not if she could help it.

She glanced about the shadowed terrace. It felt cool after the ballroom's warmth. The moon, partially obscured by cloud, cast a weak light and stars studded the night sky.

She shivered. She hated waiting, always had. Nervously, she twisted at the locket at her throat. It had been her mother's and she liked to rub it and feel that tangible connection.

The glass door into the ballroom opened, music spilling out. Rilla turned and dropped the locket to her chest.

A man stepped forward, silhouetted against the light from the ballroom.

'Lord Lockhart!' Rilla approached him, squaring her shoulders.

The man turned. Moonlight lit the hard planes of his face and square, determined jaw.

'Miss Gibson.'

'You!' Rilla stared, her mouth dropping.

'It appears you expected someone else,' Paul, Viscount Wyburn, drawled.

Rilla did not like his look or tone. Apprehension knotted her stomach. She flicked her fan against her wrist and swallowed. His eyes bore into her and she detected no softening in their glacial depths, or any lingering memory of the morning's heady heat.

'I—'

'Unfortunately—' His gaze raked her. 'I may have to curtail your…tryst.'

'My what?' she managed to say.

'I didn't realise the earl had endeared himself to you. I thought you had more sense and I cannot say that I condone your taste.'

'He hasn't.'

'Really? Yet you are here specifically to meet him. I heard you call his name.'

'I didn't,' she said.

'I had always thought you a woman of uncommon candour. Do not lie now, Miss Gibson. Nor ask me to doubt my senses.'

'I had no intent of meeting the earl. Or I had, but—'

Impatience flickered across the viscount's even features. 'Enough excuses. If you care so little for your own reputation, could you not consider your sister? And my stepmother?'

'It is for my sister that I am here—' Rilla tried to speak for the third time. Her lips had dried and she breathed raggedly. She'd thought she'd seen him angry before. She hadn't. That had been a pale imitation of the emotion now hardening his features.

'Obviously you are truly the impetuous hoyden I first thought.' He stepped forward and now loomed above her. Goodness, he was tall.

'I am not—'

'And immoral, a trait I did not suspect.'

'I am none of those things!' The words exploded

from her. It hurt that he could say or think such things.

'It would serve you right if I left you here to meet your suitor, but my stepmother deserves better.'

'If you're quite done ranting and raving, may I speak?' Rilla cut in, her hands tightening into fists.

'For that you do not need my permission, but you can say nothing that would interest me.' He eyed her with a lazy, heavy-lidded gaze as though she were a closed book for which he could summon little interest.

'Too bad. It's my turn now.'

'Your turn? I was unaware we were playing a game, Miss Gibson.'

'We're not. But I wish to speak and you are going to listen.'

'Then pray continue with your *turn*, by all means.' His lips twisted mockingly.

'I'm not here to meet the Earl of Lockhart. Or I am, but not for the reasons you assume. I found this.' Rilla rummaged in her reticule and pulled out the letter.

Paul took the crumpled page. It rustled drily. He glanced over the bold script.

'It is addressed to Imogene,' Rilla said.

'Quite so. I have mastered the art of reading.'

'My sister dropped it. He is planning to meet her here and I won't have it!'

'You are telling me you have come to protect her reputation?' he asked.

'Yes. Contrary to your opinion, I can judge a man's character. And the earl is an...an odious toad. I know he's a member of the *ton*, but he's loathsome—a snake, a viper.'

Paul watched the expressions flicker across her mobile face. He met the grey-green fire of her eyes. It blazed at him, igniting the night. He'd never seen her so angry, or met anyone so fearless of his own displeasure.

A tingle of admiration flickered through a cold, hurt part of him and he recognised ridiculous relief. Miss Amaryllis did not seek the Earl of Lockhart's company. Moreover, she found him to be a toad, a viper and all manner of reptilian creatures.

His lips twitched and an inappropriate desire to laugh bubbled upward. He tamped it down. 'Whatever the earl's character, your latest exploit was hardly safe, appropriate or effective.'

'I had to come. Don't you know what would happ—?'

'Yes, I do. But do you?' He stepped to her, so close he smelled her scent and heard the inhalation of her breath. 'What if he had come and I had not? Did you think about your own reputation? Your own safety? Did you confide in me or Lady Wyburn? No, you acted with blind arrogance. You decided that you, a twenty-year-old innocent, could handle this situation alone.'

'Twenty-one.' Rilla bit her lip. Suspicious moisture shone on the sweep of her lashes.

His anger lessened. A lone tear trickled down

her cheek. Ridiculously, his hand itched to soothe the very hurt he'd caused.

'Here.' He thrust a handkerchief at her. 'No need to cry.'

'I'm not,' she said, blowing her nose loudly, which made him want to laugh again.

Heaven help him, he belonged in Bedlam. He'd never experienced such emotional extremes. Nor did he like it.

'You see,' Rilla continued, her words punctuated by an occasional sniff, 'Lady Wyburn might not like the earl, but she fails to properly discourage Imogene. And you…well, I didn't want to give you an opportunity to think worse of us.'

'You didn't trust me, you mean.' That hurt. A lot.

'I wanted to protect Imogene. Besides, you've been closeted in that card room since your arrival. I could hardly invade that masculine domain.'

'You didn't think to speak to your sister?'

'Indeed, I would have,' Rilla admitted, looking down at her hands. 'Except it seems that my dislike of the earl only makes her the more determined. Truthfully, that was part of my plan. I hoped he might be angry with me and that Imogene would see him for what he is. He has a wicked temper. Of course, she should know that from our school days, but she was young and he only took lessons with us a few summers.'

Paul watched her throughout this speech. The woman was defiant vulnerability. Her eyes shone with tears and anger; her chin trembled but was still held at a defiant angle, and those lips...

'Well, Miss Gibson,' he said briskly, 'it appears neither party has ventured out, or we've frightened them away. I suggest we move indoors. I will look into this matter, and you need worry no more.' He crumpled the paper in his fist.

'You'll not duel him or do anything foolish?'

'Concerned for my welfare?' he mocked, yet he was aware of a pleasant warmth at the thought.

'I would not wish anyone to be hurt on my own or my sister's account. Lady Wyburn cares for you very much.'

The breeze gusted and Rilla rubbed her arms. She was cold; he could see her nipples outlined against the fabric's sheen and her skin prickled with goosebumps.

'I would have helped you,' he said, very gently touching his thumb to her cheek to wipe away a tear. 'Without judgement.'

'I know,' she said with a quick intake of breath.

He liked that soft gasp. His hand trailed along the contours of her chin. A tendril of red hair fluttered against her cheek. He reached for it, letting its silkiness curl about his finger. She bit her lip. He tucked the curl behind her ear and heard again that quick gasp of surprise.

And pleasure.

They stood so close he could feel her body's warmth and the movement of her ribcage with her breath.

From inside, the strains of a waltz could be heard...subtle ghostly music.

He bowed. 'May I have the honour, Miss Gibson?'

'Pardon?'

'Dance? I heard tell the orchestra is much improved over my stepmother's warble.'

'I—' She broke off.

'I'll take that as a yes.'

Hesitantly, she placed her hand in his and looked up, her eyes luminous in the moonlight.

The moment reminded him of that morning, only more perfect.

A gold locket nestled between her breasts, glinting softly. Silver light caught the iridescent threads of her gown, making her shimmer like a water nymph.

The cloth rustled. He heard the shuffle of her slippered feet and felt her legs nudge his own. Her body swayed into him.

There was a rhythmic quality to her movement. No counting this time, rather a yielding to the music and to the sensuality of the moment.

*She'd be like that in bed.* The thought flashed unbidden. He pulled her closer. She smelled of lemons.

For a man who seldom relaxed, he felt a peculiar easing of his muscles, a feeling of comfort and of belonging.

When the music ceased, Paul did not step away. Instead, his arms tightened. She did not resist.

Slowly, he tilted her chin, rubbing his thumb along the line of her jaw. He heard that quick pant. Her lips parted.

Groaning, he leaned into her and caught her lips. He felt her startle, her muscles tautening. He gentled his touch, playing with her lips, nibbling until she swayed into him in instinctive surrender. Her mouth opened.

All restraint slipped.

He wanted her. Christ, he wanted her.

Her hand lifted. Tentatively, she ran her finger across his cheek and into his hair. With a wonderful, intuitive boldness, she arched towards him. He felt the swell of her breasts pressed against his chest.

His body hardened.

All coherent thought scattered. Desire invaded, driving and propelling. His blood roared. Paul wanted this woman. He wanted her naked. He wanted her naked and beneath him…on Lady Swinton's flagstones.

'Lockhart, I cannot see what is so extraordinary about the sky that you must persuade us into the chill. Why, the moon's half-obscured with cloud.' The strident tone shattered the night's stillness, loud as a duellist's fire at dawn.

Paul pushed Rilla from him. She gave a choked cry.

'Oh, my!' a woman said. The prim footsteps stopped.

Calming his own expression, Paul turned. Lady

Swinton stood mere feet away, flanked by Lady Anton and Jack St John, Earl of Lockhart.

'Good evening,' Paul said with a languid bow.

'Oh, my,' Lady Anton repeated. Her mouth still hung open, but the shock had passed and her eyes sparkled. 'Can it be? Viscount Wyburn and the elder Miss Gibson!'

'Dear ladies.' Paul forced his lips to smile. 'I am embarrassed. The emotions of the moment, don't you know? Please, be the first to congratulate me. Miss Gibson has just paid me the honour, the very great honour, of accepting my hand in marriage.'

# Chapter Eight

Rilla gulped.

For a second the words made no sense as though her brain needed time to piece them together as one might a jigsaw.

'I—'

Paul's glare silenced her words. Rilla bit her lip. It still tingled from his kiss. Her legs felt wobbly and she wished the earth would swallow her into its dark depths.

It didn't. She remained, flushed, flustered and furious, under the quizzical eyes of Ladies Anton and Swinton. She refused to even meet Jack's gaze and studied instead the neat, interlocking pattern of Lady Swinton's paving stones.

'What felicitous news,' Jack said.

Rilla cringed. The smug velvet of his tone grated, like nails on a chalkboard. She glanced up and saw the curve of his too-pink lips.

At that moment, Lady Wyburn stepped on to the terrace.

'The very lady!' Paul raised his voice. 'Step-mother, congratulate us. Miss Gibson has said yes to my proposal of marriage.'

If Lady Wyburn was surprised, Rilla could detect no evidence of it. Her brows did not rise, nor did her mouth gape. Instead she swept forward with a rustle of taffeta.

'Darling, I'm so happy for you, both of you. You're exactly what I would want for a daughter.' She grasped Rilla's hand.

Lady Wyburn's skin felt warm, or perhaps it was that Rilla's hand had turned to ice.

'Shall we announce the glad tidings tonight?' Lady Swinton asked.

'No!' Rilla said. The word blasted out with such vehemence that everyone's gaze swivelled to her like the mobile eyes of marionettes.

'But why? You should be delighted to share such news,' Lady Swinton's voice squeaked. She was a stout woman and the sound was incongruous with her size.

Rilla wanted to giggle.

'Delighted. We both are,' Paul spoke easily. 'I would love to make the announcement above all things, but we cannot. I have a confession.'

Everyone leaned closer. Rilla heard their eager indrawn breaths. She found herself also waiting with peculiar detachment, curious about the next development, as though anticipating another act in a play.

'You see,' Paul said. 'I have been precipitous. The moment. The beauty of the ball. Your lovely romantic decor, dear Lady Swinton, quite over-came me. But I haven't yet consulted with Miss Gibson's father. Sir George resides in the country and I must talk to him before making any public announcement.'

She watched their faces. Yes, he had bamboo-zled them all, even Lady Swinton.

'Besides, it appears that dear Rilla is quite un-done from the excitement,' Lady Wyburn said. 'And chilled. So inconsiderate of you to drag her to the terrace, dear.'

'Correct as always, Stepmother. Let us return to the ballroom. We will leave shortly.'

Between them, Paul and his stepmother engi-neered the party back through the French doors. For a second, Rilla froze, blinking, as the ball-room seemingly surged towards them, all colour, heat and chatter.

'Rilla, dear, do thank Lady Swinton for a lovely time,' Lady Wyburn prompted.

'Thank you. It was lovely. The decorations are beautiful,' Rilla said.

'You're sure you must go?'

'Afraid so. Come, dear,' Lady Wyburn said.

Rilla stepped forward and blinked, unable to take in the whole of the scene, but rather seeing bits and pieces, disjointed blobs and twirling figures.

Despite the firm touch of Lady Wyburn's hand,

she moved awkwardly, her knees wobbling as though inclined to bend backward.

The bright colours of the ballroom swam as in a heat haze.

'Don't you dare swoon,' Lady Wyburn muttered, so close to her ear that Rilla could feel the moist warmth of her breath. 'You're made of sterner stuff. You do not want to be like the Misses Eggerton. They always fainted in a most inconvenient manner.'

Another giggle effervesced. Perhaps this whole nightmarish episode was a dream, or the product of too much wine. Although surely one would never dream about fainting 'Eggertons'.

And how exactly did one faint in a *convenient* manner?

In the entrance hall, their appearance caused a buzz of activity. The viscount, his countenance shuttered and his lips tight, shot out instructions with artillery-fire rapidity.

Liveried footmen hurried to fetch Rilla and Lady Wyburn's cloaks, their carriage and Imogene.

Rilla watched this flurry of activity with detached interest.

Cause and effect.

This was a classic case of cause and effect. She had kissed the viscount, setting in motion this string of events, minute details entangled within the catastrophic.

Now this *thing* had its own momentum. Like her waterwheel.

She put on her wrap. Lady Wyburn helped her with the clasp. Paul took her arm and they walked outside.

Everything was quiet. It seemed miraculous, this peace, as though she'd expected the cosmos to reflect her distress.

Instead, moonlight glistened on the rounded cobbles and a breeze made the London air almost fresh. She could smell soil, June rain and flowers.

The distant strains of the orchestra formed a subtle fairy backdrop, mingling with the prosaic rap of the footman's feet and the stamp of horses' hooves.

The coach door creaked as it opened. It needed oil. She had a can that the blacksmith had given her for use on her waterwheel. Perhaps she should offer it to the footman upon her return.

Rilla clambered inside. She could still smell Imogene's perfume, gardenias, lingering from their arrival.

'Goodbye,' Paul said, leaning in. 'I will find your sister and pay my respects tomorrow morning. Then we can discuss matters more fully.'

'Yes.' Rilla did not look at him, studying instead the tartan pattern of the travelling rug.

Imogene arrived moments later. A frown creased her forehead as she climbed into the coach.

'Whatever has occurred?' she asked, her voice sharp. 'You look dreadful. Did you have—I mean, was it—?'

Rilla said nothing. The words seemed too hard

to find. She wished Imogene wouldn't talk so loud. Her head hurt.

'Lady Wyburn, what has happened?' Imogene asked, her voice threaded with worry.

'I'm not entirely certain, but Rilla is apparently planning to marry,' Lady Wyburn said.

Imogene looked stunned. Her mouth fell open and she made a sharp exhalation as though winded.

'Do get in and close the door, dear,' Lady Wyburn said. 'You're creating a dreadful draught.'

'But she can't and who? Who is she planning to marry?' Imogene at last managed to ask, sitting with less than her usual grace.

'My stepson. Paul Lindsey, Viscount Wyburn.'

Imogene gaped. Rilla wanted to giggle. Or cry. Or both.

Lady Wyburn tapped the roof, and the coach rolled forward.

'The viscount—*proposed*—and…and you accepted!' Imogene stated, speaking disjointedly. 'But…but you've always said— And…and do you even like him?'

'I think we will leave questions until later,' Lady Wyburn announced. 'And do close your mouth, Imogene, dear. And stop stammering. I recall a young lady from my own come-out who tended to do so when overly excited.'

'Maybe he did not mean it.' Rilla spoke suddenly from her place huddled within the corner of the carriage.

'He is a man of honour. He would never back down from such an offer,' Lady Wyburn said.

'Oh dear.' Rilla shivered, although it was not cold.

'You poor child, let's wrap that rug around you.' Lady Wyburn leaned forward and unfolded the travelling blanket.

It smelled musty and had the itchy texture of wool. Still, its warmth comforted.

Tears stung. Rilla swallowed with a painful gulp. 'I'm so sorry, Lady Wyburn. I should not have gone out on the terrace.'

'The terrace? You were with him on the terrace?' Imogene said.

'Yes.'

'But what were you doing on the terrace?'

Rilla made no answer.

'I believe,' Lady Wyburn said helpfully, 'she was kissing the viscount.'

Rilla slept little that night, but lay curled upon herself, hands to her eyes as though to press out the whirl of images.

But she could not extinguish the memories of the viscount's kisses, the touch of his hands and, more shocking, the way her own fingers had twisted into his hair, pulling him closer. And then there was the feel of him—the strong, hard bulk of him against her and those peculiar, wonderful, unfamiliar sensations at the touch of his lips—

Followed by Lady Swinton's startled predatory eyes.

How could she have been so foolish? She'd accused her sister of stupidity and had herself played the fool.

Rilla tossed to the other side of her bed, her long legs mired in the sheets. Thoughts hammered at her, relentless as a smithy shoeing a horse. Groaning, she got up and padded across the braided rug to the window. It was dark outside. She leaned her forehead to the pane.

Had Paul's offer of marriage been serious? Or a ruse to quiet the meddlesome ladies' tongues?

*He is a man of honour. He would never back down from such an offer.*

'But I *can't* marry him. I don't love him. I can't marry anyone.' The thing was preposterous. They did not like each other. He looked at her with empty eyes.

Not always. Sometimes, flames banked and smouldered.

Except desire was not love.

Besides, to marry anyone would make her forever vulnerable. A husband would have the legal right to declare her mad. And a man of Wyburn's power and position would never be refused.

Her stomach tightened with sick nausea. She remembered her mother's worried countenance. Instinctively her hand touched her locket. She opened it, running her fingers against the worn gold.

When she had been a little girl, Rilla had

dreamed of marriage. Hers would be one of love and trust, she'd thought, like her parents.

Then a myriad of little things happened. When she was six, she'd foretold a coming storm. When she was seven she'd saved the cat. When she was eight, she'd known the village blacksmith had died before anyone had even found his slumped form.

And then, there was Sophie—the before and after of her life.

And from that moment, people had looked at Rilla with curiosity mixed with fear.

And her mother had stated that, as long as she experienced such moments, she must not marry.

Rilla twisted the gold chain about her neck. 'I wish someone could love the whole of me.'

A little before dawn, Rilla heard a tap at the door. She jumped, but it was only Heloise.

'I knew you'd be up, *mademoiselle*. I heard you moving around so I thought I might as well get you dressed.' As always Heloise spoke briskly, but her face had softened and her beetle-black eyes were warm.

Her French accent had also slipped, Rilla noted, much as an accident victim might notice an inconsequential detail in the street. Heloise had had such lapses before.

'Thank you,' Rilla said, suddenly glad for the presence of another human.

'Indeed, it is good I came. Wandering around in

your nightdress, you'll catch your death.' Heloise made a comforting tutting noise.

Without waiting for a response, she opened the closet door. 'This blue morning gown would be quite suitable, I think.'

Suitable—suitable for what? Did fallen women have a dress code—blue in the mornings, scarlet at night?

'That should be fine,' Rilla acquiesced.

Heloise eyed her charge, perhaps noting the pale face or the workings of her mouth. 'We all make mistakes, *mademoiselle*. And remember, you're a lady through and through. Those snooty dowagers are not a patch on yourself, if I may say so.'

Rilla smiled and blinked, conscious of her stinging eyes. 'And those snooty French maids aren't a patch on you either, if I may say so.'

'You know? That I am not from France?'

Rilla saw worry flicker across Heloise's face and her brows draw together.

'Yes,' she said gently, 'but I won't tell a soul. Anyone who can make my hair behave is a gem, regardless of nationality.'

'Quite true, I have a good hand with hair, but people do take such stock in a French maid.'

'I take stock in having a true friend.'

'I am that, miss. I am that. It'll all work out. It will all come out in the wash, as my sainted mother used to say. She was half-French, you know. Taught me the language at her knee. Well, enough to get by, plus put on the accent now and then. Now, let us do something with that hair. A veritable rats' nest!' Heloise eyed the dishevelled locks, her lips pursed in disapproval.

'You'll work wonders.'

'I will have to. Now sit still!'

Breakfast proved a gloomy affair.

It was served, as always, in the morning room. Rilla always found this chamber dark, the small windows faced north and the walls were painted an unpleasant dull shade of beige. It didn't even have mirrors to lighten the gloom.

Of course, a fire flickered, but the hearth's vastness made the blaze a small thing within a dark hole.

Lady Wyburn was not yet up, but Imogene sat at the table. Plates of bacon, fried eggs, toast and coffee filled the sideboard. The air smelled of bacon which Rilla normally liked, but today it made her stomach squeeze unpleasantly.

Rilla took coffee and dry toast and sat opposite her sister. Her chair scraped against the hardwood floor, loud in the silence.

Imogene shifted, glancing in Rilla's direction before returning her gaze to her egg yolk.

'Yes?' Rilla said.

'What?'

'I know you're dying to ask me about last night.' Anything to break the silence.

'All right,' Imogene said. 'So what happened? You've always said you'll never marry and the next thing I know you're engaged and kissing someone you don't even like. And after lecturing me about dancing twice with Jack only a few days ago.'

Rilla put her cup down with a clatter. 'If you'd listened to me, I wouldn't have been kissing anyone.'

'What?' Imogene leaned forward, her eyebrows drawn with sudden anger. 'What have I to do with this?'

'You were going to meet Lockhart.'

'Jack? I wasn't. Why would you think that?'

'I found his note. Besides, you've let him run after you like a—a pet rat,' Rilla said, taking a gulp of coffee so quickly it scalded her tongue.

'I never got a note.'

'Well, I found a note and it was opened. He invited you to meet him on the terrace.'

'But I never read it. Besides, I wouldn't meet him anywhere. He's disagreeable.' Imogene wrinkled her nose.

'You think he's disagreeable? Why didn't you say so? And why have you been so friendly?'

Imogene shrugged, flushing prettily. 'Maybe because you've been so bossy and big sisterly.'

'You encouraged him just to irritate me?'

'No...' Imogene paused, rubbing her finger against the edge of her plate. When she spoke again her tone had dropped, her cheeks flushing. 'I had a plan. I hoped that if he really liked me, he'd forgive Father his debt.'

'You know about that?'

'Yes.' Imogene poked at the yellow yoke, her voice so low that Rilla had to lean forward to hear her.

'You didn't tell me,' Rilla said.

'And you didn't tell me.'

*True.* 'So I worried that he'd toy with you, while you were, in fact, toying with him.' Rilla's lips twisted. 'I wish you'd told me.'

'I think I didn't because I knew it was foolish and conceited on my part.'

Rilla reached across the table to take her sister's hand. Imogene's palm felt warm from the coffee cup she had been holding. 'I think I understand why you would.'

Rilla did not have the sort of beauty that brought men to their knees, but she could understand wanting to use that power, any power, against Jack St John.

'You're not angry?'

'I should have confided in you more.'

The sisters fell silent, but it was no longer uncomfortable.

'The viscount will come round this morning?' Imogene asked at last.

'He said so.'

'He'll repeat his proposal.'

'Probably,' Rilla said.

'What will you do?'

'I can't marry him. I'll have to think of some reason or excuse—'

*No. Help him.*

Rilla startled. The words were so loud that she turned quickly, staring wildly about the empty room.

Nothing. The room was deserted save for her sister and the flickering flames within the dark hearth.

'What?' Imogene asked.

Before Rilla could answer, the door grated against the wood flooring and Merryweather stepped forward and cleared his throat.

'Excuse me, Miss Gibson. Viscount Wyburn has arrived.'

# Chapter Nine

Paul turned as soon as he heard Rilla's footstep. She stood an irritating few feet across the threshold, as though poised to run.

'Good morning, Miss Gibson. I thought it best if we had the opportunity to talk in a civilised manner.'

'Indeed. Please take a seat,' she said and claimed a place on Lady Wyburn's sofa.

Although pale, she seemed calm enough and not likely to dissolve into vapours.

Paul sat in the chair opposite. 'I must reassure you. My proposal last night was serious. I have ruined your reputation and will honour my obligations.'

He noted no easing of her posture. Instead, she sat ramrod stiff, her chin lifted, as though in defiance.

'That won't be necessary,' she said.

'Pardon?'

'You need not make an offer on my account.'

'I need to if we wish to salvage your reputation.'

'I can return home. My father would never turn me away and I enjoy country life. I'll not miss all the balls and fuss, so neither of us need make this sacrifice.' Her words came out in a hurried rush.

'Sacrifice? I didn't imagine marriage to me would be so abhorrent.'

Good lord, he'd spent the night coming to terms with the necessity of this marriage and she thought to refuse.

'I—um…' She paused, looking down at her hands. 'I don't actually think I am the marrying kind.'

'Every woman is the marrying kind.'

'It is not my aim.'

'Then you are unusual.'

She smiled a little wanly, but with a glint of genuine amusement. 'That is an established fact, my lord.'

*Good Lord.* He didn't know whether to be angry, amused, insulted or impressed. For a decade, women had thrust themselves or their daughters at him, but this girl, without money or lineage, seemed inured to his title and money.

'Don't tell me you're still dreaming of true love. Believe me, our marriage will be happier without it.'

'But, Paul—'

He was startled at her use of his first name. He saw her flush. 'Yes?'

'You cannot wish to marry me. You must hope to care for a wife more than you do me.'

He laughed, aware of both bitterness and a less familiar tenderness at her concern.

The bitterness won out.

'You need have no worry on my behalf,' he said. 'For me, love has no part in marriage.'

He had expected some response, but Rilla said nothing. Indeed, she appeared almost distracted, as though listening for someone or something.

'Miss Gibson?' He shifted, conscious of the taut-ened muscles within his shoulders.

She did not answer.

'Miss Gibson,' he repeated more loudly.

She looked at him now, her eyes widening as though she had momentarily forgotten his pres-ence. Her hands had balled into fists and he saw the movement of her throat as she swallowed.

'I'm sorry. I thought—I mean, I—'

He went to sit beside her, gentling his tone. 'Sorry. I was too blunt. I forget what a shock this has been. I cannot promise love, but I can promise you respect and consideration.'

She nodded.

'And if we do not marry the scandal will hurt more than only you.'

'I know that too,' Rilla replied. 'Imogene is the only reason I'd consider this marriage.'

She spoke with honesty. He should, he sup-posed, be relieved that she was not pining with unrequited love.

He wasn't. Instead he felt a contradictory need

to break through her defences, to prove that she was not as inured to him as her words suggested.

He took her hand, laying it in his own. He ran his fingers across her palm, tracing her fingers and touching the soft, white skin at her wrist. Gently, he cupped her chin with his other hand. She licked her lips. He heard her whispered gasp and felt her lean into him.

He loved that gasp.

And hated his own reaction to it.

He put down her hand and stood.

'I will leave you to consider your options and return tomorrow,' he said, abruptly.

Bowing, he left the room.

The door closed and he was gone. Rilla's breath left her body in a rush of spent air. She heard the click of his boots, his careless greeting to a footman, and finally the solid bang of the front door.

Then silence. Blessed silence.

Her breath came unevenly and her fingers plucked at a loose thread on her dress. She allowed their movement, watching idly as she picked at the cotton, pulling, twisting, winding.

Even the room seemed different, as though, once stripped of his personality, it lacked life or colour—a painting without red.

She did not doubt he was serious in his proposal. He was a man of honour. And, she was too honest to deny that his closeness—his very proximity—made her heart beat more quickly. Even now, in the harsh light of morning, she could not banish thoughts of the night before, of his lips against her own, both gentle and demanding.

A part of her wished she could accept. He excited her mind…and her body.

Such a marriage would protect her from scandal and, more importantly, protect Imogene…

Even as a child, Imogene had designed wedding dresses and penned ink-stained invitations. Imogene wanted marriage and social status above all things. Rilla had promised their dying mother that she would take care of her sister.

Any scandal would hurt Imogene as well as herself, but as Paul's wife she could help Imogene, protect her.

Unless, of course, she lost her reason.

The door opened. Rilla jumped as Merryweather entered. 'Lady Julie St John has come to call. Shall I say you are indisposed, miss?'

Before Rilla could speak, Julie rushed forward. She wore a pink bonnet of a stiff, starched material. Her face was flushed and she smelled of perfume too heavily applied.

'I'm sure I'm the very last person you want to see, but I had to come.' She grasped Rilla's hands in her own. The palms of her gloves were cool and still damp from the outside.

'Of course I want to see you.' Rilla made an unsuccessful attempt at heartiness.

'You won't when I tell you. That's what I came to say. I had to explain.'

'Explain?' Rilla asked.

Merryweather cleared his throat.

'Oh, yes.' She turned to the butler. 'Bring us coffee, please, Merryweather.'

The second the door closed, Julie spoke with breathless speed. 'It's Jack, you see.'

Rilla started. 'Jack? What about him?'

Briefly, she remembered the man's smile last night and the smug velvet of his tone.

'I overheard him talking to Mr Conway. I couldn't sleep, so I left my room to go to the library. That's when I heard them, in the study.'

'And?'

'I'm so ashamed—' Julie removed her headgear with distracted, agitated movements.

'Julie, please, just tell me.'

Julie sat without grace, throwing herself into the chair. 'Jack positively gloated. It seems Mr Conway now owes him a considerable sum because Wyburn has been forced to propose. They had a wager and Jack trapped you both.'

'What? How?'

'Originally, they had bet that Jack would convince Imogene to say she would run away with him, but Lord Wyburn heard about this and put a stop to it. Except then they changed the bet and wagered on Wyburn himself.'

'But that doesn't make any sense. I did not speak to Jack last night until…well…on the terrace.'

'You found a note?'

'Yes, from Jack—addressed to Imogene.'

'It was fake. Jack intended for you to find it. Then he made certain that the viscount overheard plans for an assignation. Of course, he knew Wyburn would assume he was meeting your sister and dash off to defend her honour.'

Rilla groaned. 'We walked into his trap.'

'Yes, he claimed himself delighted. He contrived to get you both outside. I suppose he hoped that the moon...' Julie paused and pulled off her gloves.

'Odious...toad!' Rilla stood and paced the length of the carpet, no longer able to remain still.

It was not only that he had meddled in her life, but that he had known or guessed her attraction to Paul. That was a secret. She had a deeply private nature and to know that something she was not ready to admit even to herself was known to that man...

She crossed her arms, hunching her shoulders.

'I am ashamed to call him brother. Truly, I am. This is worse than all his debts. If I could do anything—'

Rilla again paced the room, stopping in front of the empty hearth. 'There is nothing you can do.'

'I'm sorry.'

'It is not your fault,' Rilla said. 'I do not blame you.'

The silence stretched between them.

'He will offer, I am sure,' Julie said.

'He already has.'

'Then perhaps things are not all bad?' Julie asked, her voice rising with tentative hopefulness.

'No.' Rilla stood with her back to Julie.

'He is titled, rich and handsome,' Julie said.

Rilla heard the creak of the horsehair cushioning as Julie stood up, crossing to her. 'I know,' she said.

'How do you feel about him?'

Rilla shrugged, her gaze fixed on the darkness of the hearth. She should have ordered a fire. 'He is not the sort of man I should love.'

And then, from the inner recesses of mind and heart, Rilla realised with terrible certainty that she *could* love him.

And that frightened her more than all the rest.

Rilla could neither read nor sew that afternoon, but sat in Lady Wyburn's drawing room with nerves taut as whippets on race day. She'd declined an invitation to go shopping with Lady Wyburn and Imogene, but now she wished she had taken up the opportunity for distraction.

Her foot tapped, the motion vibrating into her leg and torso. Her thoughts circled.

If she refused the viscount, she brought scandal on herself and Imogene.

If she accepted, she'd spend a lifetime with a man who, for whatever reason, appeared to bring out that part of herself she most wanted to forget, ignore and destroy. As husband he would have every legal right to commit her to an asylum.

Moreover, if he felt such a decision right, he would put it into action with single-minded purpose.

Rilla stood. She pushed back the curtains and peered through the window, her eyes sore from her sleepless night.

A curricle careened around the corner, pulled by a pair of spirited greys. The animals moved dangerously fast, snorting and shaking their heads against the reins as the whip nipped their flanks.

Rilla squinted then, discerning the crest, she drew instinctively back, pushing the curtains into place.

Had he not done enough? Must he now gloat? Her jaw clenched. She rubbed damp palms against her skirt.

Merryweather was coming. She heard his footsteps in the passageway outside and the creak of the door as it opened.

'The Earl of Lockhart,' he intoned, disapproval dripping from his every syllable.

Without waiting to be announced, Jack sauntered into the room, flashing that wide, white smile.

'Will you be wanting coffee, miss?' Merryweather asked.

'No. The earl will not be staying.'

'Very good, miss.' Merryweather permitted himself a half-smile and retreated from the room.

'No refreshment?' Jack said. 'Decidedly unfriendly to an old neighbour, what? I'm sure Lady Wyburn would not condone such inhospitality.' He sat even though she still stood, thrusting his feet towards the fire.

'Unfriendly? You should be thankful I do no worse.' Her voice trembled and her jaw felt tight with anger.

'Lud, I quake within my Hessians.' He smiled and re-crossed his feet, eyeing his boots' polish with obvious satisfaction.

'I wonder you dare show your face, given your earlier villainy.'

'I am a villain now! What heady melodrama, you should take it to the stage. Or write one of those novellas you women adore.'

'It is you who write lies. I stick to the truth.'

'How frightfully dull. I see Julie was right. You have flown into the boughs. You know you really should be thanking me on bended knee. A delectable spectacle.' He lifted an eyebrow provocatively.

'Thank you?! You interfered with my life and placed me in the middle of a scandal.'

'My dear girl, I have done you no harm and much good. The viscount is bound to offer for you and it will all work out wonderfully as long as you are not too missish and refuse.' He leaned forward. 'My sister thinks that is a possibility.'

'My response is absolutely none of your business.'

'But it is. Truth to tell, I find myself a trifle short of the ready and happened to recollect that your dear father owes me a significant sum, what?' He looked at her from under hooded lids.

'My father? But I thought—I mean, you…he… made an agreement. He paid you a part of the sum and you agreed to wait until his translations were finished and Marianne and Gilbertina calved.'

'Ah, yes, your fruitful livestock,' Jack drawled. 'I was feeling generous that day. But calving can go awry. Not a sure thing, don't you know. Besides, I find it inconvenient to wait for the forces of nature.'

'It would be dishonourable to renege. You'll have to wait.'

Jack laughed. 'My dear girl, are you still under the erroneous impression that I care for honour?'

'But my father can't—he doesn't have the funds.'

'I will concede one cannot get blood from a stone—to be biblical. But I do not fancy waiting. Like you, patience is not one of my virtues.'

'I did not know you had virtues.'

'So unkind.' He took a pinch of snuff and carefully returned the case to his pocket. 'But let me be direct. I have done you a favour and I must request one in return.'

'A favour?' Rilla spat out the words.

'Thanks to my efforts you are in the position to make a most advantageous match—'

'One I do not want.'

'Unfortunate, but immaterial.' He stood and took a step towards her. 'Upon your fortuitous marriage, I'm certain you can convince your beloved to pay off your father's debts and, if he is generous with his pin money, float me a loan now and then.'

'I would rather give money to a flea!'

'No doubt. But that insect would not be in the happy position to make use of the viscount's guineas. Nor would it have certain information about your father or yourself.'

'Information? What information? My father's an open book and the only scandalous thing I've done is now brandished among the *ton*.'

'Indeed, you have led an entirely blameless existence. Indeed, it could be described as a helpful existence in many respects. One might even say you have a special way of being *helpful*.' His voice caressed that last word. He took another step closer and smiled.

She hated that smile. She hated the full, unnatural redness of his lips. She hated the even, white teeth.

She stepped back towards the hearth and felt the heat through the cloth of her skirt. Her hand reached for the mantel, tightening about the marble so that the edge bit at her flesh. 'I won't marry Paul for money.'

'"Paul", is it? How deliciously cosy. But this puritanical bent is inconvenient. I really don't know if your poor father will be comfortable in debtors' prison.'

'You wouldn't.' His breath smelled of alcohol and she fought the impulse to step back again, fearing she would set her skirts alight. 'You're a toad, a snake without morals or conscience.'

He yawned. 'I believe I heard those particular descriptions in your schoolgirl years. I had hoped you'd become more sophisticated with time. Of course, there is hope yet. Bedlam may add to your vocabulary.'

'Bedlam.' She breathed the word, releasing the mantel so that her hand fell against her skirts with a soft thwack. 'What do you mean?'

He smiled.

'Only, my dear, that I hope you will marry the viscount with all possible dispatch.'

# *Chapter Ten*

Rilla sank into an armchair the second the door shut behind him. She had no choice. She could not have stood a second longer. Her legs shook. Her heart pounded. Bile rose to throat.

Jack had always scared her. There was a ruthlessness about him. She remembered how he'd kicked his own dog and smiled at its yelps and how he'd thrown Julie's kitten into the well, laughing at her tears.

But now Rilla's terror trebled like yeast rising.

*One might even say you have a special way of being helpful. Of course, Bedlam may add to your vocabulary. Bedlam. Bedlam. Bedlam.*

The word thumped through her brain like a savage's drum.

There'd been gossip in the village after she'd found Sophie. And there had been other smaller incidents. Had Jack heard of them? Did he somehow know that she was still plagued with her 'moments', visions and knowledge she did not want?

Nausea gripped her so virulent and sudden that she fled, stumbling up the stairs and through the corridor to her own quarters. She slammed the door and, crouching, vomited into the chamber pot.

She retched until her stomach was empty and, still shaking, leaned against her bed, wiping her mouth with her handkerchief.

It had been her mother's nightmare that someone would find out. And that this person should be Jack.

She cursed the man.

She cursed all men.

She cursed the vulnerability of her own mind. And the ludicrous fascinated attraction that the viscount held for her. Even more, she cursed that she should feel this ludicrous fascinated attraction with the very man who seemed most connected with her 'moments'—the very man she should avoid.

Pushing herself up from the floor, Rilla poured water into her tooth mug. The liquid splashed, splattering on to the polished wood of her dressing table. Her hand shook as she dabbed at the small puddle ineffectually with her handkerchief.

She must think...

Still shaky, Rilla went to her waterwheel. She touched its wooden frame, rubbing her finger against the grain.

If she chose not to marry Paul, Lockhart might put her father in prison and spread rumours about her own sanity. Imogene's chance of a happy marriage would be ruined.

If she chose to marry Paul, she would avoid scandal. She might save her father from imprisonment and help Imogene.

But she would still be vulnerable to the earl's blackmail. She would still be vulnerable to the vagaries of her own mind.

And she would have a husband—a husband who would have the power to declare her insane—just like her great-aunt.

She could not win.

Exhausted, she flung herself on to the spongy softness of her bed. The ceiling had been freshly painted with white paint and was thus without the hairline cracks which patterned her own ceiling.

For a long while she stared up at the white ceiling until her eyes smarted and then, at last, she dozed.

When she awoke, the warm light of late afternoon touched her room, forming weird elongated shadows. Strangely, the mind-boggling confusion had lessened, the whirling thoughts calmed and a peculiar tranquillity prevailed.

Rilla lay quite still.

She knew what she would do.


Paul strode into the drawing room next morning with an air of effortless elegance and masculine sophistication.

Rilla straightened, an instinctive response. He looked irritatingly at ease while her own heart thumped as though to escape her body.

'Good morning,' he said, making his bow. 'I trust you slept well.'

'Not very.' She managed a weak grin.

'Ah, that predilection for free speech.' His jaw loosened and she saw the merest hint of a smile.

He sat beside her on the low sofa. 'I will follow your example and also be blunt. Have you reconsidered my proposal?'

'Yes.' Rilla gulped, twisting at the corner of a cushion.

'And?'

'I will marry you. I mean...if the offer still stands.'

Emotion flickered briefly across his face before his usual implacable mask slid into place. 'I would be honoured to be your husband.'

*Husband.* Nervous tingles slithered down her back.

The grandfather clock ticked. She was conscious of the size of him, his proximity, the exhalation of his breath and the tangy scent of male cologne.

'Well, I—'

'I need to tell—'

They spoke at once and then stopped. 'Pray, after you,' he said.

'It is nothing. Please continue.'

'I was merely going to suggest that I give you this. I know it isn't customary, but I wanted to emphasise the seriousness of my intent.' He pulled out a velvet jewel case.

'Oh—'

He'd got her a ring—as though this betrothal was real. Although, of course, it was. Terribly real.

She extended her left hand.

The tiny hinges whined as he lifted the lid to show a glittering emerald. He took her hand. His fingers were warm, the touch gentle. Again, she felt that tingle, a *frisson* of awareness, excitement, now mixed with anticipation.

The ring slid into place.

'How did you know emeralds were my favourite?' She studied the jewel with its life and fire.

'Green's your colour. A diamond wouldn't do. It is too cold and impersonal.'

Something squeezed under her ribs. It touched her that he'd wanted to give her jewellery and had given its selection such thought. 'Thank you.'

'Thank the poor jeweller who I forced from his bed at an unearthly hour.'

'I thank you both. You look tired. You needn't have risen so early.' She reached, touching her hand to his cheek. The skin felt soft, but with a hint of stumble.

She felt his jerk of reaction.

He lifted his hand. For a moment, he hesitated as though uncertain. Then with a groan, he pulled her close and she felt a dizzying influx of sensation: his musky, masculine scent, the closeness of sculpted lips, the warm strength of his arms about her.

He caught her mouth.

Heat, instant and molten, surged. Instinctively,

she opened her lips to him. His tongue invaded, his hands winding through the thickness of her hair.

She could feel the ridged firmness of his chest as her body arched against him, the movement both innate and shocking.

His hands spanned her back, pulling her closer. She felt the warmth of his fingers through the flimsy cloth of her dress.

Her nipples hardened. As though recognising her need, his hands moved from her back, cupping her fullness, while his lips trailed kisses down her throat and to the base of her neck.

Then, with another groan, he almost pushed her from him. 'We can't,' he said, his breath ragged. 'I apologise.'

Her cheeks burned hot. 'I—it is all right,' she said with inherent honesty.

'It isn't. I lacked appropriate control.'

He walked to the windows as though needing to physically distance himself from her.

After a moment, he turned. 'Let us move on to more practical matters and discuss the wedding.'

'The wedding?'

'Yes, most women have filled their childhood with dreams about it.'

'I didn't. Except I do not want anything big. We don't have to have a big society do at St George's, do we?'

'I'd imagined you would want one.' His eyebrow quirked in surprise.

'Oh, no,' Rilla said. 'I'd much prefer something

quiet in the country. I mean, unless it's absolutely imperative that you marry with great fanfare, being a viscount.'

'Being a viscount means that very little is imperative,' he said wryly. 'Small is fine. However, we must make an announcement in *The Times*, given the situation. I will make the appropriate arrangements and speak to your father, as is proper.'

Rilla nodded. Somehow these practical details made everything seem firm and inevitable. More so even than the heavy emerald. Marriage was no longer an abstract. It was a concrete entity, a fact.

'It seems you've thought of everything,' she said.

'I hope so. A marriage is much the same as any other business arrangement. Success rests in the details. The only thing left to determine is the date. You're sure you wish it in the country?'

'Yes.'

'We'll say six weeks perhaps.'

'So soon?'

'There is little point in delay. It will stop the wagging tongues and help Imogene's prospects.'

'If it is to be done, it is best done quickly,' she quipped.

Paul seemed to view his upcoming nuptials as a general might a military campaign.

'Perhaps five Saturdays hence? July the eighteenth? I will arrange for the banns to be read.'

'That would be fine.'

'Good, I'll leave you to break the news to Lady

Wyburn.' He rose, a faint smile curving his well-sculpted lips.

Rilla grinned back. 'Leave me the hard work. You know a wedding in six weeks will flummox her. I'll be lucky if she does not have the vapours.'

'Hopefully, relief about my impending nuptials will mitigate her distress. She has been suggesting various spouses for the last umpteen Seasons. She worries I will die without an heir.' His smile widened just a little.

'Indeed, she did mutter dire predictions about some dreadful cousin awaiting your imminent demise.' Rilla rose also.

'In this he will be disappointed, as I am feeling much alive.' He bowed over Rilla's hand, touching it with his lips. His breath warmed and tickled her skin. It was a chaste caress, yet she felt a growing, spreading, tingling heat.

She lifted startled eyes.

'I'm afraid it is tradition that we go to my estate at Wyburn immediately after the wedding.'

'Wyburn?' She whispered the word as the image formed, eerily superimposed on Lady Wyburn's furnishing.

The lake appeared. She saw the shimmer of its water and the velvet-green lawns stretching towards rocky shores.

'It is beautiful,' she whispered.

'Pardon?'

She pulled herself back to the room. 'I've heard it is beautiful.'

He shrugged. 'I spend little time there, but the tenants will expect to see you.' He spoke in clipped tones as he stepped towards the door.

At the threshold, he turned back to her. 'You do me a great honour, Miss Gibson. And I will do my best to make your life pleasant and comfortable.'

'I hope to make you happy.'

His eyes gleamed with a bleak humour. 'We cannot expect the impossible.'


'It can't be done. It cannot be done,' Lady Wyburn repeated for what seemed to Rilla to be the thousandth time.

Rilla sighed. She sat with Imogene and Lady Wyburn in an open carriage, surrounded by the beauty of Hyde Park, now rich with summer green.

It might have been very nice without Lady Wyburn's one-track discourse and Rilla's unpleasant recognition that *she* was the subject of speculation by every passer-by.

It was a fashionable time for a promenade and they'd stopped frequently to accept well wishes. Rilla scarcely knew these people and hated the way they eyed her with open curiosity. Indeed, by the end of the half-hour, her teeth were on edge and her shoulders felt strung about her ears.

She had broken the news to Imogene and Lady Wyburn in the forenoon, shortly after Paul's departure.

It was now six.

In the intervening hours, Lady Wyburn's emotions had veered from elation to irritation and now rising panic.

'There is Lord Alfred with Julie,' Imogene said, nodding to a high-drawn curricle pulled by matching greys. She winked at Rilla from under the brim of her bonnet. 'I wonder if they will make a match of it?'

Rilla smiled back her thanks. Such gossip was bound to distract their companion, if only briefly.

Diverted, Lady Wyburn looked towards the vehicle, bobbing her white fringed parasol in that direction. 'He is eminently better than Lady Lockhart deserves given the way she dresses the poor girl. Certain people should not wear ruffles, at least not in pink or in such quantity. But back to the subject at hand. The man is not sensible.'

'I'm sure Lord Alfred will gain sense when he is less concerned about his ties,' Rilla said and dipped her own parasol in her friend's direction.

'I am not talking about Lord Alfred and well you know it, young lady,' Lady Wyburn said with severity, her soft wrinkled face drawn into a frown. 'How does Paul expect us to pull together a wedding in six weeks? Six weeks!'

'We are only planning a small event.'

'Which is not sensible either. Oh, there is Lady Pettigrew with her lapdog. Did you know that she gives him sweetmeats every morning and then wonders why he is flatulent all afternoon, although it is hardly a fit subject for discussion.'

Lady Wyburn again nodded and waved her parasol towards a high-sprung phaeton moving with a brisk *clip-clop* of hooves and whizzing wheels.

'And what does he know of weddings! A man!'

'I would have it done with, as well,' Rilla said.

'"Done with!" You're not having a tooth extracted. This is your wedding day. A woman has only one—God willing. It must be special and wonderful and beautiful.'

'I hope it will be, but...' Rilla paused, looking past the carriages towards the glistening silver ribbon of the Serpentine River. 'But we're not attached to each other. It would be foolish to pretend the sentiment.'

'Pish-posh. There is definitely something between you. The air fairly sizzles. Besides, the *ton* never marry for love. Why, if that stopped every bride from traipsing down the aisle bedecked with jewels and flowers, St George's would be a desert. No, I mean, deserted, because you couldn't really have a desert in London as it is not sufficiently warm or dry. Look at Lord and Lady Chatterbox—'

'Chatterhelm,' Imogene amended.

Lady Wyburn nodded in the direction of a young gentleman and lady strolling along the footpath. 'He is in love with her land and she with his title. A match made in heaven. You're sure you would not like St George's? It really is quite small.'

'No, a simple country wedding.'

Lady Wyburn tut-tutted. 'It seems that you and my stepson have convinced yourselves this is in the nature of a business contract—which, if you ask me, is no way to start a marriage.'

'But very fashionable.'

'As though you give a fig for fashion. Have you thought whom you might invite?'

'The people I love best—you, Imogene, Father, Mrs Marriot and some of the villagers, the people I've known since childhood.'

Lady Wyburn rolled her eyes, but a smile softened her expression. 'Well, it's your wedding. What have you to say about this simple nonsense, Imogene?'

'Mother always said that it is useless to argue with Rilla once her mind is set. In general, I've found this to be true.'

Rilla met her sister's eyes and grinned.

'Your mother was a woman of some sense,' Lady Wyburn conceded.

'But you'll still help us? I have no idea what to do.'

'Of course.' Lady Wyburm beamed. 'I love a wedding. The dress is, naturally, the first priority. We'll go to Madame Aimee. She's incredibly busy and Paul will have to throw considerable blunt her way. The very least he can do. Such a lucky man to be marrying you. Not that he knows it. But he will. He will!'

Rilla's lips twitched. She strongly questioned whether the viscount would come to this conclusion, but she couldn't squash Lady Wyburn's enthusiasm. Instead she leaned over and touched her gloved hand. 'Thank you, for everything.'

'I am only glad I am guaranteed such a delightful daughter-in-law, if somewhat obstinate.'

In her enthusiasm, Lady Wyburn waved her parasol so energetically at a passing acquaintance that Rilla feared it would sail off over the Serpentine.

As promised, Paul had gone to Sir George Gibson and returned to London, reporting that good gentleman's baffled consent.

On hearing this, Rilla knew she must visit and explain the situation to her remaining parent. She'd tried to write but, other than a brief note of her intent, had managed nothing which had not ended crumpled and splattered with ink.

Besides, she needed to talk to him about his debt to Lockhart and she could only do this in person.

Therefore, three weeks before the wedding, Rilla, Heloise and the model butter churn travelled to Sir George's estate in the comfort of Lady Wyburn's well-sprung carriage. Her ladyship and Imogene would come later to make final arrangements and prepare for the wedding breakfast.

Despite the vehicle's luxury, the journey took for ever and Rilla knew she drove Heloise distracted as she squirmed, humming childhood ditties and fiddling so constantly with her cloak that the clasp almost broke.

As they turned on to the rutted drive, Rilla stilled and, holding her breath, pressed her face silently to the vibrating glass of the coach windows.

The pane was cold, damp with condensation and vibrated against her cheek as the wheels moved over the cobbles. Even the horses' hooves sounded impatient, their cadence quick as if eager to arrive.

And then as the vehicle swayed around the last bend, her home appeared    shabby and dear.

Rilla could not wait for the coachman to open the door or lower the steps. The second the vehicle stopped, she pushed wide the door and jumped into the freshness of the country air.

Home.

Everything smelled of grass and hay and horses. She took a huge breath before running across the drive, up the stone stairs and through the front door.

'Papa! Papa! I'm here! I'm here!'

The door banged against the inner wall as Rilla stood, blinking, her eyes adjusting to the hall's dim light.

The study door opened.

'Papa!' Rilla threw herself into her father's arms and held him tight, perhaps a little tighter than before, inhaling the familiar smoky scent of him.

He wore a nankeen jacket, the cloth rough against her cheek and chin.

'Oh, Papa, I'm glad to see you,' she whispered. 'I've missed you dreadfully. And Mrs Marriot.'

Extricating herself, she turned to the older

woman who had come from the kitchen, still in her apron and smelling of cinnamon.

'Truly I am glad to see you both. I've missed everything: this house, the cows and even Thomas.'

Smiling gruffly, her father pulled out a kerchief. 'Never heard of a London beauty pining for a cow. But the house has seemed a tad quiet. You have a way of filling a place. Come into my study.'

Rilla followed him. The room was unchanged. The grandfather clock still ticked its rhythmic count of time. Sly sunbeams played in the dust on her father's desk, the shabby couch sagged, books were heaped in haphazard piles and papers littered the floor.

Doubtless Mrs Marriot would clean on Friday, her dusting day, and Father would spend the weekend cursing that everything had moved and he could find nothing.

Rilla sighed. It seemed wrong that this world should remain unaltered while her life had been turned upside down and shaken like a baby's rattle.

Following Sir George's distracted wave, she sat in an armchair beside the fire while he made himself comfortable in the chair opposite. He moved, she thought, with a slowness she had not noticed previous. His joints cricked and he wheezed as though short of breath.

'Had a visit from that young viscount the other week,' Sir George said, never one to beat about the bush.

'I know.'

'Was surprised by the content of our discussion. Quite surprised. I am not a man easily surprised.' He placed his fingers together to form a steeple and studied them with apparent intensity.

'I should have explained things to you better in my letters. But I couldn't find the words.'

'Ah, words. Our language is rich with 'em and yet I too am tongue-tied. Your mother would have known what to say, eh.' His gaze wandered to her mother's portrait over the mantel.

Rilla looked also. It had been painted about ten years ago while her mother's face was still plump and rosy. She looked like Imogene, but with the worried eyes of the perpetually anxious.

'But back to the matter in hand,' her father continued. 'The viscount asked me for my blessing regarding your upcoming nuptials, and he is a hard man to refuse—a hard man to refuse. However, I need to know that this is what you want. I'll not have you pushed into anything, viscount or no viscount.'

Rilla reached over, clasping his hand between her own. His skin had the dried feel of an autumn leaf. 'I think so. But I should tell you the whole of it. There was a scandal brewing which forced Lord Wyburn to propose. I did not do anything wicked, but I was foolish and impetuous.'

She waited.

'So you are marrying him to avert scandal?'

'In part and to help Imogene.'

'And that is all?'

'Yes,' she said, then knew with sudden clarity that this was not the whole. 'But I—we like each other and I want to.'

The words hovered in the stillness. Voiced, they frightened her. Would 'liking' be enough? Was it even true? Could this complex mix of physical attraction, intellectual interest and apprehension be termed 'liking'?

'Is liking enough?' Her father eerily echoed her own thoughts.

'I think so.'

'It is what you want?'

'Yes,' she said, more positively.

It was true. Jack, for all his bullying, could not have forced her to do something that was abhorrent. Rather, she realised, he had given her the excuse to ignore sense and reason.

'Then there is nothing more to say. I give you my blessing and hope you will be as happy as I was with your mother.'

'Thank you, Father.'

'I am glad also. In a way.'

'Glad?'

'I worried…' He paused as though searching for the right words. 'I worried that you would let your mother's fears deter you from even considering marriage. I knew you to be set against the notion. But I thought, well, I thought that the right man would soon quieten such concerns.'

*The right man?* Briefly, silence filled the room. Rilla knew the words she longed to say. She wanted to tell him that her second sight, or whatever it was, had worsened, that the viscount made it worse and that he was not the right man, but the worst man.

But she didn't. She could not willingly take away her father's optimism with harsh reality.

Then the moment was gone. Sir George straightened, releasing her hand.

'Anyway,' he said briskly, 'I must speak to you on another matter. My finances, or lack thereof. I've made mistakes, Rilla, I won't deny it. Haven't been much of a father, I sometimes think.'

'You've been the very best of fathers! Who else would teach me Greek? Or let me climb trees? Or engineer peculiar contraptions?'

'A dowry might be considered more beneficial than tree-climbing,' he said, wry laughter threading his voice.

'Not to me.' Rilla stood and impulsively leaned forward to hug him.

'Anyhow, not having a dowry is one thing, but no son-in-law is going to pay off my gambling debts. So I contacted that young scapegoat, Lockhart. You knew I was in debt to the fellow?'

'Yes.'

'Told him I'd be well paid for my latest translation. He'll get his money sooner as opposed to later.' Sir George pushed his spectacles further up his nose.

'He has agreed to wait?'

'He has.'

She exhaled. 'I'm glad. I was going to ask Paul,

but I'm glad I needn't. And, Father...' she reached again for his hand, '...promise you'll not gamble again. I know Lockhart may urge you.'

'I'll gainsay all temptation,' her father said and, removing his hand, promptly took some snuff.

# Chapter Eleven

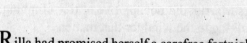

Rilla had promised herself a carefree fortnight before Lady Wyburn and Imogene's arrival with the resultant flurry of wedding preparations.

She kept that promise.

Fields beckoned, and she went to them, striding through grasses heavy with seeds so that they yellowed her skirts and freckled her stockings.

She inhaled the country air, ran with the wind and flung herself, exhausted, to the ground to stare upwards at the infinity of blue.

When Mrs Marriot and Heloise were not looking, she climbed her tree, smelling its lushness and savouring the dark, green translucence of its canopy. She'd hidden here during her mother's illness, brief moments of respite from the sickroom with its bottles and airless hopelessness.

Later she'd come to nurse her grief until it had softened to an ache mixed with the sweetness of fond memories.

But Paul's pain, she knew, had never softened. It was raw and festering. Time had not healed.

'Am I doing right? Can I make him content?' she asked aloud.

The wind brought no answer. No whisper, no touch half-felt.

Clambering from the tree, Rilla strode towards the back of the house thankful that Mrs Marriot had not seen her.

Mrs Marriot did not approve of tree climbing. Nor talking to the wind for that matter.

Perhaps she should make herself useful. She'd gather flowers from the back garden. A few bouquets would brighten the place. This proved easier said than done, but Rilla found a few roses amongst the weeds and had soon arranged them within a vase.

Hardly a masterpiece, but adequate, she supposed, as she carried them out of the kitchen. Imogene was really better at flowers.

She entered the dining room which was, as always, dark and cool. Mustiness scented the air and the curtains were tightly drawn to prevent sun damage.

'Good day,' a deep male voice stated.

Rilla almost dropped the flowers.

She blinked, momentarily dumbstruck, unsure if the looming figure was real or an illusion. 'My lord, I didn't expect—must you always startle me?'

She put down the vase.

'I apologise. Your lad Thomas let me in.' Paul

made his bow, then closed the space between them and pressed her hand to his lips.

That was real enough.

He straightened and she found herself breathless, the rhythmic thumping of her heart suddenly loud.

In the intervening weeks she'd forgotten the breadth of his shoulders, the length of his legs, the muscled thighs so clearly outlined in his breeches.

Everything—the room's shadows, the flowers' scent and the hushed solitude—brought back those moments on the terrace.

Her gaze went to the wry curve of his lips. She remembered their touch and with that memory heat flared.

'I'll just open the...the curtains. It's so dark.' She stepped across the room, almost stumbling over the footstool.

She pulled the curtains aside with a rattle of rings on the rod.

Sunlight flooded through the smudged panes with painful brightness. She exhaled.

Turning back, she found him still standing, his expression quizzical as though seeing too much.

She glanced down. His hands rested on the chair back. She remembered their strength and the feel of them, spanning her back.

The room felt airless.

'Right,' she said with determined briskness. 'We'd best not dally. Were you wishing to talk to me about something in particular?'

'I had not realised we were observing a tight timeline. But, yes, I did have a special purpose for my visit.' He picked up a jewellery box which he must have placed on a table nearby. 'I've brought something for you.'

'Thank you.' She took the box and sat so that it was balanced on her knees. The wood felt smooth and imbued with polish which had turned golden with time.

A bubble of anticipation effervesced. She'd had few presents. 'Should I open it?'

'Unless you can see through solid wood.' Paul sat in the chair opposite.

The hinges moved easily and the lid dropped open. 'Oh,' she breathed.

A magnificent diamond-and-emerald choker nestled within folds of faded blue-grey satin.

'May I?' Gently, she picked up the heavy, glittering gems. They caught the light, each rock flashing in a mix of fire and ice. 'They are...*beautiful*.' Never had she felt the word to be so inadequate. 'Magnificent. You came all this way to give them to me?'

'It was worth it.' His voice sounded strange, husky almost. He cleared his throat. 'Shall I help you to put them on?'

'Please.'

'I thought you might like to wear them for the wedding.' He stood and walked behind her.

Bending, he placed the jewels around her neck.

Her breath caught at the touch of his fingers, warm with a tingling roughness at the tips. She felt a ludicrous desire to lean her head against him or to reach up and touch his fingers with her own.

Perhaps he felt it. As the fastener clicked into place, he slowly trailed one fingertip across the nape of her neck and along her collarbone.

'London is not the same without you,' he said.

For once giving way to impulse, she leaned against him, feeling the firm strength of him behind her. He stroked her skin, tracing her collarbone, circling and dipping under the modest neckline of her dress.

Excitement mingled with lazy languor. She didn't move. She didn't want to move. She wanted only to fall under this spell.

Then, as a cloud sneaks up on a summer sky, unease prickled. The necklace became weightier. She felt its presence as though it were a separate entity.

'Your mother wore them.' The words blurted from her.

The mood broke, shattering. He removed his hands. She straightened, stepping from him and turning.

She touched the gems, her fingers tight about them. She could feel the other woman's emotion. She could feel her giddy, childish excitement and wild moments of happiness intertwined with melancholy.

'As did my stepmother. They won't bring ill

luck, if that is what you fear. They have been given to every bride for generations. Most of whom were quite content.' He spoke with clipped tones, his expression shuttered.

'I didn't mean—they're beautiful.'

But the moment had passed, the intimacy between them spoiled.

'Shall I return the necklace to the safe in my stepmother's house?'

'Yes.' She tried to keep the eagerness from her voice. But the feeling of being in another's skin still lingered and she longed to pull the necklace from her neck. He stepped behind her. She heard the click as he undid the clasp and felt the necklace lift from her skin.

Thank God.

'I will go to Wyburn tomorrow,' he said, 'to ensure that all is in readiness for our arrival. I plan to return to Lyngate shortly after Lady Wyburn has taken residence. Naturally, I will call on you immediately upon my return.'

'I will look forward to it.'

'No doubt,' he said drily. The tension dissipated a little.

'Thank you for bringing me the necklace. It is beautiful,' she said, again recognising the inadequacy of the word and that her own reaction had been inadequate.

Seconds later, she heard the solid bang of the front door and muted *clip-clop* of horse's hooves.

He was gone.

\* \* \*

Rilla found Sir George sitting on a lawn chair in the shade of the overgrown back garden.

He was smoking. The amber glint of his pipe resembled a slow-moving firefly and wisps of tobacco smoke perfumed the air.

'Didn't Thomas tell you the viscount was here?' she asked. 'He will think us very unusual, Father.'

'Knows that already and doesn't seem to mind,' Sir George said laconically. 'I like your viscount.'

'He's not my viscount,' Rilla sat next to him, frowning with irritation.

'You'll be married soon. Then he'll be yours right enough.'

She wriggled in the seat. 'We're not like that—'

'Perhaps you should be. You'll be spending the rest of your life with this man.'

She shivered, although whether it was with excitement or apprehension she did not know.

'Have you told him?' her father asked abruptly, looking at her with his still sharp gaze.

'About what?'

'Your taste in hair ribbons. About your moments, second sight, ghostly visitations or whatever you want to call them.'

'No,' she said.

'I knew your mother better than anyone else in the world and she knew me inside and out, the good and the bad.' He exhaled a grey balloon of smoke.

'It's not the same.'

'I don't hold with secrets between man and wife.'

'You know he'd…he'd think me mad,' she said in a low voice although there was no one about save trees and birds.

'Might be more understanding than you think.'

She shook her head. 'Not about this. He doesn't mind my inventions or my love of history, but he wouldn't like this.'

'His mother took her life, as I recall.'

'You know?'

'Old gossip,' he said with a diffident shrug. 'His father was never the same afterwards. Drank heavily.'

'I think Paul fears any emotion or sign of moodiness.' Rilla looked down, rubbing the fabric of her gown.

'As I recall, Olivia Wyburn was a woman of highs and lows. Damned hard to live with, if you'll forgive me my French. But you are nothing like that. Good Lord, you're less moody than your sister or your mother, God rest her soul. And more sane than either of 'em. Maybe he needs to understand that. Maybe you need to explain it.'

'How could I? How could I say that I'm perfectly sane but see dead people? How could I when—' she swallowed and her voice dropped low '—when I don't—when I don't believe it myself?'

He said nothing for a moment, carefully tapping ash on to the ground from his pipe. 'Then maybe you need to start believing.'

Rilla stood, pushing her chair back, tired of the conversation. 'There's nothing to believe and nothing to tell. My peculiarity is a—a remnant of childhood, a childish foible. It will not recur. Or if it does, I will control it.'

'God doesn't take away his gifts.'

'The devil might.'

Lady Wyburn's retinue arrived at Lyngate Estate and consisted of so many servants, trunks, crockery, linens and hardware that Rilla, who had gone to greet her ladyship, thought it resembled a military campaign rather than the preparations for a wedding.

News of the arrival spread through the countryside and Rilla found her peaceful days abruptly ended. Visits and teas became a constant everyday event. Moreover, she had never realised that a wedding involved so many decisions—about the menu, the guest list, seating plan, decor and other minutiae—that Lady Wyburn thought terribly important.

'Let's escape. Let's leave this stuff,' Rilla said a few days later with a sweeping gesture towards the neatly stacked presents and last-minute wedding invitations. 'I am tired of this wedding. I do not want to talk about it, write about it or drink another cup of tea. I'm drowning in tea. Let's go, Imogene. Walk with me, just the two of us, like we used to.'

Imogene frowned and tapped an embossed

sheet of writing paper with an impatient finger. 'We should complete these invitations. They are late enough already. I don't know why Father didn't remember these two professors weeks ago.'

'Just one walk,' Rilla wheedled. 'The woods are beckoning. Besides, I doubt those professors will have any interest in a wedding unless it is for the food.'

'And our father's conversation.' Imogene giggled. 'Although I shouldn't encourage you by laughing, I think you're entirely too frivolous.'

'I have only one week of frivolity left.'

'Gracious, it's your wedding, Rilla, not your funeral.'

'Then walk with me and convince me that everything will be fine.'

'Very well,' Imogene said in gentler tones. 'It will, you know.'

They strolled down the familiar woodland path. The soil felt spongy under Rilla's feet and the chestnut trees had grown together so that their overarching branches formed a green roof of light and movement.

In London, noise was as omnipresent and oppressive as the smoke from the city's coal fires or the smell of the Thames. Here, peace pervaded. Rilla heard her own breath, the tread of their footsteps and the rustle of their gowns.

It felt good to be with her sister as though, just for a second, they could revisit the past.

'Shall we go to Mother's grave?' she asked, as

they approached the small church in which the Gibson family had worshipped for generations.

Imogene nodded and they skirted to the left of the building with its single spire and stained-glass windows. Slates had fallen from the roof, giving it a checkerboard appearance, and the northern walls shone green with moss.

The graveyard was a shady, tranquil place, the grass punctuated with neat headstones, well-tended graves and three ugly monuments erected to Lockhart ancestors.

Their mother lay in the south corner under a beech tree. Father or Mrs Marriot must have visited recently. A vase of flowers had been placed neatly beside the headstone. Rilla sniffed the blooms. 'Mother always liked sweet peas.'

'She said they were a friendly flower.' Imogene smiled wistfully. 'Not ostentatious like roses and carnations.'

Rilla crouched, tracing the inscription's chiselled words: *Beloved wife and mother*. A thin layer of moss had rooted and its soft fuzz tickled her fingertips. 'I loved her so much.'

'She had a kind word for everyone.'

'And a poultice or herb tea.' Rilla grinned. 'Remember how old Mr Foster used to hide whenever he saw her coming down his lane? He even tried to sneak out the back door while she was knocking at the front.'

'She was certain ginger-root tea would aid his

digestion and he was equally certain he needed something stronger.'

They both laughed. Then Rilla sighed and sat suddenly and inelegantly on the grass beside their mother's grave. Tension knotted her shoulders and the horrid bubble of uncertainty that had been growing since the moment she'd said 'yes' ballooned. 'Imogene?'

'Hmm?' Imogene knelt to rearrange the sweet peas in the vase.

'I need…I'm worried and I must talk to someone.' Rilla looked at her mother's headstone, the stone dappled with shifting splashes of sunlight. She wished—but if wishes were horses… 'Paul visited a few days ago.'

'That was nice of him.' Imogene spoke absently, still rearranging the sweet peas.

'Imogene.' Rilla rubbed her fingers across the stone. 'I hadn't had a single moment since I'd returned here, not one.'

'That's wonderful!'

'Yes, but I had one during his visit. I think—I know this sounds crazy—but I think there is something about him or his mother that worsens them.'

'Lady Wyburn?'

'No, his real mother.'

'She's dead,' Imogene said.

'I know.'

*'No.'* Imogene spoke sharply. She sat on the grass, her movement unusually awkward. 'No, you are nervous or fatigued, but nothing more.'

'Imogene, I'm…afraid. I fear I am marrying the worst person—the very person who might make them worsen?'

Imogene pulled out a weed. She looked intently at its roots, shaking the loose dirt fiercely. 'Mother hoped you'd outgrow your feelings and Father has never been concerned about them.'

'Father is seldom concerned about anything except his Greeks and Romans and I fear Mother's theory was wishful thinking. She also recommended that I not marry should they persist.'

'She wanted to protect you.'

Rilla looked down at the headstone, running her fingers across its soft layer of green and listening to the crisp rustling of the beech leaves mingled with birdsong. 'But no one can protect me. They're part of me. Like Mother's cancer.'

Imogene turned. 'Rilla, that was an illness. You mustn't think—'

She looked so stricken that Rilla repented her words. She reached forward and squeezed her sister's hand. 'I'm sorry, Imogene. Truly, I didn't mean to upset you. Maybe the graveyard makes me maudlin or, like you said, I'm merely nervous.'

'Yes, yes, I am sure that is right. And you've been working too hard.' Imogene spoke eagerly and stood, brushing the grass from her skirt with brisk movements. 'Once the excitement is over, you'll find you have no more of your moments. Come, we'd best get back to those invitations.'

'You believe that?' Rilla asked. 'That it's only the excitement?'

'Yes, yes, of course,' Imogene said, but she looked away, intent on removing a stray leaf from her skirt.

Rilla stood also, trying to smile, her lips wobbly. 'Right, let's get back. No doubt Father has recalled another long-lost friend.'

'At this rate, he'll have sufficient numbers for a lecture on the antiquities immediately after the wedding.'

Rilla laughed, but her humour was forced.

Even before they'd reached the house, the late afternoon sun had disappeared behind the hills, leaving the landscape darkened by shadow.

## Chapter Twelve

Paul returned to Lyngate on the day before his wedding and found Lady Wyburn in the orangery, a glassed-in structure that jutted into the garden like an afterthought. It had a red-brick floor and was filled with vibrant vegetation.

The heat met him in a damp, earthy wave. Even Lady Wyburn, who usually loved heat, looked flushed, her ringlets limp from humidity.

'Paul, dear, lovely to see you.' She glanced up from the plant she was pruning and gave him a dangerous wave with her secateurs. 'Although I had expected you yesterday.'

'I visited Lord Marpole. I am trying to convince the landed gentry to oppose the Corn Laws, before this country ends up in as big a mess as France.'

'That won't happen, dear. We are so much less excitable than the French. Indeed, teatime would arrive and we'd go home for a cup rather than storming prisons and the like.'

'I hope you are right.' He spoke grimly. His conversation with Lord Marpole had only proved to him that the landed gentry were as intractable as ever.

'However,' Lady Wyburn said with a second wave of her secateurs, 'your interest in reform might be laudable, but your timing could be better. It would have been wiser to arrive yesterday, given that your wedding is tomorrow. It is not sensible to leave things to the last minute. I recall my cousin could not decide which tiara to take to court and ended up with neither, which was rather a shame as her husband later took her to Yorkshire and she had limited opportunities to wear tiaras at all.'

'I presume the Gibsons dine here tonight?' Paul interjected when his stepmother paused to draw breath.

'Yes, I expect them in an hour, so you just have time to change.'

He nodded and absently eyed a small orange plant with undersized fruit. He'd rather hoped to talk to Rilla alone. Their last conversations about the necklace had been...

Unsatisfactory.

Every woman he had ever known adored jewels and by her own account Rilla had a fondness for emeralds. Initially she'd seemed happy enough and yet later the necklace appeared to discomfort her and she could not wait to remove it.

He sighed. As usual, his fiancée proved unpredictable.

Moreover the fact that he even cared irked him

more. He could not remember a time when he'd cared how a female received his gifts.

'That one isn't doing very well,' Lady Wyburn said, recalling his thoughts to the undersized plant.

'Maybe it needs water?'

'No, the soil is moist enough. I might try talking to it. Mrs Evans, who always wins at the village flower show, advocates that strategy.'

'Then I'll leave you to it,' Paul said, and strolled away, although he could not resist sneaking a glance at Lady Wyburn now gravely conversing with the orange plant in question.

Paul descended to the front hall after dressing for dinner to learn that the Gibsons had arrived, but were no longer in evidence.

Sir George had already disappeared into the library, while Imogene and Lady Wyburn had gone to his stepmother's bedchamber, no doubt to examine some frippery from London.

Merryweather suggested that Miss Gibson might be found in the rose garden. Therefore, Paul sauntered into the early evening towards Lady Wyburn's roses.

Of course, 'rose garden' was a misnomer as it consisted of only one flower bed in a star-shaped design bordered by a short box hedge.

In point of fact, Amaryllis was found in the dead centre of this single bed, apparently studying the sundial. She had stepped over the box hedge and had her back to him, presenting a fetching rear view.

'Were you hoping to improve the sundial's design, Miss Gibson?'

She straightened and turned sharply. 'My lord, you're back.'

'In the flesh.'

'I was actually looking at the engravings. Lady Wyburn said she thought it was the goddess Hera who was depicted, but I knew it to be Athena. I was right. I've always liked Athena.'

'May I help you on to the grass or do you still wish to examine the sundial?'

'No, I'm finished.' She placed her hand in his. She had stripped off her gloves. Their fingers touched, her skin soft and warm.

Awareness flickered—peculiar and oddly irksome that she should have such an immediate impact on him. Good Lord, he had known many attractive women and had never found his attention unduly captured by the smallness of a lady's hand.

She stepped over the bed, her hair brushing his chin. She smelled of lemons.

He still held her hand.

'Thank you, my lord,' she said, glancing up.

'Given that we are to be married tomorrow, you might call me Paul?'

Her colour deepened. 'Yes, Paul.'

'Much preferable.'

'I…um…need to talk to you.'

'I too wanted a private moment. Shall we sit for this discussion?' He glanced back to a stone bench.

'If you'd like.'

He did like. Once seated together he was remarkably aware of her body's proximity and the warmth of her thighs beside his own.

However, Rilla wasted no time. 'My l—Paul, I must clear the air. I was not sufficiently appreciative of the necklace or the trouble you had taken to bring them to me.'

'It's no matter.'

'It is.' She shifted so that she faced him more squarely. Her chin jutted out with stubborn determination.

From this angle, the manner in which the turquoise cloth clung to the soft roundness of her breasts proved quite fascinating.

He frowned, shifting his gaze.

'We're getting married tomorrow and I don't want to feel that there are misunderstandings between us. I worry that you might think I am ungrateful. You see...' she inhaled '...the diamonds are beautiful, but I need to wear this.'

Her hand went to her throat. She held out a golden locket and flicked open the clasp.

The tiny heart parted to reveal a painted image of a woman bearing a strong resemblance to Imogene, but with Rilla's grey-green eyes.

'Your mother?' he guessed.

'Yes, I would like to wear it on my wedding day. I hope you are not disappointed.'

He shook his head and took her hand between his own. He looked at the glittering emerald he'd given to her. 'No. You must wear whatever you wish on your day. Besides, I'm certain there will be other occasions for the Wyburn diamonds.'

Again, he felt her reaction, a shrinking within herself, a discomfited movement. 'Yes, of course,' she said.

'Only if you want to.' He glanced at the sky turning pink in the sunset.

Good Lord, women were complicated creatures.

'So,' he said before the silence could become awkward, 'how have you occupied yourself since my departure?'

This time she looked at him and smiled, her countenance transformed by her wide grin and mischievous eyes. 'Discussing the weather and drinking tea. Gallons and gallons of it.'

'How awful. I hope our nuptials will be worth such tortuous activity.'

'But there is more. Mrs Banks, who owns the village store, has promised to bring in three new varieties of tea leaves. I am to select my favourite and she will sell it as "her ladyship's tea".'

'What honour.'

'But you have not been forgotten. Mr Banks has developed a new variety of rose and plans to name it "Lord Wyburn" He has aspirations that it might place first at the village fair.'

'And what does this paragon of a flower look like?'

'Dark, like your hair, which is admirable in hair, but perhaps less so in a rose.' She gave him a slant-eyed humorous look.

'Then I will not set my hopes on "Lord Wyburn".' Paul laughed. Odd how often he laughed in her company and how infrequently in her absence. It was as though the world had more flavour…more tang.

'I missed you,' he said.

The words popped out, surprising him and, once said, could not be recalled.

She looked at him, then away as though confused. Her eyelashes cast lacy shadows against her cheeks and he noted three freckles sprinkled on her nose like flecks of brown sugar.

She shifted. The silk of her dress rustled. 'You're making me feel as though I have a smudge again.'

'No smudge,' he said huskily. 'Only three kissable freckles.'

'Imogene says that freckles are not ladylike.'

'I like your unladylike freckles.' He leaned into her, pressing a kiss on the tip of her nose.

'It is because I always forget my parasol and my sun hat.'

'Hmm.' He kissed her cheek.

'Mrs Marriot suggests I put lemon on them.'

He kissed the base of her throat.

'I mean my nose, not my hat or parasol.'

He kissed the little hollow at the very base of her neck and along the smooth line of her collarbone.

'But it only made it pink. My nose, I mean.'

He kissed her shoulder.

'And—and the sun also makes my nose pink—and—and freckled.

'I believe,' he said, trailing kisses up the column of her neck, 'that talking can be highly overrated. Particularly about the weather.'

She swallowed. Her eyes widened and she bit her lip again.

'You look,' he murmured into her ear, 'like a frightened rabbit.'

'Hardly a complimentary analogy.'

He chuckled.

'I believe you like to irk me,' she said.

'I believe I do.'

His fingers traced the contour of jaw. Bending, he touched his mouth to hers. Briefly, he felt her hesitate and waited for that wonderful, familiar, erotic gasp.

It came and what had started as teasing pulsed to neediness. He pulled her closer.

She hesitated. He kissed her gently on the lips, stroking her back until she relaxed, her body soft and wonderfully yielding against his own.

His hand shifted, moving to cup the fullness of her breast. He felt her tremble of reaction—not resistance, more like surprise—and then again that wonderful pliable yielding…

His heart thundered.

She arched towards him. Her response was instinctive, ardent and unschooled.

He groaned. She pushed the limits of his control more than the most skilled paramours. His fingers moved to her shoulders, pushing almost roughly under the cloth. The fabric rasped as it shifted.

Her lips opened to him, accommodating the intrusion of his tongue...

Something—a noise or a clatter—jerked him back to reality, back to the rose garden warmed by afternoon sun, to the grandeur of his stepmother's house behind them, to the fact that he had been so ludicrously close to losing control.

He set her aside and stood.

'I apologise. I seem to do that quite frequently in your company.'

'I didn't mind, so very much.' She still looked wanton.

Every muscle tensed. Why did she affect him so much more than any other woman, so much more than was sensible or reasonable?

He would not, he could not, allow it. It was not rational.

He stepped away. 'My actions were not respectful to you. It will not happen again. Straighten your gown, please.'

She did so, her colour deepening, although whether in anger or embarrassment he did not know.

'If our marriage is to be a success, it is important that we follow proprieties,' he said.

'In that case, I am certain you will ensure that our marriage is proper in all respects.'

She sat very straight and pulled on her white gloves with quick, abrupt movements. Her cheeks were flushed and her gaze sparkled with hurt or anger. She stood also. 'Shall we go to dinner? Would that demonstrate suitable propriety?'

'Indeed. May I?' He offered her his arm.

She placed her hand on his arm. Her fingers trembled. He'd hurt her again, he realised, and she had done nothing wrong.

Again he felt that peculiar, contradictory need to make her smile and ease the hurt he'd caused.

'But that was,' he muttered into her ear, 'infinitely more interesting than the weather.'

And tomorrow he need not stop. Tomorrow he could bury himself in her and expunge this driving, needful lust.


Rilla did not expect to sleep on the night before her wedding, particularly after the incident in the rose garden.

Men were so complicated. One moment it had felt as though nothing and no one existed in the world save themselves and within the next, he appeared displeased, distancing himself behind that wall of his own creation.

She longed for her butter churn, but the original was in the shed and the replica had been packed ready for its journey to Wyburn. It would have been nice to study it. Machines worked on principles, cause and effect, while her emotions...

However, despite this confused muddle of thoughts, she had slept soundly and woke to sunbeams slanting through the lace curtaining and a house filled with early morning silence.

Slipping from her bed, she padded to the window and looked across the overgrown garden to emerald fields and hills.

All was ready. Her portmanteau stood packed and waiting in the hall. The table at Lyngate was set for the wedding breakfast. Her wedding dress hung against the door on the iron hook where Heloise had placed it last night.

Rilla went to it. It hung luminescent in the morning's grey light, a shimmering fairy tale of a dress. She touched the pearl-encrusted bodice and rubbed her cheek against the swishing silkiness of the cloth. She inhaled. It smelled of Madame Aimee's shop—a mix of gardenias with the faintest hint of mothballs.

She squeezed her eyes shut and tried to visualise herself walking to the altar, placing one foot in front of the other, approaching ever closer.

In her mind's eye, she could see him. Tall and immaculate, that cool autocratic veneer masking smouldering fires.

She shivered. Her heart beat fast with apprehension...anticipation...

Tonight...

The rose garden had convinced her of two things: firstly that she would enjoy her wedding night and secondly that retaining control of heart, mind or body would be no easy task.

'Ah, good, you're up,' Heloise said, knocking while simultaneously pushing open the door. 'I've brought you your morning chocolate. Lady Wyburn and her maid, Hillis, will be over from Lyngate any minute. Not that I want Hillis touching your hair. It's awkward, your hair. It needs a familiar hand.'

Seconds later, Imogene entered and sat on Rilla's bed, her dainty feet tucked beneath her like a child. She looked excited—a genuine excitement, not the horrid fear that lined Rilla's stomach.

And before they'd even finished their chocolate, Lady Wyburn's sing-song voice warbled up the stairs, audible long before she poked her head around the door.

'Imogene, Rilla, do not fret,' she called jubilantly. 'The cavalry is here. Not that dear Hillis is a horse or even rides a horse, but she is invaluable, particularly with hair and such. I thought she could work on Imogene's coiffure in your mother's boudoir.'

'That sounds wonderful. Thank you for your help,' Rilla said as Lady Wyburn entered.

'Oh, I am glad to do it. Indeed, I am most excited. Oh, I do hope the vicar doesn't have chilblains.'

Rilla blinked. 'Is he likely to? It is summer.'

'That is true, which is a good thing as I do not hold with winter weddings. They are too wet. Except in the north where it would be white—prettier, no doubt—but still dreadfully cold. No, I was merely recalling Mrs Burke's wedding. The vicar had chilblains and became so distracted by his feet that he read the funeral service. He came to his senses soon enough but I don't think poor Mrs Burke ever felt properly married.'

Rilla giggled. 'I'll make sure the vicar knows I'm alive.'

'That is as well. Right, Imogene, come with me. Let us leave Heloise to do her magic.'

And Imogene and Lady Wyburn were gone, their chatter replaced by quiet and the lingering scent of gardenias.

Rilla sat in the rose-print armchair. 'Heloise,' she said, stretching slippered feet towards the empty hearth. 'Do whatever you wish with my hair but, please, please, do not talk.'


Imogene and her ladyship stood in the Gibsons' shabby drawing room when Rilla entered. Lady Wyburn wore a perfectly cut grey-silk dress of simple design. Dark purple amethysts sparkled at her throat and grey curls clustered about her ears and forehead.

It was a warm day and sunlight streamed into the room, lighting the shabby damask chairs and butter-yellow walls.

At Rilla's halting entrance, Imogene and her

ladyship turned, their chatter silenced. Rilla swallowed. She felt ludicrously nervous. Lady Wyburn stepped forward and took Rilla's hands in her firm, warm grasp.

'You look truly beautiful,' she said gently, her words for once slow.

'Thank you.' Rilla pressed a kiss against the softness of her cheek. 'Thank you for…for everything.'

Lady Wyburn's eyes glistened. She hastily produced a handkerchief. 'I would so love to embrace you, but I'd ruin your hair and Heloise would never forgive me. We live in such fear of our servants. Dear me, I am an absolute nitwit.'

'You are wonderful, as always.'

'I must think of something uplifting because if I cry my nose will go all red and splotchy. Wet noses are so unappealing, unless one is a dog. I had one once, a beagle. He absolutely refused to hunt, which was quite irritating because really there are limited other uses for a beagle.'

Rilla laughed but felt her eyes sting. She turned quickly to her sister. 'Imogene, you've said nothing. Do I not pass muster?'

'Of course you do. You look beautiful and regal.'

'Regal? That's a stretch. I rather feared I resembled a snowman with a bonfire on his head.'

They laughed, breaking the tension.

'Fiddlesticks,' Lady Wyburn retorted. 'The lace of your veil looks lovely and mitigates the red hair most wonderfully. Now, is "mitigates" the right word? No, "mellows" is better. "Mitigates" sounds too much like a solicitor. And where is your father?' Lady Wyburn looked around vaguely as though expecting Sir George to appear from behind the curtains. 'I do hope he has remembered to dress.'

Sir George entered at this moment, moving awkwardly in the formality of his old-fashioned morning suit.

'Right, are we ready?' he asked, rubbing his hands together with a chafing sound. 'Best get this done with, what?'

'I suppose.' Rilla shivered, also rubbing her arms. 'I feel like I did when I went swimming as a child. I could never decide whether to tiptoe in or just jump.'

Sir George smiled as he peered over his half glasses at his nervous daughter. 'On this occasion, my dear, I rather think you might be jumping.'

# Chapter Thirteen

The viscount looked across the pews of the pint-sized country church. Parishioners watched him, their faces unknown but with the universal appearance of the English farmer or shopkeeper: strong, sensible and kindly in a no-nonsense way.

The organ's volume rose, played by a nervous, spinsterish woman who stared at him like a frightened rabbit and hummed several beats behind her own music.

Sunlight filtered through the single stained-glass window, splashing blobs of colour on to the pews and upturned faces. Grass, flowers and the mustiness of an old building scented the air.

Then the murmur of voices hushed and the wooden pews creaked as the parishioners turned, angling their bodies towards the rear of the church.

She had come.

The back doors were swung wide. Sunlight splashed in, dappling the floor gold. The music grew louder and more jubilant as though competing with the fast, rhythmic beat of his heart.

His bride stood silhouetted briefly against the brightness outside. Her body swayed as she stepped forward and the doors shut behind her. Her father stood beside her. He wore his best coat, cut in the fashion of ten years previous, and looked faintly puzzled.

Paul's lips twitched. Rilla had no such look. She walked steadily, not fast exactly, but with a businesslike determination which seemed typical.

And she looked beautiful—no, nothing as bland as beautiful. She looked resplendent. The ivory dress clung to her slim form. The cream veil softened the red of her hair, while the unusual square neckline exposed creamy skin and the tantalising swell of her breasts.

He was glad now that she hadn't worn the diamonds. They wouldn't have fitted with the warm simplicity of this country church. The locket, nested between her breasts, suited her far better.

Then he frowned because he saw that, despite her brisk movements, she was scared. He could see it in the tilt of her chin, the angular straightness of her carriage, the way one white-gloved hand gripped the fabric of her father's arm, squishing the cloth into folds. She held a posy of wild roses, the sort that grow on hedgerows. He saw them tremble.

The music ended. A thick silence filled the church, well remembered from childhood services and his mother's funeral.

But he must not—would not—think of that.

Rilla stood beside him. Her father had gone to the pew. Paul heard the quickened intake of her breath and the rustling movement of the veil. Their eyes met and she smiled, a tentative twist of moist lips.

He smiled back, conscious of a tender warmth, a need to comfort, and to promise a happily ever after even when he knew it could not be.

She made that breathy gasp.

The warmth turned to heat.

The ceremony blurred for Rilla into a series of vibrant but strangely disconnected moments—the strength of her father's arm, the sheen of moisture in Mrs Marriot's eyes, her sister's hug, tight and fierce.

She remembered the scent of the flowers decorating the church, sweet peas in honour or her mother, the organ music, jerky under Miss Plimco's nervous fingers, and Thomas's dropped jaw as he twisted his cap between hands red raw from scrubbing.

She remembered the shuffling noise of her father's feet as he stepped from her at the altar.

And then she stood alone.

With Paul.

Paul wore a dark coat and breeches and looked handsome, unbearably handsome. When he smiled, a pain stabbed beneath her breastbone and a heady heat pulsed through her.

The vicar cleared his throat. A fly buzzed. Someone coughed and a child whispered, his voice quickly shushed.

'Dearly beloved, we are gathered together in the presence of God, and in the face of this company, to join together this man and this woman in holy matrimony...'

Timeless words pronounced in that familiar baritone that she'd heard since her earliest moments. At least Lady Wyburn would be happy. The vicar had started with the right service and she was still among the living.

The fly returned to the vicar's bald pate, circling with an irritating whine. The vicar turned a page and the gold-edged paper glinted in the light.

She startled. She must have missed something, because Paul was speaking.

'I will,' he said.

His tone was strong and resolute. That would please Mrs Marriot. She did not like mumblers.

Now both Lady Wyburn and Mrs Marriot would be happy.

Paul took her hand, holding it as he removed the glove. His hands were warm but not sweaty. She watched their fingers entwine.

'Amaryllis, wilt thou have this man to be thy wedded husband...'

'I will.' Her voice sounded clear too, as though she knew what she was doing, which she didn't.

Making their vows was not, after all, so very difficult. Indeed, it proved less taxing than performing in the annual Christmas pageant. She need not even memorise lines, but merely repeat the vicar's words.

*Quite easy*, she thought. A giggle bubbled.

'In sickness and in health.'

She heard him say the phrase and recalled with horrid clarity her mother's words. 'Of course, my poor aunt was sick in her mind. Her husband had to put her away.'

'Put away' as though one were a sugar bowl or a milk jug.

Paul took her hand again, his warm touch jolting her back to the present. 'With this ring, I thee wed.' The ring slipped over the nail, to the first knuckle.

'In the Name of the Father and of the Son…' he pushed it to the second knuckle '…and of the Holy Ghost, Amen.'

The gold lay snug against her skin. She looked at it in a curious, detached way.

'You may kiss the bride.'

Paul bent and lifted the veil. He touched her lips with his own, the kiss modest, chaste, brief.

It was over. They walked down the aisle while Miss Plimco pounded on the organ with sudden confidence. Bells pealed. People began to speak, not loudly, but with a happy murmur.

Emerging, Rilla blinked in the sunshine. Villagers gathered, kissing her, grasping her hands, throwing rice and flowers so that petals rained, tickling her face, sticking to her hair and splattering against the silk.

It was a dream—not a delightful, childish daydream nor yet a nightmare. Rather Rilla knew an academic curiosity, as though watching someone else's story and wondering if it promised a happy ending.

Her voice answered the well-wishers. Her arms hugged. Her lips kissed. Her mind whirled.

The wedding breakfast would come next. It would be held at Lyngate, a small gathering. Then they'd drive to Wyburn. Lord Wyburn's travelling coach stood ready—no, *her husband's* travelling coach stood ready.

*Husband...husband.* The word clamoured in her head, loud as the pealing bells.

The portmanteau had been carried from the Gibson residence and now waited somewhere within the bowels of Lady Wyburn's home. The model butter churn would come too, although Heloise had said that no one with a husband like the viscount would require a butter churn for entertainment. Rilla did not follow that thought to its conclusion, her mind skittering away with a mix of both fear and excited anticipation.

The breakfast seemed to Rilla like one of those peculiar events that are interminable, but conversely, once ended, seem to have happened within a blink of an eye.

At times Rilla thought herself a marionette, nodding her head and raising her cup as if twitched by unseen strings. And then, as suddenly as it had started, the meal ended and Lady Wyburn leaned over and whispered, her breath warm and laced with coffee, that Rilla should change.

That's when everything sped up like a galloping horse.

Rilla excused herself from the table and went to the bedchamber upstairs which had been put aside for her use. Heloise removed the pearl-encrusted fairy tale of a dress and placed it on the bed, its moment of splendour already passed.

Rilla donned her travelling clothes. Heloise fixed her hair, gave her an almost motherly pat on the shoulder, and bustled about the room looking for a bottle of scent, her beetle-black eyes moist.

'I do not need perfume,' Rilla said. 'Indeed, it is likely to make my nose drip.'

'Just as well, as I cannot seem to find it. I will bring it with me when I join you at Wyburn. You are sure you will manage, my lady?'

'Absolutely. I want you to help Mrs Marriot pack the rest of the items I wish to take to my new home. I'm sure there'll be a maid who can look after things until your arrival.'

'She'll probably be some country girl who does not know the first thing about hair,' Heloise said morosely.

'Making your eventual arrival doubly welcome.'

Paul greeted Rilla in Lyngate's marble entrance and they walked together into the brightness outside. Rilla hugged her father, who stood with Lady Wyburn, Imogene and Mrs Marriot. The latter dabbed her eyes with her apron, which for some reason she had put on.

'Don't you be pestering the viscount's servants with them contraptions of yours, or they'll think you irregular,' Mrs Marriott said.

'I'll save my contraptions for you, as you already know me to be irregular.' Rilla tried to laugh, but her lips wobbled.

The coach stood opposite. Its black-lacquered paint gleamed and the crest glittered. The liveried footman swung open the door, which moved without even the whine of hinges.

She had never given the oil to Lady Wyburn's coachman, Rilla recalled.

Then she hugged her sister and kissed Lady Wyburn's soft, wrinkled cheek, before settling into the opulent interior.

This proved even more luxurious than Lady Wyburn's vehicle. Its cushions were of blue velvet, decadently plush and so well padded that Rilla sank into them without a creak.

Paul followed. She watched as he stretched his long legs across the floor in comfortable elegance. He was so big he seemed to fill the compartment. In repose, he reminded her of a lazing lion, a combination of beauty and danger.

The footman closed the door. Rilla caught her breath. There was something very final in that metallic click.

Saluting smartly, the man sprang to his podium.

Rilla wondered if it took practice to jump with such surety and if he'd ever stumbled.

He must have urged the horses forward because the coach moved. It lumbered across the cobbled courtyard towards the tree-lined drive, the light flickering through the carriage window as they travelled between shade and sun.

Now that the final moment had come, Rilla wanted to cling to every second, to slow time, to grab it and hold tight.

Pushing down the window, she hung out and waved to the group clustered outside. Sir George lifted his hand in mock salute. Mrs Marriot fluttered her best lace hanky. Lady Wyburn went so far as to brandish her new bonnet and Imogene blew kisses.

The horses trotted, quickening their pace. The wheels *click-clack*ed smartly over the cobbles. The carriage swayed. Family and friends were dwarfed into tiny figures, waving miniature stick arms.

The coach rounded a corner and the stick figures, with their stick arms, disappeared.

Rilla raised the window. It banged shut.

Everything fell quiet, even the horses' hooves and the normal rattle and creak of transportation muted.

Rilla looked towards her newly married lord. He leaned back, his eyes half-closed, although she surmised he was aware of her every movement and expression.

*Husband*—her mind still stumbled.

'How long to Wyburn?' she asked.

'Four hours.'

Four hours in this no man's land, no longer Miss Gibson but not yet properly his wife. Four hours before she saw Wyburn, the place he hated.

The place where his mother had died...

'Tell me about the estate,' Rilla, his bride of but a few hours, asked. Her voice was loud and her tone brittle.

For a second, reluctance pulled at Paul—he had little fondness for Wyburn and little wish to speak of it. He was only adhering to this wedding-night tradition because it would hurt the tenants if he did not.

Yet he saw her need for conversation, a clinging to normality and the pushing back of fear.

'People say the house is beautiful. The park is large and well stocked with deer and other game. It's old and has much history,' he said.

'You've made improvements?'

'Yes, it is now prosperous.'

It had taken some doing. His father had been the worst kind of landlord. He had taken from the estate but had never invested in it. Lady Wyburn's money had helped, but too much of it had gone into gambling and not crops.

But now Wyburn stood proud, its cottages neat and its fields productive.

Although, of course, he still hated it.

'Lady Wyburn said you'd introduced many innovations. Tell me about them?' She leaned forward.

Paul looked at her doubtfully, questioning that any woman would want to discuss agricultural reform, but her interest seemed genuine. He liked that aspect of her character, that thirst for knowledge, the quick wit and inventiveness.

'Well.' He stretched his legs even further beneath the seat opposite. 'The land had been overworked. We left some fields to lie fallow and tried different crops. It is important that we make our land profitable. Currently the landed gentry are riding on the backs of the cities.'

'How?'

'I don't wish to bore you with politics.'

'I'd like to know.'

'Have you heard of the Corn Laws? Perhaps your father mentioned them?'

'If they were not enacted by Caesar, he'd pay little heed.' She gave that wide, generous smile. 'What are they?'

'Laws that impose tariffs on foreign products. All very well for country estates, but it makes food so expensive that our townspeople starve.'

'Are those the laws you are working to repeal?'

'Yes, but progress is slow. We are a Parliament made up of landlords.'

She nodded, then leaned back, staring from the window with her brow creased. He wondered what she might be considering with such intent.

'Perhaps my butter churn will help with your improvements?'

That he had not expected. He grinned with sudden spontaneity. What other woman would come to his estate bearing a milking machine—correction, a butter churn?

'I'm sure my staff will be happy to promote scientific discovery.'

Rilla pulled a wry face. 'I'm afraid most domestics are not enthusiastic. Mrs Marriot was not interested in my bread maker. And you already know about my experiment with the churn.'

'The one that flooded the dairy.' And this time he laughed. She was fresh air, as unaffected as her wild-rose bouquet.

He wondered if it was dangerous to feel pride for a wife, but decided not. Pride was not love.

And what about respect for her intelligence? Surely that would only serve to ensure that their children were not dolts and that they might have something left to say to each other in the years to come.

And physical desire? Was that dangerous? Might it push him into affection? But, no, he had seduced and enjoyed many women. This would be no different.

Besides this all-consuming, driving desire would lessen once their marriage had been consummated. Right now it obsessed him. Good Lord, he wanted her here and now in this travelling coach—except she was his wife and deserved better.

With measured movement, Paul turned to the window and concentrated on the scenery outside, the brown of fallow fields and the puddles of muddied ditch water.

He studied them for so long that when he finally looked back, his wife dozed. His breath caught at the sight of her. She looked so young in repose with her mussed hair and the delicate fans of her eyelashes pressed against her flushed cheeks.

Gently, so as not to disturb her, he leaned forward and pulled the travelling rug about her shoulders. She sighed, cuddling into its comfort. He smelled that clean fresh scent of lemon soap. He brushed a silken red strand from her cheek before staring again through the mud-splattered window.

But this time, he knew a feeling he could not pinpoint. It was different from lust or physical desire, stronger than intellectual interest.

And more unsettling than either.

# *Chapter Fourteen*

Rilla stirred as the carriage's rocking motion and the wheels' *clack-clack*ing slowed. They must have neared their destination.

Still heavy with sleep, she pulled herself upright and stretched her cramped body.

Outside, twilight had fallen. She could discern the tall, dark shapes of the trees which stood on either side of the road, like giant sentries on patrol.

'Almost there,' Paul said as they swung between two pillars, white in the dimness.

She pressed her face to the pane. Her breath misted the glass.

Wyburn would be visible soon. Her new home. Olivia's home.

She pushed the thought away.

The carriage lurched as they pulled to stop at a massive stone structure hunkered at the end of the drive. Torches, at least a score of them, flickered, whispers of smoke rising from their flames.

Curious, she peered through the dusk towards

the house. It was a two-storey structure with a stone turret and porte cochère. The sun had set, but its glow still touched the sky, turning the stone walls and turret to polished pewter.

'What do you think?' Paul asked.

'It's magnificent.'

The carriage jerked to a stop. Silence descended, muting the rattling wheels and the *clip-clop* of horses' hooves.

The footman stepped down. The carriage door swung open.

Moving stiffly, Rilla clambered out. The wind blew surprisingly strong and cool, and she pulled her cloak more tightly about her. The torches flared.

At close quarters, the house proved neither ugly nor beautiful. Rather it had presence. She could feel it in the proportion of the turret, the intricate masonry about the doorway and the wide arch of the porte cochère.

'Welcome to Wyburn,' Paul said. 'May I present your staff, my lady.'

Looking away from the building, Rilla stared at a row of servants lined up like Father's tin soldiers. She wondered that she had not noticed them before.

'How long have they been standing here? They must be chilled.'

'Half an hour or so. As is their duty. It is a Wyburn tradition that they greet you, as their new mistress.'

'But outside? Could they not do so inside?'

'It is tradition,' Paul said.

An older man, the butler most like, with dark clothes and stooped back, stepped forward. 'Welcome, Lady Wyburn. I am Edison, my lady. If you care to follow me, I will make the requisite introductions.'

'Thank you, Edison.'

The servants bowed or curtsied, their well-schooled faces blank. They reminded her strangely of a toy she'd had as a child with chickens that had bobbed in unison.

Rilla also realised that she'd neglected the obvious. She'd been so worried about her role as wife that she'd given no thought to her role as mistress.

Names rushed at her. Lud, she'd never remember half of them. If only she could talk to each person and learn their stories.

As for Edison, his teeth concerned her. Even in the dim light, his jaw looked swollen and the skin stretched and inflamed.

'That is the sum of us, my lady, and we are very pleased to meet you and pledge to serve you faithfully,' Edison said, his gravelly voice intruding into her thoughts.

'Er...thank you. I am...certain I will be very happy here,' she said.

Paul touched her arm and led her towards the entrance. Their feet tapped softly. The stairs were shallow, worn by constant usage into curved bowls.

As she stepped over the threshold and into the front hall, Rilla's eyes widened and she forgot to breathe. She'd seen many splendid places in London, but this was different. It was not beautiful, but magnificent.

Iron chandeliers hung from a domed ceiling. Thick stone columns, wide as an oak's trunk, supported the roof and the grey walls were interrupted only by heavy tapestries and suits of armour.

The air felt cold and their footsteps echoed, rebounding from the walls and making the space seem even more cavernous.

'This is the medieval part,' Paul said. 'Quite frigid, particularly in winter. It dates from the thirteen hundreds. Other parts are more habitable.'

'Frightening…intriguing, and *wonderful*,' she said in breathless awe.

'I forgot your love of history. I might be able to scrounge up a Roman remain or two. As a child I discovered a coin in a vegetable patch.'

'That would be perfection.'

She had thought she loved history, but her experience had been with dusty texts or neat exhibits. There was a rawness here, something uncivilised which seemed bigger and more overwhelming than the present.

'No doubt you will want to rest and refresh yourself after the journey. The housekeeper, Mrs Lamprey, will show you to your room,' Paul said.

A large woman, big boned and strong, bobbed a curtsy, the movement made awkward by her sizeable frame.

'Certainly, my lord. The bedchamber is, of

course, ready,' Mrs Lamprey said, her accent thick with the country.

'Excellent. I will leave you with Mrs Lamprey, my lady, but I'll join you shortly for a light supper.' Paul bowed and turned, the tap of his footsteps reverberating through the hall.

'If you'll follow me, my lady?' Mrs Lamprey said.

'Yes, yes, of course.'

They clambered up the stone staircase that followed the curved contour of the wall. Of course, it had no banister and Rilla found herself instinctively clinging close to the wall so that she brushed against the faded tapestries, doubtless shifting the dust of the ages.

At the landing, Mrs Lamprey moved to the right, stepping into the narrower confines of a corridor. At first this small hallway remained of stone, but further on the rock changed to wood panelling and pine floorboards. Lit sconces punctuated the darkness, providing weak, intermittent puddles of yellow light.

'This wing is much newer and dates back only a hundred years. Ah, here we are, my lady.' Mrs Lamprey stopped, thrusting open the door.

Rilla stepped inside and looked around, almost giggly with relief. The chamber was beautiful. Undeniably so. At some point, as they'd traversed the ancient structure, she'd imagined a medieval room with stone floor, walls and a gaping black mouth for a hearth.

But this chamber proved to be all things comfortable. A blue-wool rug covered the floor, white walls brightened the room and long blue curtains obscured the window at its far end. The fire, already lit, provided cheery warmth.

It even smelled nice, a smoky scent, pleasantly mixed with flowers and furniture polish.

'Why, someone has arranged a bouquet for me. Was it you?' Rilla stepped towards the red blooms carefully placed on the bedside table beside the four-poster bed.

Mrs Lamprey blushed, bobbing another curtsy. 'Yes, my lady. A little welcome. His lordship ordered a light supper and after that I'll send Molly up to draw a bath. I'm sure you must be fatigued from your travels.'

'I am a little.'

'My lady…' Mrs Lamprey hesitated, her large hands moving nervously against her apron so that the white cloth made a starched rustle. 'My lady, we're that happy you're here. We'll do everything possible to make you comfortable. If you can make the master happy, well, we're grateful. That we are.'

Rilla smiled, touched that they cared so much for Paul, who must seem an austere master at times. 'Thank you. I'll do my best and I'm sure we'll all get on very well.'

'The footman will be up with your trunk, your ladyship. Do you need anything else?'

'No, thank you.'

Mrs Lamprey curtsied and withdrew.

As the door closed, Rilla allowed her breath to escape in a long, grateful sigh. She was alone, truly alone, perhaps for the first time since those pre-dawn moments in her chamber. Her shoulders, which had been hunched around her ears, lowered.

Stepping to the fire, she warmed her hands, listening to the flames' crackle and the rhythmic ticking of the mantel clock. An oblong mirror hung over the hearth and she went to it and studied her reflection.

'Lady Wyburn.' She practised saying the words, rolling them in her mouth as though tasting fine wine. She did not feel married. The wide-eyed girl in the mantel mirror with the haystack hair did not look married.

But she was. Married. Soon he would come. After all these traditions, civilised introductions, warm baths and light repasts, he would come. She almost wished it now, before her stomach knotted and she stopped breathing altogether.

She was afraid.

This fear was not maidenly apprehension. She'd enjoyed his kisses and had felt her body stir and respond to him. Rather, she too well remembered the urgency, the need, the desire which overwhelmed all else: logic, sense and self-control.

And Rilla prized reason and feared, above all things, that which she could not constrain.

Paul stood beside the hearth in his quarters, a large room with a massive bed, fireplace and bay window. His wife, he knew, was mere feet away, separated by the oak door connecting the two chambers.

They'd finished supper and he had withdrawn so she might have privacy to bathe and prepare for the night, as was right and proper.

But now, he thought, she'd had time enough.

He had waited long enough.

He took a final sip of his brandy and, after knocking softly, Paul pushed open the door.

It rustled over the rug's thickness as he stepped inwards.

His wife sat at her dressing table, attired in a voluminous robe of deep forest green that covered her more completely than the most intricate dress. A bathtub still stood in one corner, partially encircled by screens. The air was steamy and the room scented with floral soap.

'My lord.' She stood, jarring the dressing table so that the scent bottles clinked, their glass glinting in the light of the long tapers.

Emotion flickered across her mobile features. He saw her swallow and her breathing quicken.

Slowly he went to her and raised his hand to brush her cheek, rosy from the bath. Her hair hung long and loose, dry except for a few tendrils which curled damply around her face and at the nape of her neck.

He'd waited so long to see her like this, with her hair unrestrained by pins or clips, a molten, fiery mass. Gently he lifted his hand and ran his fingers down its length. It was soft, as he'd known it would be and thick, falling through his fingers like molten gold.

He moved closer. Her hair tickled his chin and he dropped a kiss into its scented silk.

'Oh,' she said.

'Did you require any further refreshment or assistance from your maid?' He must not be selfish or give way to ludicrous schoolboy haste.

Briefly she looked as though she'd grab the reprieve. Her mouth opened, but she closed it again, shook her head and squared her shoulders.

His lips softened into a smile. There was such inherent bravery about her, as though determined to get the worst over with expedience.

But he'd have her eager yet.

'Then, my dear,' he said gently, touching her robe, 'I suggest that you are overdressed for the occasion.'

'Oh,' she said again, biting at the pinkness of her lip. 'I...I'll get undressed.'

He liked that she did not play coy, but raised her gaze to meet his own. Curiosity, apprehension, anticipation—*yes*—and excitement tangled together in her grey-green eyes.

'Allow me.' He slowly unfastened the tie of her dressing gown. It undid with a swish of silk.

The cloth of her robe fell open, falling off her shoulders to reveal...

*My God.* A flannel monstrosity.

'You were expecting a blizzard in July?'

'Blizzard?'

'Flannel?' He raised an eyebrow.

'I thought it might be draughty.' Her breath came quickly. He could see the rise and fall of her breasts under the cloth.

'I will protect you from any draughts.' He caught her hand, uncurling the fingers and bending to kiss each pink tip. She smelled not of perfume but soap.

'And—and rheumatism,' she said.

'Pardon?'

'Mrs Marriot always promises rheumatism if one sleeps without flannel.'

'You, my dear wife, are not going to sleep.'

'Oh,' she said again, blushing delightfully.

With sudden urgency he pulled her to him. He felt her tense, but she didn't shy away. Instead, she leaned into him. Hesitantly, she reached for his shoulders, her hands sliding under the fabric of his robe.

Her fingers felt cool as she eased across his flesh, pressing her palms to his chest and tangling her fingers into the fine hairs. He liked the feel of her fingertips. He liked, even more, her growing confidence as her body pressed closer to him and her touch became bold.

'Kiss me,' he murmured.

Instinctively Rilla seemed to know what he wanted. She placed her lips on his, opening her mouth in a way that was both innocent and unbearably erotic.

He caught her lips.

His hand found the soft, heavy fullness of her breast. He cupped it.

For a second, she stiffened, but with a spontaneous knowing she arched towards him, her nipple puckering.

But he didn't want to feel flannel. He wanted skin. He wanted her naked beneath him, had wanted it since the moment she'd tumbled from the tree on him.

Impatiently he pulled at the primly tied blue ribbon of her nightdress, and heard the rasp of the fabric.

It stuck, knotted.

He tried to untie it. It wouldn't give. With a muttered curse, he ripped at the flannel.

'My night—' she started.

'Is a monstrosity!' He tore it clear through and tossed it in a perfect arc so that it landed with a muted plop in the bathwater.

He felt a pang of conscience and studied her expression, hoping he had not scared her. He was unused to virgins. He was unused to this level of need. He'd always had control.

But Rilla was laughing. 'I would have undone it for you if you'd asked.'

He looked at her as she stood, naked, making no attempt to cover herself. A goddess with red hair.

'Goodness,' he muttered, need drowning all restraint. 'You're magnificent.'

Bending, he touched his lips to the pink tips of her breasts and trailed kisses to the hollow of her neck where he could feel a ragged pulse. Eagerly, he stroked the length of her spine, caressing the smooth skin and cupping the soft, generous curve of her buttocks, pulling her tight to him.

And he could wait no longer.

Scooping her up, he laid her on the massive four-poster bed, stretching out beside her, his hands roaming her satin skin. His body demanded speed, but he made himself slow, coaxing and caressing until she relaxed, becoming pliant as her fingers moved along his arms and muscled torso.

Shifting his weight, he eased his body on to her. 'Shh,' he soothed and something in his chest squeezed and softened. His desire did not lessen, but changed. 'Don't think. Don't talk. Just feel.'

Gently with teasing slowness, he kissed her lips, her neck and her nipples. His fingers circled her belly, dipping lower.

But only when he heard that wonderful hic-cupped gasp and felt the instinctive parting of her thighs, did he give way to his burning, driving need, feeling sated at last.

The air washed cool against his torso as Paul slipped from the bed, his footsteps silent except for the floorboard's creak. Rilla slept.

He went to the window. With a shushing sound of velvet, he pushed back the curtains and stared at the dim contours of his land.

Darkness shrouded the lake, but he could feel its presence. He knew its every mood, the sound of its waves, its shiny inky blackness and the cold, penetrating damp of it.

He had hoped that making love with Rilla would release him from the constant thoughts of her which had plagued him for weeks.

It hadn't.

Their coupling had been like nothing he'd experienced previous.

It had touched him and released some part of him, causing a joy so intense it was pain.

And Paul knew, without question or doubt, that he'd made a terrible mistake.

# Chapter Fifteen

Rilla dreamed she was underwater. Darkness surrounded her. She didn't know which way was up. She gulped for breath, thrashing wildly.

Fluid filled her lungs.

*I don't want to die. I don't want to die. I don't...*

Jolting awake, Rilla bolted upright, staring around the shadows of her room.

Someone had called out for her. She'd heard... she knew...

But the details of the dream were already fading, leaving a sadness, a sense of loss too big, too all-encompassing to be contained in sleep.

Freeing herself from the linens, Rilla stood.

The room was empty. Paul had gone.

Grabbing her robe, she went to the bay window and fingered the lush softness of the velvet curtaining, conscious of a heavy scent.

Lavender.

She shivered, quickly drawing the curtains and pushing open the pane. Cool morning air

and light flooded inward, bright with the promise of a fine day.

Outside, green lawns sloped down to the lake
which lay, smooth and unruffled, resplendent in
morning glory.

Strangely, she felt no curiosity or surprise, but
rather a sense of coming home. She knew this lake.
She knew the small jetty and rowboat. She knew
that the eastern shore was rougher than the south
and that its shores were thick with wet clay.

She didn't ask how she could know these things,
just as she didn't ask why she could smell lavender.

Because she already knew.


A maid brought Rilla chocolate, but she drank
it with little enjoyment. Last night had been wonderful and yet it had frightened her—not in a missish, virginal way—physically sleeping with Paul
had felt right, instinctively, wonderfully, fantasti-
cally right.

But in its rightness there had been something
which eclipsed rational thought or control.

It touched the primal and Rilla did not trust the
primal.

Nor did she feel like Rilla Gibson any more. She
wasn't Rilla Gibson.

But who was she?

And who was he? She'd hoped that last night's
intimacy would bring answers and emotional content. It hadn't.

Instead, their physical intimacy had made her

long all the more for emotional intimacy. Yet how could she expect any true closeness when she must hide her soul? And how could she expect trust when she could not give it?

Frustrated by her circuitous thoughts, she thrust the chocolate aside and stood up. She would find something practical to do. She would lock away sick fancies and romantic dreams. Focus on that which was sensible and scientific had always soothed the mind.

The house proved as massive in morning light as it had seemed the night previous, a vast collection of corridors sprouting from its medieval core like the limbs of a mythical monster.

Fortunately, a footman guided her to the dining hall which proved as huge and medieval as the Great Hall with two iron chandeliers, a high stone ceiling and mammoth fireplace.

Good lord, the knights of old must have been giants of men. Was there no smaller apartment in which two people might eat? At this rate they would need to shout out the niceties of the day.

'Breakfast, my lady?' A footman pulled out a chair from a table which looked to be at least twelve feet in length.

There was no sign of Paul.

'His lordship has gone to view the estate. He said he would be back for lunch.'

'Thank you.' She sat. 'And your name?'

'Geoffrey, my lady.'

He poured coffee. Wisps of steam spiralled from the dark liquid. Its aroma mixed pleasantly with the smell of bacon, sausage and egg.

'Thank you, Geoffrey. There are many names to remember, but I promise to do my best. By the way, I must see Edison. I'm quite positive he suffers from toothache.'

'I will inform Mr Edison that you wish to see him, my lady,' Geoffrey said, his young face impassive.

Rilla nodded. *Action*, she thought as she sipped her coffee. A practical task would disperse this prickly gooseflesh feeling. Of course it was totally logical that Wyburn would make her nervous. Anyone with an ounce of imagination would feel nervous, surrounded by stone walls, faded tapestries and huge wrought-iron chandeliers.

And what if the lake seemed familiar? Lakes generally resembled each other. Moreover, lavender was hardly an uncommon scent in a lady's boudoir. The servants had probably splashed it about or some such thing.

Edison entered. He bowed, his forehead wrinkled in concern. 'You wished to see me, your ladyship?'

'Yes, I noticed last night that you had a toothache. I wanted to ask after it.'

'How—it's much improved, my lady.' Edison quickly hid any astonishment.

'Your jaw is swollen to twice its size. And it's

red—very red. It must be painful,' Rilla said with blunt sympathy.

'*Er*...just a little, my lady.'

'Well, I've finished here, so I'll make you a poultice.' Rilla stood abruptly. 'Which way to the kitchen?'

'The kitchen, my lady?'

'Yes, we must go there now.'

'This way, my lady.'

The kitchen, like everything else, was immense— double the size of that in the Gibson residence. It had a red flagstone floor, a ceiling studded with dark beams and a grey stone hearth taking up a good half of the far wall.

But it smelled like a kitchen right enough and had a vibrant energy absent from the rest of the house. The air was moist and warm, scented with a mix of onions and yeast, and Rilla could hear the rhythmic chopping and clatter of dishware.

Upon her entrance, the cook and kitchen maids stopped as one, heads swivelling and jaws slack. Then, as though perfectly choreographed, they curtsied, their anxiety palpable in their flushed faces and the flustered movement of their hands.

'My lady, were you looking for Mrs Lamprey to review the menus? She's in her room at present.' The cook rubbed her palms across the starched white cloth of her apron.

'Indeed, no. I'm looking for chamomile and a whole host of other herbs.'

'Er...I'm—I'm sure I could make anything you would like, my lady,' the cook said.

'Good. I'm making a poultice for Edison's tooth. We'll work together. What is your name again?'

'Mrs Green, my lady,' the cook replied, looking, as Mrs Marriot would say, flummoxed.

Rilla would have found Mrs Green's facial expression funny except she knew the moment to be important. At some point since arriving, she'd determined not to be a guest in her own home. She had tiptoed about Lady Wyburn's house, but she refused to do so here. She might never claim Paul's heart, but she would claim the hearts of these people.

'Right, Mrs Green, do you have a large pot?'

'Yes, my lady.'

'Good. You boil the water and I'll go outside and pick the herbs.'

'I'm sure Elsie, the scullery maid, could pick the plants, my lady,' Mrs Green suggested, her round face settling into unhappy lines.

'But she might not know a dandelion from a parsnip and I need the right things if the poultice is to work. Edison should have gone to the tooth extractor long ago.'

'He would not. You know, gentlemen are not as tough as they would have us believe, my lady.'

The cook flushed slightly and Rilla wondered if she might have feelings for the butler.

'Right, we'd best get started,' she said, heading briskly into the kitchen garden.

Rilla inhaled. I⸱ felt good to get out of the immense stone structure that was Wyburn and into the fresh air. She liked the view, the expanse of rolling countryside, the rich, dark furrows of soil. She liked the smell, the scent of earth and vegetation.

Staring at the garden, she felt a need to get her hands dirty. She wanted to plunge them into the soil, to dig and weed and connect herself with all that was mundane, ordinary and practical.

To all that was alive.


When the viscount stepped into the front hall, he found it deserted. He frowned, tapping his hand impatiently against his breeches. It appeared that Edison and both footmen had vacated their posts.

Worry flickered. His shoulders tensed as he hurried across the Great Hall.

Had something happened?

His servants would never have left their posts except in an emergency. He stopped. A trill of laughter sounded from the depths of the servants' quarters. His jaw tightened. He pushed through the baize door and descended with measured steps. He loathed sloth or disorder.

Halfway down the servants' stair, he froze, surveying the scene before him.

*Good Lord Almighty.*

His butler sat on a high stool in the centre of the kitchen, a towel draped around his neck and shoulders. Meanwhile, the cook and his own wife appeared to be applying greenish slime to the man's chin. The other servants had ceased their work and hovered close as though expecting a miracle of biblical proportions.

'My lady,' he said, his tone quiet but with an edge.

Rilla started and the servants instantly dispersed with a rustle of bobbing curtsies and shuffling feet.

'My lord, I'm so glad you've come. I've made a poultice for Edison,' his wife announced.

'So I see.'

'Now, Edison, keep that on for at least ten minutes and reapply it this afternoon. I'm sure Mrs Green will see to it.' Rilla nodded and stepped back as though to admire her handiwork.

'Yes, my lady.' The cook's gaze skittered towards her master and away.

'Do I take it your work here is complete, my lady? May I escort you to our quarters?' Paul questioned politely.

Rilla nodded and smiled brilliantly at the staff. Only the challenging tilt of her chin showed that she recognised his ill humour.

Again the woman confounded him and he was quite undecided whether to scold, laugh or ravish.

As she placed her hand on his arm, the latter option seemed most delightful. Still, he must talk to her. She could not go about causing domestic chaos.

'My lady, if you will grant me a moment in my

study?' he said as they reached the top of the servants' stair.

'Naturally, my lord.'

He led her past the knights with their shining, sightless visors and down a smaller passage.

Of course, his London study suited better. It had fewer memories. He'd spent little time at Wyburn, and consequently little had changed since his father's day and the study seemed particularly timeless. The fire had not been lit and its only windows were narrow and faced northward on to the front drive.

Thankfully, not the lake.

Rilla stood a foot past the threshold. He watched her take in every aspect of the room's appearance with the intelligent curiosity which was typical of her.

'Right,' she said when she'd finished her surveillance. 'I'm ready.'

'Pardon, my lady?'

'Isn't this where we stop "my lording and ladying" for the benefit of the servants and you give me the peal?'

He found himself wanting to smile. 'That had been my intent.'

'I am sorry if I've displeased you,' she said, although she did not look particularly repentant. 'I am aware that it's not quite proper to go to the kitchen—'

'On that we agree.'

'But, you see I needed—need—to do this. In London I tried to be proper—'

Paul made a slight snort.

Rilla raised those well-marked brows, placed her hands on her waist and thrust out a mutinous chin.

'I beg your pardon. Pray continue, my lady,' he said.

'Yes, well, I did my best to comport myself in a way that was proper and conventional. But I really am not very proper—'

'You do surprise.' He smiled. He could not help it.

'And I refuse to turn myself into something I cannot be.'

'That's all very well,' he said, determined to regain control of the interview. 'But the servants have their duties. Too much familiarity discomforts them.'

'Walking around with a toothache discomforts them.'

'A toothache?' he asked.

'Edison. Did you not see the man's jaw?'

'I'm afraid I tend not to examine my servants' anatomies. But if he has need of medical attention, we'll send for a physician or whatever he needs.'

'He is fearful of having his tooth extracted.'

'Fearful!' Paul sat in the chair his father had used. The leather creaked. 'Did the man give you his life history?'

'Mrs Green confided in me. I think she likes the butler.'

'You think she likes the butler?' Paul looked at her blankly.

'Indeed, she appeared quite flushed.'

'That—that is beside the point.' He spoke with effort and started to drum his fingers on the top of polished oak. 'The point is that it is neither necessary nor appropriate for my wife, my *viscountess*, to masquerade as ministering angel and cover our servants with slime. I mean a delivery of oxtail soup to a tenant is one thing, but—'

'The point is that it is neither necessary nor appropriate for a man to suffer when I can help.'

The viscount glowered. Rilla glowered back.

'Rilla,' he said, taking a deep breath. He would not lose control. He drummed his fingers relentlessly. 'I will be blunt. I do not hold you to blame. You are inexperienced, but you must not allow such familiarity. I have a staff of hundreds, not just one, as in your father's household.'

'Two,' Rilla corrected. 'Mrs Marriot and Thomas. Plus Kate came up from the village sometimes.'

'Very well, two. I am sure they were devoted to you and would put up with all manner of eccentricity. It's different with a staff of this size. Respect is key. The servants will not respect you if you go traipsing about like a maid.'

'People respect others who treat them with caring, who treat them like people.'

Paul met her gaze. She looked good with such high colour in her countenance. The strength of her will impressed him along with the independence of her thinking. Indeed, he enjoyed these heated moments far more than the blandishments of other women.

*Damn.*

With tightened jaw, Paul looked down to the papers piled on his desk awaiting his attention and forced his tone to chill. 'I will not interfere in your domestic arrangements, of course, but I ask that you do not behave in any way that will discredit my name.'

'I do not think that helping another human being is likely to do so.'

'And that's the problem,' he said sharply. He picked up his pen and dipped it into the ink. 'You do not think. You act without thought—'

'I'm not averse to thought.'

Goodness, she had more fire in her than the French cavalry.

'I prefer,' he said grimly, 'not to be interrupted— if you could remember that for our next conversation. For now I will bid you goodbye.'

He stood in curt dismissal.

Rilla frowned, angling her chin upward. 'Fine, but I must say marriage has not had a happy effect on your manners or temperament.'

With this parting shot, Rilla exited, allowing the door to close noisily. Paul sat down, pulling a second ledger towards him.

It was somewhere down the long column of figures that he remembered Edison, his face adorned with green slime and surrounded by ministering females.

At first, Paul's lips twitched. Then he grinned, and finally a full-bodied laugh burbled to his throat.

# *Chapter Sixteen*

'Domineering, rude, autocratic...' Rilla muttered as she pounded up the curved stone staircase to her chamber.

The interview had upset her. It proved that she and Paul saw everything differently and that he wanted her to mould herself into the image of a proper viscountess.

For some stupid reason, she'd thought he might accept her or at least this aspect of her, even though he could not love her. Besides, if she were entirely honest with herself, acceptance of the unconventional might augur well for his tolerance of...other things.

But, no. He wanted her body, admired her wit and even credited her with intelligence, but he did not value her spirit.

Few people had ever accepted her. Her father, perhaps, although he did so in an absent-minded way, noticing her on an infrequent basis between Roman relics.

At the top of the staircase, Rilla had intended to go directly to her bedchamber, but found herself halting on the landing. It was an abrupt movement, not quite of her own volition. Rather it was as though she'd been jerked to stillness like a chained dog.

A door stood ajar.

She turned, oddly unsurprised to see it open. She touched the handle. It was fashioned of cold iron. She pushed against it and the door swung inwards. The hinges whined. The door grated over the stone floor.

Her skin prickled.

She stepped inside a long, narrow chamber with a stone floor, a high ceiling and tall leaded windows. From the opposing wall, Wyburn ancestors stared back at her. Men in satin, armoured knights, ladies clutching lapdogs and wide-eyed children laced into tight brocade. The pictures came in every size, small portraits and huge fulllength masterpieces. Rilla scanned the dull gleam of gilt frames and the stiff, solemn faces, immortalised in oil.

A breeze came from somewhere, cool and sufficiently strong to stir tendrils of her hair. She glanced about, confused, because the windows appeared fast shut.

Despite the cold wind, perspiration prickled under her armpits and dampened her palms. Rilla rubbed her hands against her skirt, the rustle of cloth loud within the quiet room.

The silence itself seemed oppressive, like a separate physical entity within the still air of the portrait gallery.

Then Rilla saw her.

Olivia, Paul's mother.

The painting occupied a large portion of the end wall. It was almost life-sized and encased within a heavy gilt frame intricately carved. Olivia wore a blue-silk dress, cut in the fashion of twenty years previous. She stood on a red-brick terrace and clutched sprigs of lavender.

Rilla moved forward, stopping only inches from the painting. Her hand lifted. She placed it on the frame and looked downwards, oddly fascinated by her own fingertips outlined against the gilt. She watched as she touched the wood, running her fingers over the gritty film of dust.

'Olivia,' she whispered.

She stepped back to better view the painting and then everything changed. At first, the difference came subtly, like the shift of morning sun to the gold of afternoon. Olivia grew larger. She came closer, as if walking forward on the painted terrace. The very essence of the portrait altered. It looked no longer flat, but had depth and movement. Rilla felt the breeze. She heard the rustle of leaves and the soft intake of the woman's breath.

And lavender. She smelled lavender.

Awkwardly, Rilla's hand inched to Olivia's painted gown. With shaking fingers, she touched the cloth. It was silk and felt as silk should, soft and warm as if heated by a woman's flesh.

'I need… He needs… He mustn't think…'

Rilla heard the whisper, quiet as the breeze. The gallery darkened. Rilla spun towards the windows and saw that the leaded panes had turned black.

Looking back at the portrait, she saw that Olivia had brightened to luminescence, her eyes shining in their painted sockets. A raw, childish neediness pulsated through the room. Olivia's pink lips parted.

Then the room rocked, and with a muted cry Rilla slid, quite slowly, to the floor.

'Rilla! What are you doing here?' Paul's voice roused her. Rilla blinked and felt his touch on her shoulder, rough with concern but comfortingly human and warm. Her back hurt and she was shivering from lying on the stone.

'It's light again,' she said, as she pulled herself to a sitting position, her gaze moving to the windows.

'Light? Of course it is. Rilla, are you all right?' He crouched beside her.

'What…what happened?' she asked.

'You tell me. I've been looking for you. It's past luncheon.'

Indeed, she saw that the sun had shifted and now poured directly into the chamber.

'I must have slept,' she said inadequately.

He was not satisfied. She could see it in the

clench of his jaw and the nervous tic flickering across his cheek.

'You must be ill. Come!' He thrust out his hand. 'Let's get you out of here.'

'She didn't do it.'

'Pardon?'

'Kill herself. Your mother didn't kill herself. It was an accident.' Rilla placed her hand on his arm and felt him jerk away from her touch or her words.

He pressed his hand to her forehead. 'You're delirious.'

'It was an accident,' she repeated.

'And maudlin. Come,' he repeated, putting his arm around her shoulders. 'We will get you warm and away from this place.'

'She didn't mean to do it.'

'It doesn't matter.'

'It matters to her.'

'She's dead, for goodness' sake. There is no *her*,' Paul said, almost shouting.

Rilla wanted to speak, to explain. Indeed, she felt drawn to do so by some force greater than herself, but she forced the words down, clamping her mouth shut.

'Stand up,' he said more gently. 'Let's get you some hot tea.'

Rilla nodded. Her thoughts moved slowly, like treacle in winter. She stood, still unsteady, brushing the dust from her gown.

'Tea will do you the world of good,' he repeated,

his voice soft with almost a rhythmic, sing-song quality.

As though talking to an invalid or child.

Unease slithered through her. She liked the anger better, but she complied. She stepped into the hall, grateful when the heavy wall banged closed, shutting in his dead Wyburn ancestors and Olivia.

It had been an unpleasant afternoon. Paul sat astride his horse, looking across the fields and listening to the drone of his manager's voice. The image of Rilla lying on the floor beneath his mother's portrait still flickered before his mind's eye. His stomach tightened and he twisted the reins, tapping the leather against his palm.

'We've put up a new fence and I thought to cut a road through here. If you approve, that is, my lord?'

'What?' Paul stared at poor Sorely as though the man spoke a foreign tongue.

'The new road, my lord. I thought to put it between these fields. I wondered what you thought.'

'How the devil should I know? Put it where you please.'

'Yes, my lord.'

'Sorry, Sorely,' Paul said, instantly regretting his rough tone. The man was a good worker and honest soul. 'The road would do well there. And tell me about those new cottages you're planning.'

'Yes, my lord. The villagers wished me to thank you for the renovations to their existing cottages and also send their felicitations on your nuptials.'

'Thank you.' Again Paul spoke too curtly, but he had little wish to be reminded of his newly married state. Already the woman occupied his thoughts too much.

Still frowning, he watched Sorely swing off his horse to study a fence post.

At some point, Paul had expected to safely catalogue his wife within the appropriate compartment. He'd hoped that the physical act of love would satisfy him so that she no longer occupied his mind to an unreasonable degree. But last night had brought no lasting peace.

Moreover, this morning's behaviour worried him. Of course, she'd seemed recovered enough when he'd left her an hour back. Her colour had returned and she was quizzing Mrs Lamprey about Edison's teeth. Still the question remained, a nagging, prodding presence like a mosquito late at night: Why had she been collapsed in front of his mother's portrait?

Even now, he could see her strange, blank, sightless look. He'd seen that expression before, he realised, in the library while clutching his mother's miniature and when he'd put the Wyburn jewels about her neck.

Sorely mounted his horse, and by common accord they started back, silent except for the *clip-clop* of horses' hooves.

Restless, Paul shifted in the saddle. The animal whinnied. 'Sorely,' he said with sudden decision.

'Do whatever you need with the estate. Lady Wyburn and I will be leaving for London tomorrow.'

Rilla chose the gown of topaz silk with unusual care. It suited her, she knew. Its low neck exposed the swell of her breasts, and the colour made her eyes glitter and her hair turn molten. She pinched her cheeks to give them colour and bit her lip.

Her efforts were not about vanity, but something more important, more vital. She wanted, *needed*, to ensure that she in no way resembled the pathetic figure crumpled on the floor.

The dining room proved even more impressive at night than morning. White damask covered the massive table. Silverware glinted. Flowers scented the air and the huge iron chandeliers shone down flickering puddles of light making the cut crystal sparkle.

Paul stood at the table's head, immaculate, handsome, every inch the gentleman.

Her heart did a funny, wobbly leap.

'My lady,' he said, bowing.

'My lord.'

His expression softened in appreciation of the topaz-silk gown, but then his face settled again into remote lines like a shuttered house.

Edison pulled out her chair, which had been set at Paul's left for family dining.

'Edison, your jaw looks much improved,' Rilla said as she took her seat. The chair was a large medieval affair with a back higher than her head and ornately carved arms.

'It is better, my lady.'

'Did Mrs Green make you another poultice?'

'Yes, my lady. She has been most kind.'

Edison flushed and Rilla was glad because it made her husband smile. Not really a smile, but an infinitesimal slackening of the jaw.

Edison left to bring in their first course and Rilla ran her finger across the damask cloth.

'Paul,' she said, aware of a nasty, nervous tightness in her stomach. 'I need to apologise for falling asleep in the gallery this morning. I realise it was more appropriate for a child than a viscountess. But…you mustn't worry about it. I am not ill or…or anything.'

Paul nodded, his face politely blank. 'That is reassuring. I hope you are refreshed now.'

'Absolutely.'

Edison served the fish, sole smothered in a fragrant parsley sauce, and poured the wine into long-stemmed glasses.

Rilla commented on the taste of the fish and wine. Paul agreed that both were delicious.

Rilla commented on the weather, and Paul agreed that it had been pleasant.

And still those moments in the portrait gallery hovered between them—huge and unspoken. Indeed, Rilla did not think they would ever have ventured past polite inanities had not Paul mentioned the threshing machine.

The wonderful news that the estate owned such a marvel made Rilla forget all else so that she leaned towards him, elbows propped on the table.

'Really, you have one? Lud, I cannot wait to see it in operation. No one had one near us,' she exclaimed.

Her husband smiled, the humour even reaching his eyes. 'I forgot your enthusiasm for such things. Or I would have mentioned it earlier.'

'Have you seen it in operation?'

His lips twitched. 'From a distance, but I have not examined it scientifically so to speak.'

'I will have to do so.'

'Indeed, we must return during the harvest so you can see it in operation.'

'I would love that. Mr Meikle must be a genius. Sometimes I wonder what he was doing when the idea struck him and if he realised that it might change the whole way we farm.'

He leaned towards her, a teasing smile tugging at his lips. 'What were you doing when you first thought of a butter churn?'

'I was in my bath.'

'Ah, those baths.' His gaze darkened. 'And your kneading machine? Another bath?'

'No.' She looked down, and rubbed the heavy silver cutlery with her thumb. 'I saw Mother in the kitchen. She was ill. Her arms were so thin, yet she insisted on making her own bread and I thought if I could find a way of lessening her labour…'

Those had been bad weeks. Her mother had not

yet accepted the inevitable and had fought a horrid losing battle.

'It must have been hard.' His gentle voice interrupted her thoughts.

'Yes, Imogene and I became very close. I looked after her. Of course Imogene is only two years younger, but it seemed so much more in those days.'

'We'll make certain that you still see a lot of her in London.'

'Thank you.'

The moment lengthened. She was aware of his proximity, of that dark gaze and his lean fingers curved about his utensils.

She remembered their touch and swallowed. 'I wanted to ask about Heloise. She hasn't arrived with the rest of my luggage. Have you received word?'

'They came earlier. I directed them to change horses and proceed to London as we're leaving tomorrow.' Paul sipped his wine.

'We are? But we were supposed to stay a week.' Rilla laid down the massive fork with a clatter.

'I altered our plans.'

'Without talking to me?'

'I do not make decisions about my household in committee.'

'"In committee"? We are not in Parliament. I am your wife and you're moving me around like so much baggage!'

Anger blossomed, although it was less about his

autocracy and more about that tiny unacceptable *frisson* of relief.

'I would not use that unflattering description,' Paul said. 'But, yes, I will make the travel arrangements for my household as I see fit.'

'Perhaps I don't want to go to London.'

'I thought you'd be glad.'

'Because…' Her stomach lurched. The incident sprang huge between them.

'I thought Wyburn not salubrious to your health.'

His admission made her angrier. She balled her hands to fists. Her jaw tightened. 'My health is robust. Besides, my parents discussed—' She stopped. Her parents spoke about everything—village doings, their children, their hopes and dreams.

But this was no such union.

'We are not your parents.' His voice, though soft, cut.

'No,' she said.

They continued eating in an uncomfortable silence, broken only by the clinking of knives and forks.

Irritation at him and at her own vulnerable relief tangled in Rilla's mind. She wanted to leave this place. Yet his choice to do so perversely annoyed.

Edison refilled their glasses, cleared the plates and served a sweet, fluffy concoction for their pudding. Then he left and silence again enclosed them.

'I think I will retire and leave you to your port,' Rilla said at last, rising from her chair.

Paul stood, but made no effort to detain her.

'Rest well. We leave after breakfast. I hope that is convenient.'

She nodded. He offered her his arm and she placed her hand on his sleeve, conscious of taut muscles under the cloth and the smell his cologne.

They moved towards the door, stopping at its threshold and she was suddenly aware of their solitude, of the warmth of his breath and the height and strength of him.

He fastened his gaze on hers, placing his hand against her cheek. She tingled at this touch. Her anger dwindled, turning into something else.

She bit her lip. His breath quickened. With a quick, almost violent movement, he possessed her mouth with heat and power and need.

Stepping back abruptly, he allowed his hands to fall from her. 'I apologise. That was not appropriate.'

'We're married.'

'And therefore must restrain ourselves in the dining room.'

'Perhaps you are too ruled by restraint,' she said softly.

'Or you are too swayed by emotion.'

She flinched at the words. Was it always to be thus—this guarding of words and actions? This fear of sentiment?

'Rather that than to be a statue,' she retorted.

As she left, she glanced back. Paul stood by the fireplace. He gripped the mantel with both hands, his head bowed low, a solitary figure.

\* \* \*

Paul came to her that night.

Rilla had dismissed Molly and stood only in her chemise, brushing her hair. She heard his step. She paused, brush suspended in mid-air.

His footsteps slowed, then stopped. She held her breath and stood so still she could hear the beat of her heart and the lone cry of a distant owl. The door creaked open.

'My lord?'

'I am no statue.' He spoke the words in low strained tones as if they were ripped unwilling from him.

She put down the brush and walked to him.

He pulled her against his body and captured her mouth with his own, tangling his hands in her wild, unbound hair.

'I can't be slow,' he said.

This was different from the night before. He used no finesse or expertise, but came to her with wanton urgency.

This, Rilla realised foggily, was lovemaking based not just on pleasure but on desperate need. She had thought he did not need her. She was wrong.

And yet, even as their bodies fused, she knew he wished it was not so.


Later, half-asleep, Rilla felt her husband move away, carefully disentangling his limbs from her own. Through lowered lids she watched him slip from her room, again a solitary, lonely figure.

Shivering, she turned away, cold despite the weather's warmth and the blankets piled upon the bed.

# Chapter Seventeen

They left for London next day. Rilla made no complaint. She wanted to leave, although it shamed her to admit it. Wyburn had an eeriness that oppressed.

Paul rode Stalwart and Rilla did not blame him. She herself would have preferred fresh air to the stuffy, lurching confinement of the coach.

Often she allowed her gaze to drift outside so she could study the man—*her husband*. There was a luxury in watching with no fear of observation.

Once, he urged Stalwart into a gallop and the duo took on that mythical quality she'd first noted in the garden at her father's home. Man and beast moved in wonderful accord, but with urgency reminiscent of a chase—or an escape.

She sighed, tracing his outline against the pane. She wished she might understand him.

But how could she hope to do so when she knew she must for ever hide herself? No, they had companionship, a shared intellectual curiosity, physical passion and a sharpness of wits.

And it would be enough. It had to be.

Their first weeks in London tested this theory. Paul's passion persisted. Indeed, he loved her regularly, but with equal regularity returned to his own chamber so that she woke each morning alone. As for companionship, that also seemed in limited supply with long hours alone while the viscount visited his club and other pursuits.

Meanwhile, while Olivia's ghostly presence seemed weaker in London, Lockhart's earthly one became a constant. The man was everywhere like a bad smell. She saw him in the theatre, the opera, the park and at a crowded assembly.

And always she felt a threat. It was in his stance, the jut of his jaw and his tone of voice when he made even the most innocuous remarks.

'You are staying inside too much,' Imogene said one morning after arriving with Lady Wyburn to entice Rilla for a shopping trip. 'Besides I overheard two ladies mention that on Tuesday you were wearing last month's bonnet.'

'Gracious, there must be dearth of interesting conversation if people must discuss my bonnets.' Rilla laughed.

'As a viscountess you are expected to be fashionable.'

'But I don't even care for fashion.'

'Exactly—that is why you have me,' Imogene said.

After feeble protest, Rilla allowed herself to be taken to Bond Street. It wouldn't do to become known as a recluse or eccentric and truthfully she'd grown to like shopping with Imogene and Lady Wyburn. They both took such delight in their purchases and Bond Street itself interested with fascinating books shops, perfumers and coffee houses spilling their enticing aromas into the street.

'And now for your new bonnet,' Imogene said, tucking her hand in Rilla's arm as they exited the bookshop.

'Honestly, I do not need another,' Rilla protested.

'Fiddlesticks,' said Lady Wyburn. 'One always needs a new bonnet.'

With these words, her ladyship steered her two companions towards Madame Bertrand's millinery store. As Rilla entered this elegant establishment, she felt, as always, the need to whisper. It was a place of sophisticated quiet, the hush all the more marked after the bustling street outside. A plush rug muffled their steps. Rainbow prisms from the chandelier danced across mirrored walls and the air was redolent with perfume and flowers.

Imogene went to a central table on which headgear of every description was displayed, decorated with feathers, fruit, flowers and tulle. She tried on a straw bonnet festooned with fruit and eyed herself in one of the long mirrors.

'At least you are not like to go hungry,' Rilla said.

Imogene pulled a face. 'Lady Alice Fainsborough was wearing something identical last week.'

'Perhaps she expected a famine.'

'You have no sense of fashion.'

'None,' Rilla agreed, picking up a fan. 'Although I have noted that ostrich feathers seem all the rage this year. Every dowager sports them. There must be some very chilly ostriches somewhere.'

'Dear child, you are not supposed to create a gale,' Lady Wyburn admonished, glancing up from a bonnet she had been studying. 'Or are you feeling faint?'

'No, not faint.'

'Nauseous? In the mornings?'

'No,' Rilla said.

'That is a pity.'

'Pardon?' Rilla put down the fan.

'Well, time enough for that. Though I hope it will occur sooner as opposed to later. That dreadful foppish cousin won't do at all.'

Rilla blinked. 'Do? For what?'

'Paul's heir, if the dear boy were to part from his mortal coil, which of course I hope he won't, as I am certain he would waste Paul's entire fortune on neckties. Of course, I really should not talk about such things in front of young girls. Ah, Madame Bertrand is beckoning. She mentioned that she had set aside a perfectly exquisite bonnet in her back office for me. I'll take a look.'

With these words, Lady Wyburn disappeared into the inner sanctum.

'Gracious, I think her conversation has become more convoluted than ever,' Rilla whispered to her sister.

'I believe she becomes less coherent when she is happy.'

'She must be positively euphoric.'

The shop door's bell jangled. Rilla turned, then froze.

Jack St John stepped into the shop, bringing with him both cool air and the noise and clatter of the street.

'Lady Wyburn,' he said to Rilla, 'I saw you through the window and wished to offer my congratulations on your felicitous marriage. I have seen you about town, but have not managed a private word.' He bowed. 'I hope I find you well.'

'Yes, thank you.'

'And marriage suits you?' He took another step forward.

'Absolutely.'

There was a subtle difference about him even from the week previous when she had seen him at a dance. He looked less kempt, his cravat stained and lines of strain bracketed his mouth.

'Your husband is truly fortunate.' His voice was a soft purr.

Rilla resisted the impulse to step back. She could smell his cologne, a cloying scent, now mixed with his sweat as though he had not washed.

'You put me to the blush.' She laughed, but her laughter sounded tinny even to her own ears.

'You are too modest. Indeed, you are a woman of both beauty and talent.'

'Pish-posh. You know well enough I cannot sing or play well.'

'But miracles. I believe you specialise in miracles.' He dropped his voice on that last word, caressing it and rolling it about his tongue. 'Such that only a saint or...'

He allowed his voice to trail to nothingness, giving a slight insouciant shrug.

*Witch*—the word he had not spoken reverberated about the shop, bouncing off the mirrors, the displays of ribbon, the centre table with its ostrich feather hats, the windows and the mannequin.

Rilla feared she'd gag. She rubbed her sticky palms against her gown.

'La, 'tis Madame Bertrand who works miracles,' Imogene said, appearing at Rilla's side. 'Her work is quite wonderful. Rilla, I have spotted the perfect bonnet for you. Come, I'll show you. If you'll excuse us, Lockhart?'

She took Rilla's elbow, but Rilla did not move. She couldn't. It was as if her feet had grown roots and were planted within the soft pile of the mauve carpet.

Lockhart smiled, bowed and turned to the exit. 'Until we meet again, Lady Wyburn.'

Rilla stayed frozen. She heard the pad of his footsteps across the plush carpeting, the whine of the door and the merry ring of its bell.

'He's gone,' Imogene said, as the door shut.

'He meant Sophie,' Rilla said jerkily.

'No, no. What would he know of that?'

'Village gossip. They spoke of it for months. They spoke of witchcraft and insan—'

'Shh,' Imogene said, her gaze darting about the empty shop.

'I need to go. I must—'

Rilla turned, looking wildly for Lady Wyburn. Then she froze, her hand clutched tight about the ostrich-feather fan she still held.

Olivia.

Olivia stood beside a display of artificial flowers. She looked real. As real as the glittering chandeliers. As real as Imogene. As real as the plush carpet.

One hand reached out towards Rilla as though seeking help.

Rilla did not scream or faint. She didn't even smell lavender.

Instead, she felt a resignation. Perhaps it was, as her father said, a gift. Perhaps it was madness. Or the work of the devil.

It did not matter because, whatever it was, wherever she was, Rilla knew with absolute certainty she could never escape.

\* \* \*

Approximately one week following the abortive shopping expedition, Paul came home early. He'd been lunching in his club and listening to the prattle of a foppish character with a yellow necktie too intricately tied.

At some point during this man's discourse, Paul realised both food and conversation would be improved at home. Besides, he felt worried about Rilla. During her first week back in London, she'd gone out frequently with Lady Wyburn and her sister, but now she was reluctant.

It must, he recognised, be no easy task for a girl with her upbringing to adjust to his social milieu. Moreover, he'd spent little time at home. This was, he recognised, a purposeful decision. He'd wanted to prove, to himself as much as to his bride, that this marriage was one of mutual respect but of no undue attachment.

Not that his mind had cooperated one iota. Sometimes it seemed as though he merely survived, sleepwalking through his days, until he could come to her at night—

The entrance hall was quiet when he entered and he felt foolishly disappointed. However, on enquiry, Edison said that Lady Wyburn was at home. 'In the music room, my lord.'

Paul frowned. Rilla had never shown an ounce of musical talent or much interest for that matter. Besides, he could hear no pounding keys or ʷ︐ʸt-ing arias.

Nodding, he walked towards that chamber and pushed open the door. The room contained a baby grand piano and straight-back chairs set in neat rows. The room had no windows and Paul blinked, adjusting to the low light of the candles.

Rilla did not sit at the piano and there were not any other ladies present to enjoy a musical afternoon. Instead, she sat on the floor, hunched over an apparatus. It appeared quite large, approximately three or four feet in height. The central part was a waterwheel with a trough-like structure angled over it and supported by two posts.

Clearing his throat, Paul moved forward.

'My lord.' Rilla paused, looking up.

'What are you doing?'

'Nothing inappropriate,' she said. 'Or, at least, well-concealed impropriety.'

'I did not mean to sound abrupt. Is that your butter churn?'

She smiled fondly, like a mother gloating over a child. 'Part of it. This is the waterwheel that powers the churn. I asked Edison to store it here because I thought it out of the way. Of course, I have a scale model as well.'

*Of course?*

'So is it still likely to flood the dairy or have you improved its design?'

'I haven't had quite sufficient time to solve the problem regarding the regulation of water flow,' she explained, frowning and tapping the wooden structure with her fingertip.

He sat down, eyeing her creation with interest. It looked well-constructed and obviously much thought had been given to its design. 'So this is what you have been about. My stepmother mentioned she had not seen you for several days.'

She looked away as though discomfited, her fingers fiddling with the waterwheel nervously. 'I—um—found the social whirl a trifle busy.'

She looked pale, he now realised, with dark shadows circling her eyes as though she'd not slept well. He remembered her face after that crazy ride on Rotten Row, suffused with a red-cheeked, open-mouthed joy.

He felt a start of guilt, mingled with apprehension. Did marriage to a Wyburn deprive one of strength or joy? Like a family curse?

'You need to get out. It is too stuffy in here,' he said abruptly.

'But I must work. And perhaps someone will call—'

'Let them.'

He realised suddenly how much he wanted to see her vibrant again. He wanted to see that wide generous smile and hear her laugh.

'Let us go for a walk in the park.'

'Now?' she asked in obvious surprise.

'Yes. It is a fair afternoon.'

'It is. But many fashionable people might be about.'

'That concerns you?'

'Only if—no, actually I have had an idea. If we

went to an unfashionable area I could make use of the excursion and test my waterwheel—'

'You want to take your waterwheel?' He had not expected this.

'And my churn to see if the wheel actually powers it. The replica works, but I would love to see the real apparatus in action. And perhaps we might stroll by a pond?'

'A pond?' he asked.

'An unfashionable pond. For the water.'

'I believe Hyde Park boasts the Serpentine Lake and Round Pond, a part of which should be sufficiently obscure, if that would suit?' Paul said.

'Absolutely and I'll need a bucket.' She stood, smiling, and with sudden energy.

'I am certain our establishment runs to a bucket. I'll ask Edison. I should have known that it would be no ordinary expedition.'

'But it will be most exciting. I haven't been able to work on my inventions. Except in my baths.'

'Those baths again. Perhaps we'd best not mention your baths, if we hope to get out this afternoon.' Grinning, Paul strode from the music room to announce their imminent need of a bucket.

# Chapter Eighteen

Paul could smell the fresh mown grass and feel the sun's warmth as it slanted in sparkling diagonal rays through the clouds. A much pleasanter way to spend an afternoon than in his club.

'That would do wonderfully,' Rilla announced, waving her hand towards what Paul presumed was a part of the Serpentine Lake.

The carriage stopped. Rilla grabbed the bucket while Paul took the trough and Heloise managed the waterwheel. Burdened with the churn, Giles took the rear, a rhythmic clanging accompanying his every move.

The lake lay in a secluded area and had been left in its natural state, with muddied shore, weeds and lilies. A green scum circled the rocks and the air smelled marshy.

The party stopped. Heloise put down the waterwheel and Giles set aside the churn, his brow speckled with sweat.

'I'll get the water.' Rilla hurried with the bucket towards the shore.

'Whatever are you doing?' Paul asked, catching up to her with easy, fluid strides. 'Give that to me or to Giles, for goodness' sake.'

He took the bucket and went to fill it at the water's edge. His feet squelched in the mud and he didn't like to think about his Hessians.

'What next, my lady?' he enquired, turning back with eyebrows raised.

But Rilla was already directing. 'Giles, you'll need to put the waterwheel down just so, and, Heloise, if you could hold the trough over it...so.'

He had to smile. Rilla had a remarkable way of getting people to do exactly as she wished and to enjoy the doing—not matter how eccentric her plan.

Shoving a wet hand through her hair, Rilla knelt on the ground to affix the trough on to the stand. 'Now, I'll just attach the pulley to the churn and, Heloise, if you could come and steady the churn. My lord, if you could pour the water into the trough so that I can better observe the wheel's motion.'

'Aye, aye.'

Paul took the water and poured. He heard the quick catch of her breath and saw that her eyes sparkled. He smiled. Truly, he hadn't fully understood the excitement, the passion she had for these things.

Peculiarly, it pleased him. 'Is it performing?'

'Yes—you see, it's important that the wheel provide the right amount of force or it will not make butter in a month of Sundays. Of course, considerably greater power will be required when we actually have cream in the churn. Oh dear, I do not think there is sufficient water. Oh, for a bigger bucket. Is the trough properly attached?'

Paul put down the empty bucket, intent on checking the trough, which did not seem to be resting properly on the stand.

'Lady Wyburn, you shouldn't—'

Paul turned at Heloise's cry.

'Rilla!'

The fool girl had taken the bucket and now hurried towards the muddy shore, intent on refilling it.

'It won't take me a minute. I'll use this as a stepping stone,' she called back.

The round rock was set about a foot into the lake. Before he could yell, she stood on it, stooping to dip the bucket into the lake.

Perhaps her shoes slipped, or maybe she was momentarily dizzy. Whatever the reason, Rilla lost her balance, crying out as her arms waved wildly.

The bucket flew in a perfect arc back towards the bank and with a peculiar slowness of motion Rilla slithered forward.

She landed face down in the lake.

Paul lunged after her, sloshing into the grimy waters.

'Rilla!'

Although not deep, the water totally covered her

body, except for her skirts, which billowed across the pond's surface in huge crimson air pockets.

His blood froze. He'd seen this in his worst nightmares. Night after night.

'Rilla!' He grabbed at her and she came up, wet and spluttering.

He hauled her roughly back to her feet, running his hands across her back and pulling her wet head to his chest. He could hear the crazy hammer of his heart. 'Are you all right?'

'Wet, but none the worse for wear.' She laughed, shaking her head like a sheepdog, obviously finding the situation wildly humorous. Wet strands tickled his chin and he could smell the water's dankness.

'What were you thinking? What a crazy, idiotic thing to do!'

'My lord, can I help in any way?' Giles asked tactfully from the bank.

'No. Stay there.' Grimly, Paul picked Rilla up and carried her to shore. Her gown hung loosely, flapping about his legs while drops of water plopped and splattered in dismal duet.

Grim-faced, he put her down on the grass, where she stood with dribbles of murky water running down her forehead and into her eyes.

'Are you all right, miss?' Heloise asked.

'Of course she is. Though soaked. Put on my coat before you catch a chill,' Paul said.

'I'm not cold,' said Rilla, starting to shiver.

'Must you argue on every point? Take my coat.'
Paul removed this garment, draping it about her.

Turning, he directed Giles to get the blanket from the carriage and informed the footman that they must return home immediately. 'Leave this clobber here. You can get it later.'

'Not clobber. My churn,' Rilla said.

'And you.' Paul rounded on her as soon as the servants had withdrawn. 'Do you never take care? Do you never think?'

'My lord, I am merely wet,' Rilla said with an arch of handsome eyebrows that seemed to Paul supercilious. Infuriatingly so.

'You could have drowned.'

'In three feet of water?'

'It's happened.'

'To a babe perhaps. I assure you I was in no danger. At home I swam quite often in our pond.'

'I do not care what rustic or aquatic activities you enjoyed previous. You are now my viscountess. These ludicrous, risky behaviours must stop. Do you understand?'

She stared up at him, belligerence glittering. 'Being a viscountess hardly means I need be wrapped in cotton wool.'

'Being a viscountess means you have responsibilities. You must look after yourself. You can no longer act the hoyden or…or play in the mud.'

'I have not acted the hoyden since Rotten Row,' she retorted. 'Besides, a minor mishap hardly impugns my character.'

'A long litany of minor mishaps is ample proof that you act without care.'

Anger pulsed through him. He could feel the vein throbbing in his temple. It seemed that all the tension of the last few weeks ballooned. His hands had tightened and the muscles in his shoulders turned to solid bands.

Good Lord, he wanted to lock her up and throw away the key. He wanted to shake her until her teeth rattled. He wanted to hold her and kiss her. He wanted to cast her away and, conversely, he wanted to keep her fused to his side.

Why, Rilla wondered as she descended the stairs to the drawing room after the disastrous excursion, had she brought the churn in the first place? Why hadn't she agreed to a nice, normal stroll or carriage ride?

It was, she knew, both a driving urge to avoid any chance encounter with Lockhart plus her own foolish and illogical thinking. She still clung to the belief that her ludicrous impractical inventions were a shield, that they could save her from Olivia and her moments. She was a child clinging to a good-luck charm and in her drive to avoid insanity she'd become just plain odd.

Her thoughts had circled in this manner throughout her bath and she now felt thoroughly out of sorts. No doubt Paul intended to berate her again for the mishap. He had done so on their journey home and, when not actively berating, had sat grimly taciturn.

Upon her entry into the drawing room, however, the viscount stood politely. He had already arranged a sofa for her beside the fire and looked none the worse for the excursion. His wet and dirtied clothes had been removed and he was again resplendent in spotless beige pantaloons and a well-tailored jacket.

'I hope you're feeling better. I wouldn't want you to catch a chill,' he said.

'Indeed, I am fine, my lord. It is not the first time I have taken an unexpected dip.'

'That I do not doubt. Here is some tea to warm you. I took the liberty of adding a measure of brandy. Purely medicinal, of course.'

'But I don't—'

'Today you do.'

'Truly, the incident was not serious. Why, I've fallen into deeper water tons of times. I would suggest the pond at home is twice as large and triple the depth.' Rilla sat on the watered silk of the low sofa.

'Then I pity your father. No wonder his hair is all but gone.'

Rilla watched Paul as he crossed the floor, seating himself in the chair opposite. His tone was light and he seemed again the languid gentleman. Yet she suspected the mishap had upset him more than she would have thought reasonable. She could see tension in his shoulders and noted a muscle twitching under the skin of his cheek.

She sipped her tea. It was hot, with obvious bite.

'I am sorry if I spoke harshly earlier,' he said after a moment.

'An apology, my lord?' Her eyebrows rose.

'I make them on occasion. I have not set myself as God.'

'Only a domestic icon. However, I know I—it was somewhat foolish to bring my churn,' Rilla conceded. 'I apologise also if I behaved inappropriately.'

He looked abstractedly into the fire as though not fully attending. 'Look,' he said abruptly. 'I owe you an explanation for my uncharacteristic rudeness and…extreme reaction.'

Rilla waited, catching her breath. The atmosphere had changed, any suggestion of frivolity dissipated. He had more to say and she knew that this was no longer about the pond or her ludicrous fall. He had, she realised, lost his self-control in a way that was out of his character.

'Paul? What is it?'

'The pond was reminiscent of an episode in my childhood.'

'Your mother.' She breathed the words, the image of dark, rain-splattered water flickering before her mind's eye.

'She chose to kill herself by jumping into a lake.'

'I'm sorry.'

'When I was seven. On July the twenty-seventh. We pulled her out some hours later.' Paul spoke with total composure, his voice steady, as though reading a dictionary definition or Parliamentary motion.

'I'm sorry,' she said again.

'No need. I merely mentioned it to excuse or explain my earlier tone.'

'You're sure she meant to…to kill herself?' Rilla asked because she had to, as though compelled by a force outside of herself.

'My father was convinced. He'd accused her of being unfaithful a few hours previous. She was an emotional woman.' His hand rested over the arm of the chair, elegantly poised except for the tension evident in the clenched white of his knuckles.

'Emotional? You think she was unbalanced in her mind?'

'Yes. She should have been committed for her own good.' He spoke harshly.

'You mean into an institution?' Her stomach knotted.

'She'd have been safe.'

He stood, the motion abrupt as though no longer able to contain his restless energy. He stood with his back to her, his hands on the mantel.

'A prisoner?'

'For her own good,' he repeated.

Rilla stood also, taking a step towards him. 'I don't think she was mad.'

Again she felt a compulsion to speak.

He inhaled. She saw his shoulders rise and fall. 'Whatever the reason. It is done with now.'

'Is it? When it hurts you still.' Stepping closer, she placed her hand over his so that their fingers entwined, outlined against the mantel. The fire heated her legs.

Olivia had not chosen to die. She knew it with a deep certainty. She wished she could tell him, convince him…

'I don't think she chose to die,' she whispered.

Gently he took her hand and pressed it to his lips.

'You are sweet. You can't understand. She had moods.'

He spoke with such surety. Rilla stared at the handsome face and dark eyes and saw no doubt. His mind was made up and all she could offer was an illogical feeling that Olivia, the portrait lady, did not want to die and that, despite her moods and needy childishness, she would not have chosen to leave her son or her husband.

'But enough talk of bygone things,' he said, his mood changing abruptly. He picked up her hand, kissing it. 'Come away from the fire, my dear.'

'Pardon?'

'I want to kiss you and I'll not run the risk that your skirts will smoulder.'

'Oh.'

He led her away and, encircling her waist, he kissed her nose, her chin and the column of her neck.

'I like your churn,' he muttered, kissing the soft hollow where her pulse beat.

'You—you do?'

'Yes. And I like you because you are alive and vibrant and interesting,' he muttered, kissing her again.

Waves of pleasure started to build, warming, swamping and engulfing. Rilla slipped her hands under his jacket, rubbing her fingers against the fine linen of his shirt, feeling the warmth of his skin and the bunch of hard muscles.

She smiled, pushing her body against his, embracing the heat and the pleasure which made only the present—this moment of consequence.

Everything else...every uncertainty...every mood...every feeling fell away like so much discarded clothing.

With nimble fingers, Rilla undid the buttons of his shirt, pushing it open. She stroked his skin, its smoothness mixed with the tickle of fine hairs.

His eyes closed and he made a guttural sound. She knew she pleasured him and with that knowledge came a heady power. She pressed her lips along the angular line of his jaw and against the tiny crease of his one dimple. Her hand moved to his chest, circling his small, flat nipples.

With muttered oath, he eased her down to the watered-silk sofa. 'Do you know what you do to me?'

'I'm learning.'

He kissed her, his hands moved to her shoulders,

pushing the cloth away. He kissed her shoulder and moved the cloth lower to uncover her breast.

Then, all restraint lost, he shoved up her skirts so that the cloth formed voluminous folds at her waist. His fingers pushed aside her petticoats, seeking the smooth skin of her thigh above her gartered stockings.

'I need you,' he said.

Quickly, urgently, he pulled off his garments and, kissing her with a greedy, unsated eagerness, he spread her legs.

She arched to him as he thrust into her. She gave him everything. She wanted to give him everything and his cry, as he came in her, spoke not of the ritual partnering of husband and wife but of love, possession—a meeting of souls.

Later, as he lay spent against her breast, Rilla smiled, tangling her fingers into his dark hair and listening to the rhythm of his breath.

For once, her husband, this peer of the land, had lost restraint, relinquished control and forgotten propriety.

# Chapter Nineteen

The days passed pleasantly.

The excursion to Hyde Park, despite its drama, had given her new hope for their marriage. Paul spent more time with her now and, while he might never love her, they had…something. It was evident in the way they talked and laughed and made love.

Moreover she refused to let a ghost or a feeling or anything else, for that matter, take it from her.

As always, she fought her wayward mind with common sense and logistical thinking. Her butter churn continued to make progress and she started work on a second contraption resembling a dumb waiter.

Lady Wyburn also kept her busy and seldom let her stay at home, dragging her out for tea, musical evenings, shopping and any number of other events. Moreover, as she'd had no other chance encounters with Lockhart, Rilla started to relax into the routine of town living.

About a week after the misadventure at Hyde

Park she found herself sandwiched between Lady Wyburn and Imogene at the Theatre Royal.

'A wonderful performance. I am certain you are thankful you did not stay at home,' Lady Wyburn announced with happy confidence as the curtain descended for the intermission.

'It is well acted,' Rilla agreed. 'But the problem with Shakespeare is that one knows the ending.'

'Gracious, you are not here to see the play, but to watch the people and to be watched. Talking of which, I wish Paul were here. He is much too busy with his Parliamentary committees. I mean, few members even put in an appearance never mind sit on committees and the like. And is it sit "on" committees, or does one sit "in" them? I never know and neither seems entirely accurate, and I don't think he should do either.'

'Paul wants to make life better for the poor in this country. That's one of the things I like about him.'

'I suppose everyone has an eccentricity or two. Anyhow, let us mingle. I am longing to chat with Lady Richmond. She is always a fund of wildly humorous gossip.' Lady Wyburn stood, managing both to arrange her finery and wave to an acquaintance in a box opposite.

Rilla declined the opportunity to mingle, claiming fatigue, and Lady Wyburn, after a sharp look, let her be. No doubt her beloved in-law was hoping she might be in the family way which she wasn't.

It was pleasant to sit in the warm theatre, to hear

the soft hum of voices and the occasional raucous laugh from the pit below. The massive chandeliers hung low, glittering with golden light. They used Argand oil burners now, a wonderful step forward from wax candles, which had tended to drip into the pit. What it would feel like to invent something like that.

Or to invent something, anything, which actually worked.

'Good evening, Lady Wyburn.'

The daydream shattered.

Rilla jerked upright as Lockhart pushed through the enclosure and into their box. She was seated which made him seem to loom, horribly close.

'What do you want?' she asked.

'So terse, my dear? I only wish to talk to you. Exchange pleasantries, don't you know.' He sat in the chair next to her.

Instinctively, she shifted away. 'I am a little tired and hoped to rest.'

'Then I will come directly to the point. I noted you have a fine brooch.'

Her hand went instinctively to the diamond attached to her dress. Paul had given it to her.

'You came to compliment my jewellery?'

'No,' he said.

'Then what precisely did you wish to speak about?'

He laughed unpleasantly. There was a wild recklessness in his face and a nervy jerkiness about his movements. 'Don't try to act the haughty with me, my girl. We both know you're scared out of your beautiful skin.'

'I—I'm not,' she said.

'Never were a good liar.' He smiled, his eyes dropping to the brooch. 'Such a shame if you were to lose it.'

She frowned. 'If I were— What do you mean?'

'Jewellery can get lost in the crush of a busy theatre.'

'Are...are you suggesting that you now intend to rob me of my jewels?' It sounded ludicrous.

It was ludicrous. After all the man, however unpleasant, was a...a...gentleman, a member of the *ton*, her friend's brother.

Rilla waited for him to laugh, to scoff or call her gullible.

He didn't.

Instead he inched closer, leaning into her. He smelled of alcohol and sweat. 'I am suggesting that you give it to me.'

'That's robbery. You can't be serious. We're in a theatre and you're a gentleman.'

'A bankrupt gentleman, at present.'

'But...I won't do it. I'll tell Paul—'

'I don't think you will.' Jack smiled, his voice dropping to a whisper. 'Because, if you do, I will tell him that you hear voices and see ghosts. Sophie, wasn't it?'

Her heart stopped, or so it felt. Her chest tightened with pain as though he had reached through bone and skin and squeezed the vital organ. Her hands clenched. She gulped, dragging in air, and felt the colour drain from her face. As though from some great distance, she heard the orchestra tuning in the pit below in readiness for the second act.

'That's blackmail,' she whispered.

'Shall we complete the transaction now or meet later?'

'I have not agreed.'

'You will. Bedlam is not known to be pleasant.'

She swallowed. Slowly, she lifted her hand from her lap. She fingered the sharp edges of the diamond setting. 'Someone will see.'

'Not if you are quick and if I stand blocking the view from the other balconies, as though to leave.'

He did so, his bulk effectively blocking her view of the theatre.

With shaking hands, Rilla unclipped the brooch. 'Here.'

He took it, the movement greedy as he closed his fingers around it. 'Delightful as always. Adieu.'

Even after he had bowed his way from the box, Rilla trembled. Her breath came quickly and she shivered despite the heat.

From behind she heard the movement of feet. She twisted, fearful that he had returned, but it was only her sister and Lady Wyburn.

'I—I do not feel well. Please, I must go home.' Her voice shook and tears threatened.

'Dear, you look dreadful—as white as snow. Well, snow in the country because London snow isn't very white. Of course we'll go,' Lady Wyburn instantly agreed.

'I'm sorry that you and Imogene will miss the second part of the play,' Rilla said.

'Do not concern yourself. By leaving now I can pretend Romeo and Juliet live, which is a much happier result.'

Minutes later, they'd pushed through the warmth of the foyer and into the evening. Rilla inhaled the cooler air, thankful for the calm quiet.

'Rilla,' Imogene whispered, the second Lady Wyburn's attention was diverted. 'I saw Lockhart leave our box. Did he upset you?'

Rilla rubbed her fingers against her reticule, shifting her slippered feet on the cobbles. Lady Wyburn stood out of earshot and was instructing a footman to bring around their carriage. 'Yes, he— he said, he threatened, that he would tell about Sophie.'

'He wouldn't.'

'And my brooch—'

Rilla's hand touched the empty place on her gown. She met Imogene's gaze and saw both her comprehension and fear.

Paul was home when Rilla returned, followed by Lady Wyburn and Imogene.

'I was going to change and join you at the theatre,' he said, pouring himself a drink with a questioning look towards the three women.

'Rilla felt ill,' Lady Wyburn explained.

Upon closer scrutiny, he saw that his wife looked white, her eyes darkly shadowed and that she stood with her arms wrapped about herself as though in distress.

'I'll go to bed, if you'll excuse me,' she said and, without waiting for an answer, left the drawing room and ascended the stairs.

'Did something happen at the theatre?' he asked after the door had closed.

'Not at all. She was just resting during the intermission. Perhaps she has something to tell you?' Lady Wyburn arched her eyebrows suggestively.

'It is more likely you are jumping to conclusions.'

Still he turned quickly and, leaving the servants to see Lady Wyburn and Imogene to the door, hurried up the stairs.

Rilla sat in her chemise, her hair braided in a plait and her face still white. He noted a frozen stillness in her posture and when she spoke a harshness in her words. 'Leave me alone. Please, leave me alone.'

'I came to make certain you were all right. My stepmother said you felt ill at the theatre.'

She turned to him now, frowning and squinting as though finding it hard to focus on his face.

'Rilla?'

'It is you,' she said as though surprised and relieved.

'Of course it's me.' Who else did she expect at her bedchamber? 'How are you?'

'Fine. It—it was the heat,' she said.

'She said you might have something to tell me.'

'Who? What?'

She shifted, the movement jerky. He saw her swallow and felt certain an expression of fear passed across her face.

'My stepmother said you might have something to tell me.'

'Oh…' She exhaled. 'No. I believe she hopes I might be with child, but I am not.'

Again with the blunt speech.

'There is time enough for that,' he said.

She nodded.

'I'll let you rest now. You still look ill.'

'I'm fine.'

He paused. She looked oddly small and vulnerable within the voluminous nightgown. Again he felt something similar to pain, but mixed with pleasure, under his breastbone.

'Sleep tight.' He closed the door softly behind him and it was only as he stood in the chill corridor that he remembered her first words and their curt desperation. *'Leave me alone. Please, leave me alone.'*

Who had she been talking to because, he was suddenly quite certain, it had not been him.


Paul's nightmare came that night. He was a child again. He wore a flannel nightshirt, his least favourite because it itched his neck.

He was stealing down the back stairs. The stone

chilled his feet. He'd forgotten to put on his slippers and his bare soles made a muted *pad-pad-pad.*

He pushed open the back door. It creaked. The wind caught it, slamming it shut behind him as he stepped into the night.

Rain slashed against his face, stinging his cheeks and blurring his vision. People stood at the lakeshore. He ran to them.

His teeth chattered. Rocks cut his feet. The mud sucked and squelched as he stepped into it.

With the distortion of dreams, no one stopped him as he neared the lake. Instead, the figures melted away, parting like the Red Sea until he stood alone with his wet nightshirt clinging to his thighs and his feet sinking into the clay-like mud.

Wind and rain patterned and pitted the lake's dark surface, but he saw something a few yards from shore. He squinted, trying to make out the shape.

He could see now that it was a woman. She floated face down and wore a red dress; its skirts billowed up, buoyed by pockets of air.

With sucking steps, he waded to her. The ice-cold water inched past his ankles, past his knees and thighs. He wanted to move quicker, but could not.

Desperately he leaned forward and grabbed the woman's arm. The skin was cold—colder even than the water that dripped from it.

Shocked, he dropped the limb. The movement

must have made the form move, because of its own volition the thing rotated.

With that same awful slowness, the corpse rolled until at last he saw its face and hair.

It was the hair he noted most.

Red-gold, and oddly brilliant even in the dim light of the half-moon.


Paul rose early.

Of course, he'd had the nightmare.

He'd known he would the second he saw his wife with that strange, white, haunted look.

Sometimes there was such a sturdy, buoyant strength about her. And at others…

He hated moods.

And he hated his own vulnerability because he could ignore the sentiment no longer—he cared for his wife. Not love, of course, but even caring felt—

He cut off the thought, dressed and abruptly summoned his carriage. He needed occupation and he might as well get something done. His man of business had sent a note yesterday requesting a brief interview.

Paul had determined to keep his mind occupied, even if it meant writing letters to every Parliamentary committee known to man.


Given the early hour, Paul made excellent time and soon strode down the cobbles towards the discreet, black-lacquered doorway of Mr Begby's chambers.

As he turned towards this edifice, he bumped against a tall gentleman with a balding head, this lack compensated by a well-groomed set of ginger whiskers.

'My apologies,' Paul said, raising his hat.

'No matter.' The man shifted aside, moving with an apparent limp and holding a black cane, a lion's head engraved in its silver handle. 'Wyburn, isn't it?'

'Indeed,' Paul said. 'Of course, Mr Hugh Whiticomb? I remember you from my days at Harrow. I have not seen you about the city for several years.'

'Fighting on the Continent, old chap,' Whiticomb explained. 'Had to put old Boney away for good, eh.'

'This country owes you a debt of gratitude.'

Paul meant it. He had wanted to fight himself, but knew his duty lay in running Wyburn and occupying his seat in Parliament.

Still he did not glamorise war. A necessity perhaps, but a bloody, dangerous and wasteful one.

'Heard you married, eh? The state suit you, what?' Mr Whiticomb asked jovially, leaning on his cane and twisting one of his ginger side whiskers.

'Quite,' Paul replied, wondering if this were true.

'Must do that myself one of these days.'

Paul nodded and started towards Mr Begby's doorway. The street was becoming busier. A cab clattered beside them and two newsboys shouted from opposite corners, their high, boyish voices cracking.

'I say, the Wyburn estate borders on Lockhart's land, eh, what?' Mr Whiticomb said abruptly, still not moving his considerable bulk.

'My stepmother's estate does,' Paul acknowledged, but warily, his eyebrows slightly drawn.

'Know much about him? Was put in a demned awkward predicament the other night. Demned awkward, I must say. The man gave me his vowels. Well, you can't turn down a gentleman's vowels. Not the thing, not the thing at all. But I'm a little worried. Gave me own vowels to Gannet. You think Lockhart's good for it?'

'I'm afraid I wouldn't know,' Paul said coolly, lifting a disdainful brow, an atmospheric change Mr Whiticomb appeared not to notice.

'Assured me he was. Had a bit of good luck himself, he said.' At this, Mr Whiticomb lifted his forefinger and patted his nose with an audible tap. The movement of his clothing scented the air with a mix of strong cologne and stale tobacco smoke.

'If you'll excuse me,' Paul said.

This time Whiticomb moved aside, although he continued to talk without interruption, or even any slowing of pace. 'Rumour has it Lockhart arranged a match between an old friend, a neighbour apparently, and a rich lord. Figures the girl will give him a bit of the ready, what?'

'That is fortunate for him.' Paul was beginning to dislike Whiticomb and remembered he'd been known to have a sly mentality at school. Foxy, they'd called him, due to his temperament and ginger hair, now represented solely by the continued existence of the side whiskers.

'Well, g'day to you, Wyburn. See you in White's, what?'

With that jocular statement, Whiticomb swayed down the street, the cane making an irregular *tap-tap-tap* against the cobbles.

The solicitor, Mr Begby, had served the Wyburn family for many years and occupied apartments on the second floor, accessed via a narrow wooden staircase. These rooms were cramped, airless and smelled of coal dust and pipe smoke.

Shelves lined every wall from floor to ceiling, except for a brief interruption caused by the narrow casement window and, on the opposing wall, a modest fireplace.

Leather tomes filled each shelf so worn that their embossed titles scarcely glinted. Wall sconces had been lit and a lamp glowed on the desk.

Mr Begby himself was short, with gold-framed spectacles sliding down a squat nose that must have been broken and badly set, giving the urbane solicitor the look of an undersized village prizefighter.

'Sit down, my lord.' He rose politely, but with dignity. At least, he was not unctuous. 'Coffee?'

'No, thank you.' Paul sat within the cramped confines of the black-leather chair.

'We'll get right down to business then,' Begby

said briskly, pulling out several papers and pushing his spectacles up his nose. 'I have the deeds for the property you wished to acquire near Wyburn. However, before we deal with that I would like to raise a matter of some sensitivity. Indeed, it was about this issue that I felt compelled to write to you yesterday.'

Begby paused and, peered over his spectacles, which had yet again slipped down his nose.

'Well, get on with it. Not like you to mince words.' Paul shifted so that the chair's dry leather crackled. He favoured Begby with a sharp look.

'Quite so. It pertains to the Earl of Lockhart, my lord.'

Paul straightened further, an irritating twitch flickering across his cheek. 'Must everyone mention that man today?'

'It is a small matter. The earl came to my office two days since. He was most agitated and demanded that you pay off Sir George Gibson's gambling debts. I would have dismissed him immediately, but knowing of your marriage...' The man lowered his eyes to the papers neatly set out on his desk, his voice trailing into tactful silence.

'Quite so. I will investigate the situation and give my instructions,' Paul said.

'Of course, my lord. Now to other matters,' Begby said with the tone of a man much relieved at having accomplished an unpleasant task. 'I have prepared the deeds for your review—'

'Which will keep well enough for another day.'

Paul stood abruptly. The chair scraped on the wood flooring.

'But, my lord, isn't that why you—er—came today?'

'They'll keep,' Paul said and, replacing his hat, strode towards the door.


Rilla sat in the music room beside her water-wheel. She rubbed the wood but diffidently, even her inventions could not occupy her mind.

Her thoughts circled between Lockhart and Olivia so that she thought she would go mad. Why had she given him the brooch? Indeed, it was the worst thing she could have done because now he knew she feared him,

Her hands tightened on the wheel and she cursed her moment of weakness.

And then there was Olivia. Rilla twisted the waterwheel moving it faster and faster. What did she want? Why did she feel her presence growing, even here in London?

The slamming of the front door interrupted her circular thoughts. Rilla stood. She faced the door, hands clenched, half-expecting Lockhart to come through, asking, demanding, threatening...

She heard Paul's voice and exhaled. Yet, within the instant, her body tightened. Something was wrong. She knew it by the sharpness of his foot-steps, the curtness of his tone to Edison and the way her stomach lurched.

The double doors opened.

'I believe—' Paul said without preamble as the doors banged shut. 'I believe I have been honest in all things connected to this marriage. Would you agree?'

Rilla nodded. She could feel the sharpness of her thumbnail against her palm as she clenched her hand.

'I now demand your honesty. It appears Lockhart has been saying things about town.'

Rilla's stomach lurched. She swallowed. She felt the blood leave her face. She opened her mouth, but found no words. The thumbnail cut deeper at her skin.

Paul looked at her. A tick flickered across his left cheek and she saw his jaw clench. 'It seems, given your expression, that you have some knowledge as to the content of his conversation.'

'I can guess.'

'So you admit it? I suppose some might call your motives laudable. Saving your father.'

'Father? What has he to do with this?'

'The motivation for your conspiracy with Lockhart, I presume. You chose to marry, thus saving your father from debtors' prison.'

'What? No! I knew he owed Lockhart money, but—'

'And you conspired with Lockhart to bring about our marriage.'

'No, I—' She understood now. Everything tumbled into place. 'I thought...' Her voice trailed into silence and she stared dazedly about the dim room.

'And *I* thought you the victim of his scheme. I should have realised the man has not the brains for such a plot. But you are well enough endowed in that area.' His lips twisted cynically. He eyed her impassively, as one might examine a Ming vase only to find it fake.

'No, I'm not! I thought—I didn't understand. I would never trick you.' The suggestion was ludicrous; he must see that.

'The scheme is advantageous to both parties.' Paul spoke in a monotone, leaning against the piano. He looked at her dismissively.

'I did not enter any scheme with Lockhart.'

'You looked guilty enough.'

'No—I thought—'

'What? What did you think?'

But of course she could not say. 'I cannot believe you'd credit the man's lies.'

Paul did not answer immediately, looking down at the piano's polished wood. 'I may not believe Lockhart,' he said, at last. 'But I must believe the evidence of my eyes.'

'Then you need your eyes checked. And your heart. I never tricked you. I didn't even want to marry you.'

'You feigned reluctance well.' His lip curled.

'I *was* reluctant. I didn't want to be married to anyone.'

'Then you are a singular female.'

'And if I had wanted a marriage, I would want one based on caring, respect, love.'

'And I wanted a wife I could trust.' He turned from her.

'No, you wanted one with whom you could find fault to make certain that you never learned to care.'

'I thought I was starting to care. I was mistaken.' Paul stepped from the piano, walking briskly to the door.

Hope, despair and anger filled her. Rilla moved forward, blocking his way, hands planted at her waist. 'I do not think you were mistaken. I think you have started to care a little and that's why you had to find some reason to condemn—' She was interrupted by a knock.

'Yes,' Paul said sharply.

The door opened and Edison walked in, his usually impassive face haggard and his iron-grey locks rumpled. 'I apologise, my lord, we have a message from Wyburn. There has been a fire and several cottages have burned.'

'Any loss of life?' Paul stepped past Rilla into the bright coolness of the hall.

Rilla followed.

'No human life, my lord. At least, not when the messenger left, although some livestock have been lost.'

'I'll go directly. Make the necessary arrangements. I'll take the curricle. Edison, come later with as many staff as possible. And provisions. Round up extra clothes, blankets and bedding, linen for wounds.'

'Yes, my lord.' Edison left, hurrying to the servants' quarters.

'What can I do?' Rilla asked.

Paul turned and looked at her blankly, as though her presence scarcely merited notice. 'Nothing.'

'But I'm coming with you. I must.'

'I can't think what earthly good you'd be.'

She hated the snide, dismissive tone, but would not be cowed by it. 'Until our marriage I was used to cooking and cleaning. I can tend to wounds. I am not afraid of hard work, whatever else you may say about me.'

'Very well, I have no time to argue.' Paul shrugged as if the whole issue no longer merited his consideration. 'Be ready within the hour. Dress warmly.'

With that he was gone. She heard his brisk booted steps retreating down the corridor's length.

# Chapter Twenty

Anger buoyed Rilla during the first part of the journey, but it had long dissipated by the time they neared Wyburn. Her spirits slumped. Even wrapped within the itchy weight of the horsehair blanket, the evening cool chilled her.

Moreover, Paul had said nothing for the duration of the ride. They'd taken the curricle and one groom, but Paul had done his own driving, with his jaw tight and expression implacable. They had stopped only to change horses and for brief refreshment.

Even before the curricle halted, Rilla sensed the fear and panic, the wrongness of the place. It was in the dense smoke which hung over the house and stables, coating her tongue and stinging her eyes. It was in the animals wandering loose on the drive, confused and bewildered. Cows lowed, and, from somewhere, she heard the high-pitched scream of an animal in pain. It stopped, its absence the more awful.

'What in the name of—?' Paul jumped from the vehicle, throwing the reins at the groom.

'Paul!' Rilla's heart squeezed as she watched him sprint across the grass towards the fields and paddocks.

At the far right of the property, close to the stables, she saw what had caused his sudden action.

The constriction about her heart tightened.

A bull stood with its back to her. Even from this angle she could see the brutish power of its thick, black shoulders and rump. Its massive head had lowered and it stamped the ground.

It was towards this creature that her husband ran.

'No,' she whispered.

One man, a domestic by his livery, stood in the bull's path, cornered between the fence and stable. He held a pitchfork, but made no use of it, standing as if frozen.

Holding her skirts high, Rilla thrust the blanket aside and jumped down, pounding across the grass. Paul had stripped off his jacket, gripping it in his hand as he neared man and beast.

Cold with fear, she slowed her pace, watching as he approached the animal, his white shirt starkly silhouetted.

She saw his plan quickly enough. By coming from behind and on the bull's right, he had engineered it so that if the animal lunged in his direction, it would run into the horse's paddock where it could be contained.

Too frightened to breathe, she saw her husband place himself level with the animal's head, although, thank goodness, some distance away.

With sudden daring, Paul shouted, flinging his coat at the beast. Enraged, the bull turned.

It snorted and lowered its head, pawing the ground, kicking up chunks of turf. Rilla could see the sharp, gleaming points of its horns.

She saw now that the animal had been hurt. She could smell its singed flesh and see a bloodied welt across its buttocks.

'Get ready to close the gate!' Paul yelled to the man.

The animal stopped, looking between the two men as if undecided which to gore. Rilla saw strings of spittle hanging from its jaw.

Then, as if catapulted, it charged Paul with wild, terrible power. Its hooves made an awful drumming sound. Paul stood motionless, directly in its line.

'Paul!' she screamed.

Just as it seemed the animal must surely impale him, he sidestepped. The animal ran into the paddock and the gate swung into place.

Rilla exhaled. Her limbs shook so that she could scarcely stand.

'Are you crazy—?'

But Paul paid her no heed, turning to the servant.

'Leave him be, as long as he doesn't look like

he's about to rip down the fence. He got hurt, I take it?'

'Yes, my lord, he were trapped when the barn caught. We got 'im out, but he went wild and came up towards the main house and the stables. I don't know how bad he's hurt. No one can get near 'im.'

'Where are the farmers?'

'Not far. At the cottages. Dousing the fire and rounding up the animals. They likely don't know as how he's here. He was that crazed. Running in circles, he was.'

'I'll go down. Fetch me if he causes more trouble. Once he calms down, we'll get someone to take a look. Or put him down,' Paul said.

'Yes, my lord.'

They walked away from the animal, which still snorted and stamped. Then, without even a backward look to where Rilla stood trembling, both men continued down the road to where the smoke hung densely, the flicker of glowing embers occasionally visible.

Rilla stood, uncertain, then shrugged and turned, walking towards the front entrance. She'd do little good exchanging stares with a deranged bull.

Mrs Lamprey must have heard her approach because the huge door opened the instant she neared.

'My lady, I'm that glad you came,' she said, her homely face revealing both worry and relief.

'Of course we came.' Rilla stepped forward and took the woman's hands in her own. They were rough and work-hardened. 'How are the tenants? Are there many injuries?'

'Minor burns and shortness of breath. The smoke, you know. I'm looking after them here in the big house.'

'I'll help,' Rilla said. 'Where will the families sleep tonight?'

'I think most will fit in the servants' quarters, my lady.'

'There is the rest of the house—'

'I think they'd feel most comfortable with us, my lady.'

Rilla nodded. 'I'll help with the bandages, and we'll see what else is needed.'

With energy she did not feel, Rilla stepped forward into the cold vastness of the Great Hall.

Hours later, Rilla headed through the hall to her bedchamber. Exhaustion made her limbs leaden. After the uncomfortable ride from London, she'd spent the evening bandaging scrapes and burns and comforting terrified, overtired children.

Now it was no longer evening but early morning. Darkness swamped the medieval entrance. No one had thought to light the wall sconces; the only illumination came from the flickering of her candle.

The fire had burned out in the hearth and the building was cold. Wind, laced with smoke, whistled through its emptiness.

Rilla's footsteps echoed and she shivered. She

had not talked to Paul since their arrival. He still worked outside, apparently. She sighed.

She hadn't yet told him that he'd been crazy to face that bull.

And brave.

And stupid to think she would ever trick him.

At the top of the staircase, she paused, uncertain. She held the candle forward and peered into the shadows beyond the weak puddle of light.

The door to the portrait gallery stood ajar. She frowned. A narrow strip of light glowed through the gloom, as though the illumination came from within.

Her hand shook. The candle flickered.

Olivia would be there. Rilla knew it by the prickling along her scalp and the dryness in her mouth as her tongue cleft to her upper palate.

She felt a physical pull towards the room like iron shavings towards a magnet. She touched the oak door, rubbing her fingers along the wood's grain and reaching for the cool smoothness of the metal handle.

Then through sheer determination she turned, forcing herself to move away.

'Leave me alone,' she whispered. 'I can't help you. I can't help him. I can't even help myself.'

Exhausted, Paul slumped in the office chair in his study.

Every muscle and every joint hurt.

They'd managed to round up most of the livestock, although some had died, trapped within sheds and barns. Cows had been milked, sheep rescued and chickens fed.

The worst had passed. The fires were out, although embers still glowed, glinting wickedly within the rubble. They'd be doused again next day.

About an hour earlier, Paul and most of the men had stumbled back to the main house. Light still shone from the servants' quarters and he'd watched the others troop down the stairs, their boots a weary tattoo.

Paul had not joined them. He knew his presence would discomfit them, although he would not have minded their company. Indeed, he found little comfort in the loneliness of his study.

Mrs Lamprey had of course hurried in with food. He'd eaten, as much to give him strength as for pleasure or appetite. Now the victuals churned inside him.

Rilla already slept. He'd gone to look at her. He'd stood on the threshold of her bedchamber, and watched her curled upon the bed, her hair braided in a thick rope of orange.

She'd been wonderful—nursing, helping, consoling. He'd seen her only in brief snatches, but every time he'd noted her calm, caring strength.

Paul sipped his brandy within the darkness of his study. He had not bothered to light the lamp or put a match to the hearth.

Through the window, he could see the sweep of

the drive, the stones shining white under the night sky. Thankfully it did not face the lake.

The fire had pushed out any thought of his last conversation with Rilla, but now his own words filled his mind.

It was his lack of logic that bothered him most. He was an intelligent man with sound reasoning and rational response. In all aspects of his life, he acted with sense.

He had always acted with sense.

But to condemn Rilla for conspiracy with Lockhart was illogical, emotional and unjust.

It also proved what he'd always known, that sense mattered not one whit once a man gave way to sentiment. He had sworn to never emulate either of his parents, with their moods and fights.

And he was failing…had failed.

Paul remembered his father's accusations and his mother's tears. He remembered how his father had lingered in this room on the morning of Mother's funeral, staring from the window, his body hunched.

'We Wyburn men are a destructive lot,' he'd said. 'A damned destructive lot.'

Later that morning, Rilla sat in bed and sipped thick, sweet chocolate. She felt tired and headachy after her late night, and her throat hurt from the smoke.

The heavy curtains had been opened. She could see the pale blue sky of morning and noted that it seemed a windless day, which was as well. Any breeze might fan the embers. The smell of smoke lingered, even within the room.

The door opened. Rilla glanced up, expecting Molly.

Paul stepped into her bedchamber.

'May I speak to you?' His voice was quiet, his expression calm.

'Yes, my lord.' Rilla put her cup on the night table. The saucer rattled.

'I must apologise,' he said.

She gaped. She had not expected this. 'Oh.'

'My behaviour was unpardonable. My accusations unfounded.'

'Well, we agree on something,' she tried to joke. Her fingers twisted in the ribbons of her nightgown.

Oddly, she didn't feel any relief or triumph. Instead, his apology brought with it a dark sense of foreboding. Something was wrong between them, worse than before. It was in the rigidity of his stance, the square straightness of his shoulders and the dark, emptiness of his gaze.

'I won't let it happen again,' he said in his polite, controlled voice.

'I should have been honest about my father's debt. I suppose we're bound to have misunderstandings.'

'No! No, we are not bound to have "misunderstandings".' He spoke abruptly as though the words had burst free without his consent. He stepped back, then said, in that same tight, controlled voice, 'We are bound to behave like controlled, civilised beings.'

'Civilised beings do not always agree.'

'Civilised beings are rational. Always.'

'We're human. We have emotions,' she said gently.

'Which must be controlled by good sense.'

'Why?' She met his eyes, her hands still twisting in the ribbon.

'Because emotion without sense is destructive.'

'Perhaps sense without any feeling is equally destructive?'

He shrugged, refusing her challenge. 'If your ladyship will excuse me—'

'Of course, my lord.'

He bowed, turning to walk away, but stopped. 'You did good work yesterday.'

'As did you, my lord.'

The silence lengthened.

'Well, I'd best get back. Again, my apologies.' He sounded as polite as a clergyman and remote as the North Star.

Rilla sat on the bed long after he'd gone. She wanted to fight, yell, scream or hurl china ornaments across the floor. She wished that she'd done one or any of those things, if only to break through her husband's polite words and platitudes.

Why was he so afraid to feel?

'Bother,' she muttered, adding in a fit of rebellion, 'and blast.'

Rilla got up and dressed. She'd help downstairs. It would at least distract her thoughts. She was halfway down the servants' stair when she remembered that she'd promised to bring wool shawls to the kitchen. Frowning with irritation, she turned and hurried back up to fetch them from her bedchamber.

She pushed open the door but halted, jerking to a stop. In her haste, she had gone into the wrong room. It was not even a bedchamber but a study, or a lady's sitting room.

Sunlight filtered pleasantly through lace curtains, imbuing the chamber with bright morning stillness.

Strangely, this room did not have any hint of the smoke that lingered within the corridor. Instead, the scent of lavender enveloped her—so strong Rilla thought she saw its heavy purple droplets dampening the air. Without conscious thought, she stepped inwards, feeling the lavender envelop her.

'My lady?'

Rilla jumped, swinging her body towards the door. Mrs Lamprey's solid bulk stood at the threshold. 'Sorry to disturb you, my lady.'

'Whose room is this?'

'His lordship's mother used it as a boudoir. We cleaned it all out—well, except the desk.'

Rilla nodded and looked towards the writing table. It stood within the curve of a turret window.

The wood was inlaid with mother of pearl and its elegantly curved legs were of French design.

Mrs Lamprey waited, her big-boned hands playing with the heavy white cotton of her apron. 'We didn't like to throw away her papers and things. His lordship's father never wanted us to touch 'er things. Of course 'is current lordship got us to clear things out smart enough. But, the papers... Well, we didn't like to.'

'Of course not,' Rilla said.

She shivered despite the morning sun. A raw, pulsing neediness filled the room.

Mrs Lamprey left and, turning, Rilla followed her, glad to return to the passage and hear the door shut behind her.

Yet even downstairs in the cavernous entrance hall, lavender still perfumed the air and Rilla could feel the dead woman's disappointment, anger and desperation.

Rilla stepped into the sunlight. She had to get outside. Perhaps fresh air might clear her head. She found a trail soon enough, a shadowy, loamy, rustling place pleasantly shadowed with trees. Perhaps it might bring her to the village and she could better assess the damage.

But the path didn't wind towards the tenants' houses or farms. Instead, Rilla stepped from under the trees' canopy towards the lake.

The trail, she realised, must have wound to the north and the lake looked quite altered from this angle, larger and wilder. Slick mud and rocks made the path treacherous. In one spot, a cliff face had formed, dropping about ten feet to the water's edge.

Treading softly, Rilla went to the narrow strip of muddy shore. She crouched and, pulling off her gloves, dabbled her fingers in the water. The liquid slipped through her hands in diamond droplets.

In that moment, it seemed as if all sensation intensified: the water's chill, the sun's warmth, the squelch of mud and the breeze's touch through her dress.

Olivia had come here. She had come here on that last night of her life.

The thought came clearly and suddenly, jagged like a lightning bolt across the velvet of evening twilight. Olivia had knelt here. She had looked across the lake to the house. She had touched this water, dipping her fingers in the chill liquid.

And, according to Paul, she had wilfully stepped into the chill dark depths. She had plunged under the gleaming surface. She had allowed her lungs to fill with water and her life to end.

Except—

'Why are you here?'

# *Chapter Twenty-One*

Paul's voice slashed through her.

'I…I…' Rilla stuttered, disorientated. She shifted her weight, twisting her body to face him.

He stood behind her, his face black against the lightness of the sky. Again, he struck her as mythical.

'I came here by accident. I do not know my way about the estate yet,' she said.

'There are more pleasant views of the lake. It is bleak here. I suggest you do not come.'

'Why? Because your mother drowned here?'

She saw him flinch. Exhilaration and fear tangled within her.

'Yes.'

'Paul.' She stood, facing him. 'Your mother died years ago. Let her rest in peace.'

'I believe you mentioned her, my lady. I merely commented on the view.' A tic flickered down his cheek.

'But she is here, between us. You fear any disagreement or attachment because of her. Paul, you—you have to give us a chance.'

'I have to act in a manner which is seemly and appropriate and that is not to discuss personal issues in this way.' He turned as though in dismissal.

'I don't think your mother wanted to die.'

She watched his back tense as he slowly turned back to her. 'May I suggest that you don't know the first thing about my mother's life or death. My father always believed she'd committed suicide after a fight with him and I see no reason to disbelieve him or debate the issue with you.'

'I see every reason. His grief was unhealthy. His view was not rational.'

'But I *know* she killed herself.'

'How? You were a child.'

The silence deepened. Rilla held her breath. The lake lapped against the rock and a bird cried, a distant lonesome sound.

'I heard.' The words were dragged from him.

'What?'

'I heard her crying that night. When I went to bed. But I didn't go to her.'

He picked up a stone and threw it violently into the water. She caught a glimpse of his face and of pain so raw she dropped her gaze.

She stepped to him, hand outstretched although she did not touch him. 'I'm sorry.'

'I could have stopped her.' He threw another rock, hurling it with vicious force.

'You were seven. You were a child. Surely you can see that.'

'Yes. I see that.' Another rock fractured the lake's calm.

Rilla paused. There had been a minuscule emphasis on the *I*. 'Your father? Did you tell him?'

'Yes.' His voice dropped so low she could hardly hear him.

'What did he say?'

'He was drunk at the time.'

'Paul.' She touched his arm.

He stepped back from her. The spell broke. Again, she saw his struggle for control. He inhaled and straightened his shoulders. With visible effort, he forced the polite mask of the implacable gentleman into place.

'Rilla, this is ancient history. It is damp here and I wouldn't want you to catch a chill. May I escort you to the house?'

'Paul—'

'It is ancient history and something I do not discuss.' His tone brooked no opposition.

They stood in momentary silence.

'I would be happy to escort you to the house,' he repeated.

'No, thank you, my lord.'

He bowed. 'Then I will look forward to your company later.'

Briefly she watched his retreat, the fluid movements and easy gait as he strode away.

* * *

Rilla returned through the copse, but she did not like it half so much as she had earlier. The trees enclosed, the pine scent overwhelmed and the thick canopy blocked out the light.

She must have taken a wrong turn, because when she stepped from the trees, Wyburn was nowhere in sight and she looked instead at open farmland.

The path had widened into a rutted road, bordered by a grass verge and low stone walls. Despite the sun she felt cold and pulled her wool shawl tighter.

Her fatigue had worsened. Her head felt heavy on her shoulders and her thoughts moved slowly. Perhaps if she rested. There was a low stile nearby and she sat with an exhalation of relief, leaning against the stones and staring across the emerald quilt of fields.

She'd not known that Paul had heard his mother crying. Olivia had not known it either, she realised with sudden clarity. And his father? Had he blamed his son?

Paul's face, his cold, hopeless bleak expression, flashed across Rilla's mind. Yes, she thought, Paul's father was a man broken by his own grief, perhaps made mad with it.

And, while he had blamed himself, he had also blamed his son.

Except, Rilla knew with an absolute certainty,

Olivia had not killed herself. She had not wanted to die. But how to prove it?

The answer came to her, a clear, intuitive knowing as real and tangible as the stones on which she sat or the grass which spread from her feet in a green carpet.

But could she do it? Goosebumps prickled down her back and arms, raising the tiny hairs on her neck.

But she loved him.

She loved Paul. It was the truth. She did not know how or when this had happened, but she could no more deny it than she could stop her lungs from breathing.

And if she loved him, she must help him even if it meant opening her mind and her soul to those forces which she feared—

'Well, if t'ain't the new mistress. I be mighty pleased to meet you, me lady.'

The broad country voice did not startle her. Indeed, it seemed as much a part of the scene as the wind's rustle or the cattle lowing.

Rilla turned and saw an elderly gentleman standing a little behind her, propped on a twisted wooden stick. His back was bent and his legs bowed.

She made room for him, suddenly glad of this human contact however humble.

He sat beside her on the stile with a grunt of satisfaction. 'Thanking ye kindly, me lady. Now there's the mark of a real lady.'

'Have you come from the village?'

'No.' He chewed something, tobacco most likely, making a squelchy noise with his toothless gums. 'I lives in my hut over there.' He nodded in the direction of the fields. 'A real lady. My mistress Olivia were like that.'

'You knew her?'

'Sure and I did.'

'You're the first person who has spoken about her.' She glanced at his lined face. 'What was she like?'

'Lovely lady. Pretty too,' the man acknowledged. 'Though a bit like a child at times. Wilful, like. Well, ladies are, ain't they?'

'Some, I suppose.'

'Her and his old lordship, they was in love. Like young children they were and about as much sense between them. Not that I worked at the 'ouse myself, but I'd go to the kitchen.' He grinned. 'They loved well and they fought well.'

'Were you there that night?' Rilla swallowed.

'Aye, that I were.' He paused. 'But you don't want to be talking 'bout that there. Too nice a day and too pretty a lady to be bringing up past 'istory like.'

'Mr…?'

'Mr Hamer. Simeon Hamer be me name, for nearly three score years and ten.'

'Mr Hamer, I really need to know about her. I think—I know—it's very important that I understand what happened.'

He turned to her. One eye was a bright blue while a white film covered the other. He shifted, studying her more carefully from his one clear orb. After chewing for several seconds, he nodded. 'Aye, I reckon you're right.'

'What happened?'

He chewed again for a time before he spoke. 'There's nobody what rightly knows. She ended up drowned in that there lake, as ye'll be knowing. 'Is lordship, the master's father, was sure she killed herself. Me, I say she couldn't have done it. She'd never 'ave left her boy—nor his dad neither. Nope, she couldna done it.'

Rilla reached forward to touch the gnarled hand. His skin was dry but oddly soft. 'Do you think it was an accident?'

'Aye,' he said. 'Aye.'

The conversation had a surrealism that removed any need for embarrassment or explanation. Indeed, it seemed to Rilla that she had always known this man, while conversely she questioned if he even existed. Perhaps he was only a figment of her mind.

'I'd best be off now.' Simeon stood with another grunt of exertion, leaning heavily on his stick. 'Wishing you well, me lady.'

'Goodbye,' she said, the word strange and hard to form.

He touched his cap with twisted fingers and turned away.

Rilla watched as he progressed up the country lane. He moved stiffly, his footsteps shuffling.

Briefly, his bent frame was silhouetted against the sky and then he was gone, disappearing over the ridge.

The wind blew cold. Rilla shivered. Maybe she wouldn't go to the village, but would return home directly.

She stood, stepping forward, but with her first step the lane changed. It blurred. The dirt buckled into waves. Rilla stared with confusion at the changing landscape.

She no longer stood on the road—instead she had been transported to the lakeshore. Waves lapped at her feet. She watched them lick her buttoned boots and wondered idly if they'd wreck the leather.

Glancing up, Rilla caught sight of a woman approaching along the rocky bank. She wore a blue dress, nipped unfashionably tight at the waist. Ringlets clustered around a peaches-and-cream complexion and childish, wide-set blue eyes. She smiled, moving quickly and impulsively, almost skipping.

'No,' Rilla shouted. 'Be careful!'

Then Rilla stood no longer. She *was* the woman. She felt herself fall forward, crashing headlong into the dark, cold lake. Her clothes weighed her down. She hadn't known the lake was so deep and now she wasn't sure which way was up. She was disorientated surrounded by blackness.

Panic surged, a wild, heart-racing fear. Her limbs thrashed. Her lungs hurt. Her foot caught in the weeds. She fought to free it. She struggled until she could hold her breath no longer.

And then the world went dark.

Voices surrounded her, worried cries prodding at her mind as hands reached for her.

She was being moved, lifted. Her body swayed, briefly airborne. Then she was lying on something hard, moving forward with a bumpy, uneven gait.

It smelled nice like hay. Rilla liked hay. It reminded her of childhood and autumn hay rides. Wheels rumbled and her body rocked.

'You'll be fine, my lady,' someone said. She did not recognise the voice, but thought the comment foolish. Of course she'd be fine. She'd tell him herself, except she felt too sleepy and the simple sentence seemed too hard to form.

They stopped. The wheels whined. Reins jingled and an animal snorted, stamping its foot.

'Johns, what are you doing with a hay cart at the front door?' The voice sounded sharp. It was Edison, an affronted Edison. Someone laughed. Edison wouldn't like someone to laugh at him. Then Rilla realised the sound came from her own lips.

She heard a noise, like the lowering of a cart's gate, a grating sound. Rilla struggled to a sitting position. Her head swam and she blinked as she looked about the wagon. It was made of wooden planks, pieces of straw stuck between the slats.

'Your ladyship?' Edison said with astonishment. 'My goodness. Very well, Johns. Thank you, we'll look after everything now. Get back to your duties. Can you walk, my lady?' He spoke quickly, worry lacing his voice.

Rilla stared at him, disorientated. His words made little sense.

Of course she could walk.

'My room, please,' she said. Her tongue moved awkwardly, her mouth dry as if stuffed with cotton batting.

But walking proved none too easy. Her legs had turned to sacks of flour, heavy but with neither muscle nor bone so that Edison and Mrs Lamprey had to half-carry her up the stairs.

'One, two, three and up we go,' Mrs Lamprey said in bracing tones she'd use to coach a child.

They passed the portrait gallery. Its door stood open. Olivia seemed very clear today, her face bright in a world thick with fog.

'You didn't do it,' Rilla said, her voice loud even to her own ears. 'I'll tell him. You didn't want to die.'

'Of course not, my lady,' Mrs Lamprey said. 'We'll have no talk of dying.'

'He thinks she did and blames himself. I need to tell him, you know. I need to prove it to him.'

'Of course you do, my lady.'

Someone hurried up behind them. Rilla could

hear the quick footsteps. They seemed inordinately loud, tapping like tiny hammers in her head.

'Be careful with her, mind,' another voice said.

It was Heloise. She sounded cross, probably irritated that she hadn't been summoned immediately. Rilla giggled. Heloise would disapprove of any crisis occurring without her permission. Another giggle. Although this wasn't a crisis. Rilla just felt sleepy. Very sleepy. Sleepy wasn't a crisis.

They entered the bedchamber. Rilla saw the lake through the window—larger, brighter than life.

'She didn't, you know. I found out. For once, I'm glad she came because I needed to know. I wanted her to come.'

'Now let's get you into a warm bed,' Heloise said, already turning down the covers. 'You'll feel better after a rest. Staying up half the night and then walking about half the morning.'

But Rilla could not stop shivering even after Heloise had tucked her into a bed and Mrs Lamprey had procured a hot brick for her feet. It seemed as if the cold came from within, from a frozen, drowned part of her.

Molly tiptoed to the door. 'Mr Edison wants to know if he should send for the doctor.'

Rilla wondered why the lass spoke quietly, in a tone more apt for a sickroom. And why would they want the doctor? Perhaps one of the burns had gone bad? Her mother used to make a poultice.

Or was it Edison's tooth? It should be pulled. His jaw had still looked red and swollen.

Frowning, Rilla tried to find the words to ask, but couldn't.

'Should have done that half an hour since. Has his lordship been informed?' Heloise asked, sharp even for her.

*Informed about what?* Rilla wondered.

'Will she be all right, *mademoiselle*?' That was Molly's voice, strung tight with nerves.

'Absolutely,' Heloise announced. 'God willing.'

Rilla wondered who was ill.

Paul watched as Heloise rinsed the white flannel in an enamel bowl. Flowers decorated its sides and a hairline crack twisted around the rim. Her hands were small, the joints swollen.

Water splattered into the bowl. Heloise, having wrung out the cloth, shifted forward towards the bed. The chair's feet scraped roughly against the wood floor.

Paul had seen Heloise sponge Rilla's face often during the last three days and he hated the familiarity of the task. He hated everything in this darkened room—the scent of sickness, the stuffy heat, the occasional whine of a fly, oddly mixed with his wife's laboured breath.

Three days. Not proper days with night and day. Rather, seventy-two hours blurred together.

At first the doctor had not been unduly worried.

'Just a touch of influenza,' he'd said. 'I'll be back in the morning.'

But by morning Rilla was no better. Her temperature had soared and lucidity had given way to dementia. The doctor shook his head, advising cooling baths. 'Keep her calm,' he'd said.

Good advice, but difficult to follow. Rilla's agitation grew. Even now she kicked at the damp, sweat-soaked linen.

On the second day the doctor advised that Paul send for her family.

True fear set in at that moment.

Now it was the third day. Paul glanced at the mantel clock. Imogene would arrive soon. Sir George was laid up with gout and would come the second he could bear the pain.

Paul walked to the window. He pushed aside the curtains so that they rattled on the rod. Bright light flooded in, hurting his eyes.

The afternoon was beautiful, cloudless. The flowers had bloomed in the August heat, filling the garden with wild colour, and the lake stretched in blue beauty.

It seemed wrong somehow. It seemed wrong that everything could continue without pause. He remembered a similar feeling after his mother's death, a furious surprise that the sun still rose and the stars shone. Stupid, of course, and arrogant.

Rilla would die. Paul knew it.

It was not only the grimness in the doctor's face, the pity he'd seen in Heloise's beetle-black eyes or the funereal tiptoeing of his staff.

It was the knowledge that he, Paul Lindsey, Viscount Wyburn, had sought to outwit fate.

And lost.

A sour smile twisted his lips. He'd known that anyone he loved would be taken from him. It had happened with his mother.

And his father.

Not that Father had died. Or, at least, he'd taken ten years to do so.

But ever since that night, he'd been dead to his son. It had seemed he'd hated Paul and the memories he'd evoked.

Or blamed him.

Paul turned from the window and looked back towards the bed.

Rilla's breaths came in rasping pants. He hated the sound, yet dreaded the moment it might stop. Heloise still sat on the chair.

He'd tried so hard not to care. Ironic because he did care and her loss would be the more intolerable because he'd squandered their time together.

'Heloise, go rest. I'll stay with her,' he said, taking his post beside the bed.

'Yes, my lord.'

The door opened and closed.

Paul sat alone beside this woman who was his wife, but in no way resembled the spirited, feisty girl he'd married.

'Rilla,' he said gently, 'I know you can't hear me, but I need—I must tell you—I love you. You wanted a marriage about love and you have it. Truly, you do.'

He held Rilla's hand, but she gave no sign that she'd heard or had any knowledge of his presence. Instead, she lay quite still.

Perhaps it was his destiny to fail those he loved best.

'Come! Come with me! Come with me now!'

Rilla's high, hysterical voice startled Paul from a fitful sleep. He bolted upright.

Night had come, but he hadn't lit a candle, and darkness cloaked the chamber so completely that he could barely discern the shape of the room or its furnishings.

She was getting up.

Ghostlike, Rilla had risen, and now she stood shrouded in sheets.

'Rilla! Stop!'

She let the linen fall and padded softly to the door. She moved with peculiar ease despite the dark, neither stumbling nor hesitating.

Paul's hands shook and he cursed. He fumbled with the match so that it dropped, fizzling on the floor and scenting the room with smoke.

He cursed again and struck another. Grabbing the candle, he hurried after her.

'Rilla, where are you going? What are you doing?'

She did not answer or look back, but stepped

into the corridor, her movements direct and purposeful.

After three days in bed he had not thought her strong enough to walk, but she did so, a strange, gliding motion with her spine unnaturally straight.

'Rilla, please…' He ran to her, grabbing at the nightgown, which was so sticky with sweat he could smell and feel it.

Twisting, she stared at him with strange eyes, either sightless or seeing too much. Perspiration beaded on her forehead, shiny in the candle's glow.

'You must come! She needs to tell you. She wants you to know.' Her voice rose high.

'Of—of course. But you need rest. Come back to bed.' Paul grasped at the thin wrists, pulling her back.

'No!' She thrashed from his hold.

Paul released her. She seemed so crazed that any restraint might cause injury. He wished Heloise were here.

Or the doctor.

Eerily sure-footed, Rilla moved down the darkened hallway, stopping at the room his mother had used for a study. She reached for the handle and he saw the whiteness of her fingers as they tightened on the knob. It rattled as she twisted the handle.

The candle flickered in the draught as the door swung open.

Rilla turned and beckoned to him, the movement grotesquely duplicated by the dark shape of her shadow. He stepped forward and the cold, stale air in the chamber struck him.

On top of the staleness, he smelled lavender.

He followed her into the room. The door banged shut.

'Rilla—'

She did not turn to him, but walked instead to a writing desk. He watched as she crouched and pulled open a drawer. It whined. She thrust her hand inside. 'Here!'

'For goodness' sake.'

'Here.' She stood, holding out a book.

'What…what are you doing?'

'Look in it.'

Paul didn't want to read his dead mother's books, yet he could not refuse his wife's frantic entreaties.

'Of course,' he said.

'Promise me. Promise!'

'I promise.' He took the book, the leather-bound covers dry and cool to the touch.

'She didn't do it, you know.'

'I know.'

At last, the madness receded, replaced with life-less calm as Rilla sank to the floor.

## Chapter Twenty-Two

Heloise returned at dawn.

'How is she, my lord?'

'Bad,' he muttered, staring at the white form that hadn't moved since he'd carried her back to her bed hours earlier.

Heloise touched Rilla's forehead, pushing back the heavy hair.

'My God,' she whispered.

'What! What is it? Is she—?' He stood. The chair crashed against the wall.

'The fever's broke—'

'What?'

'She'll recover, my lord,' Heloise said.

'How can you tell?'

'The crisis has passed. Feel her head, it is quite cool.'

'You're sure?'

'Yes.'

'Thank God.' Paul's legs, wobbly as Indian rubber, sank beneath him as he fell back into the chair. 'Thank God.'

\* \* \*

Doctor Alban arrived with his bag. He twisted the whiskers of his neat, dark moustache, drank Paul's brandy and confirmed Heloise's prognosis.

'Miraculous. Miraculous. I was a little worried, I will admit. But she'll be fine now, just fine.'

'You're sure? I cannot live through another night like that.'

'She will recover. Go rest, my lord. Lady Wyburn will like not wake for many hours. I'd suggest also a bath, shave and sustenance, if I am not too bold.'

'I think I might start with sustenance.'

Paul walked to the dining room, his gait mechanical, more closely resembling the motion of Rilla's inventions than any human form. He pushed open the door and blinked at the sunlight flooding the room.

The chamber, although vast, seemed cheerier than normal, or perhaps it was coloured by his own relief. A fire glowed in the hearth to ward off the morning chill, and the air smelled of coffee, toast and bacon.

Imogene and Lady Wyburn had arrived. He vaguely remembered Edison mentioning this fact, but still knew a start of surprise as he saw his sister-in-law sitting at the table. He pushed his hair from his forehead, wishing he had bathed and shaved.

'Heloise says she is better?' Imogene said without preamble, apparently not noticing his roughened chin.

'Yes, the doctor too.'

'Thank God.' She took a drink of coffee and he saw that her hand shook and her lips quivered.

She replaced the cup.

'I am sorry you have been so worried. I forget how young you are and how much you care for her.'

She looked down. One finger rubbed the rim of her saucer, creating a high whine. A tear trickled down her cheek. She rubbed it away and laughed. 'Foolish, aren't I? Crying when I am so happy and...and relieved.'

'It is a natural reaction,' he said gently.

'I don't know what I would do without her. After Mother died, Father started to—to drink and gamble. Rilla was everything. She was my anchor until Father got better.'

Paul nodded. He knew what it was like to lose two parents. Except he'd had no anchor. The image of his boarding-school dormitory flashed across his mind.

'You were lucky to have her,' he said.

'Yes.'

Absently, he poured himself coffee, inhaling its aroma.

'When might I be able to see her?' Imogene asked.

'She's sleeping now, but you can go to her. I'll get Mrs Lamprey to show you the way.'

'Thank you.'

Paul nodded and rang the bell. 'Imogene?'

'Yes?' She turned to him and smiled.

'Has…has your sister ever had strange dreams, or done anything peculiar?'

Her smile disappeared. Her face, already pale, whitened.

'No,' she said, her mouth tight about the single syllable.

'Must have been the delirium.'

'Fever does odd things to a person.'

He nodded. The silence lengthened until Mrs Lamprey came and Imogene stood, following the housekeeper from the room.

Paul sat and pulled his cup towards him, then reached for the toast. With the movement of his arm, something dug at his ribs. Frowning, he patted his jacket, closing his fingers about the leather edges of a book.

Of course, it was the volume Rilla had thrust at him.

He pulled it out, placing it on the table. It was a harmless volume of romantic poetry but, remembering his wife's mad eyes, he felt an illogical hatred towards it as though it contained the scriptures of hell.

With sudden violence, he pushed it away. The book skidded across the polished wood and fell facedown, its spine bent and pages splayed. A sheet of notepaper fluttered to the floor.

Paul plucked the sheet between thumb and forefinger. It was yellowed at its edges and covered with the flowing and intricate loops of a feminine fist. It smelled of mould and dust…

And lavender.

He placed it on the table, brushing his fingers across the page to smooth the creases. The letter was dated the day of his mother's death. He looked down to the signature. His breath caught. His heart squeezed under his ribs.

His mother had written it.

To his father.

*July 27th, 1797*
*Dear Allan,*

*Darling, how foolish I am sometimes. I know you wanted my assurance that I would never look at another man, but I was too stubborn to give the relief you sought. However, I have had my little weep and will give it now, without reservation.*

*Darling, I love you and only you. I have never and will never look at any other man. How could I? Life would be dreadful dull without our rows and wonderful reunions.*

*I glance from my window and see tall lilies growing by the lake. I was going to send this with Matthew to the gamekeeper's cottage. You see, I know you are not in London. But now I think I will pick those wonderful blooms and send him to you with a bouquet. Of course he'll never forgive me for making him carry a posy. 'Tis cruel, I own, but it amuses me greatly.*

*Darling, despite my moods, my highs and my lows, my love for you is everlasting. You need to know this and never doubt it.*
*Your loving wife,*
*Olivia*

Paul stared at the words.

This was not the letter of a woman bent on self-destruction. His mother had not been planning her own death. What he had heard that night had been 'her little weep'.

He was not to blame.

He had not failed her.

He had not failed his father.

The thoughts rattled through his brain.

Then a more awful thought struck him like a cannonball to the gut: if she had not thrown herself into the lake, what had happened?

Bile rose in his throat and Paul swallowed its sourness. He made himself breathe, his hands gripping the chair's carved arms so tight his fingers ached.

At last, with meticulous motions and determined calm, he released the chair, refolded the note and placed it in his breast pocket. Standing, he stared about the room, at its stone hearth and tapestry-covered walls, as though it had become a foreign landscape.

What had happened that night?

Blindly, he walked into the Great Hall, through the doors and down the front steps to the drive beyond.

More by instinct than design, Paul took the trail that circled to the north shore. He walked quickly. Sweat prickled under his arms and his heart pounded.

He stopped at the spot where he'd seen Rilla a few days previous.

Where they'd found his mother's body.

And where lilies bloomed.

To his right, the rock face sheered into the lake. In front, the waters lapped against the mud and stones.

Squatting, Paul dabbled his fingers into the lake. The water was cold. It dripped from his hand and licked at the leather of his boots. He picked up a pebble and rubbed its roughness across his palm.

He threw it, swinging it high as a child might. It hit the surface with a muted plop.

Had his mother stumbled? He looked to the rock outcrop. Tentatively, he ran his fingers across the stones, its granite roughness mixed with the slickness of moss.

Would she have climbed the outcrop? Was it possible she'd clambered up the cliff to reach the lilies and stumbled?

Why hadn't she shouted for help? How far did the human voice carry? And who would hear?

Or had something even worse happened?

Tension snaked through his shoulders. He tossed

a dozen stones towards the lake's centre so that they skipped across the surface and then sank.

Questions pounded.

He'd traded one nightmare for another and knew he could not rest, could never rest, until he discovered the truth.

Heloise had appointed herself sentry and sat outside Rilla's chamber in a straight-backed chair, sewing with a brisk and rhythmic rustle of thread.

'Is she awake?' Paul asked.

Heloise looked up at him. 'But tired still. Miss Imogene saw her for a few minutes.'

'I'll not stay long, but I must see her.'

He walked in. The room still carried the stuffy scent of sickness. The curtains were closed and the furniture took on a shapeless, lumpy look in the half-light.

Rilla appeared to be asleep, but opened those remarkable eyes and looked at him as he approached. She smiled.

'Rilla.' A bubble of joy momentarily pushed away the questions and doubts. 'Thank God. I am so glad you are better.'

'Me too,' she said. ''Tis most unusual. I am seldom sick.'

'I will not tire you.'

The chair by her bed creaked as he sat in it and leaned forward to take her hand. It looked thin in his own.

'I am a little sleepy. Everything's fuzzy. Even your face,' she said in a voice still weak.

'Just as well, given the look Heloise gave me. I have not shaved.'

'Heloise sets high standards.'

'Rilla.' His grasp tightened. 'I need… I must ask you something.'

'Umm?'

'About my mother.'

He felt a sudden stillness in her hand. She swallowed. He saw her throat move.

'I found…or rather you found a book which you gave to me. It had a note in it from my mother. Do you remember?' He leaned towards her. She smelled of liniment instead of lemon.

'I—' She frowned, her eyes narrowing. Her head moved restlessly on the pillow. 'It's blurred, like a dream. When I try to think about it, it disappears.'

'You went to my mother's desk. You found a book.'

She rubbed her forehead. 'I remember, a little.'

'Had you discovered the book earlier and found the note?'

'No. No, I don't think so.'

He paused, stroking the skin of her hand with his thumb. 'Rilla, I'm certain my mother did not wish to die. The letter I found made that clear, but now I fear someone killed her.'

'No!'

'Pardon?' He stiffened at the sudden strength and volume of her voice.

She inhaled. The hand he did not hold grabbed the bed linen, folding and creasing it in her grip.

'No,' she repeated. She caught and held his gaze. 'It was an accident. I know it was an accident.'

'You want to believe that. We all do, but—'

'No, I *know* it.'

She inhaled. Her jaw tensed and her eyes darted about the room as though unable to focus or looking for some avenue of escape.

'Rilla.' He stroked her hand. 'Don't distress yourself. I should not have spoken. Heloise will never forgive me if I upset you.'

She shook her head against the pillow, clutching his hand tightly with her own.

'No, let me speak while I still have the courage. You need to know this. You need to believe me.'

'What is it?'

'I saw it. Just before I became ill, I saw your mother fall. It was an accident and her feet were tangled in the weeds.'

'In a dream, you mean,' he said gently. 'You were delirious.'

She shook her head violently. 'No, I have these… these moments when I know things. I see things.'

'Dreams can seem real.'

'No—it's more. It is not a dream. It is a—a type of seeing, a type of knowing.'

He frowned, trying to grasp what she said. 'You

mean you think you have something like second sight?'

'Yes.' With the word, she exhaled with spent relief. Her body stilled. She met his eyes with sudden calm. 'Yes,' she said.

'Rilla, you can't believe in stuff like that? It's not scientific. It's not real.'

'It may not be scientific and God knows I've fought it, but it is real. I've never told anyone before, I mean other than my family. But you need to know. It might help you find peace.'

'Peace?' He laughed shortly and stood with a jerk. 'You want me to believe that my mother's death was accidental because you dreamed it so?'

'Yes.'

'Then you are still ill or fevered.'

'In that case, I have been ill or fevered all my life. Paul, please listen. This isn't new. It didn't start with your mother. It has always been there. I recognised its force, its strength when I was very young and found a child. The little girl was visiting Lady Wyburn with her mother. Her name was Sophie. She got stuck in an abandoned cottage and I knew it. I *knew* it. Then there was a cat I knew was down a well and numerous other things. I may hate this power, but I believe in it. And I believe, I know with absolute certainty, that your mother neither took her life nor was she murdered.'

'Sophie was a third cousin or something. I remember my stepmother talking about her.' Paul paced to the window, pushing aside the curtains to look at the mocking sparkle of the lake.

He couldn't take it in. His brain felt stretched, the way it used to when he contemplated the motion of the earth and the mysteries of physics. He wanted to believe his mother's death was accidental. God knew he wanted to believe that. But second sight? It was not reasonable. It was not the belief of a rational or sane mind.

'I've told you this because you have to believe your mother's death was an accident or she will never find peace,' Rilla said from the bed behind him.

Turning, he let the curtains fall. 'My mother is dead. There is no *she*. This is a figment, a fancy, derived from your morbid interest in her.'

She stiffened. He saw her hurt.

He bent towards her, taking her hand. 'It is not your fault. It is this gloomy place. Between that and the medicine, you are not yourself. I should not have talked to you about this.'

She removed her hand from his. 'I am fine. It is not the medicine.'

'Try to rest,' he said.

He stood, needing to leave the closed air of the sickroom. He could not accept what she said. He believed in science and reason.

This was, at best, superstitious poppycock brought on by illness and imagination.

At worst, madness.

# Chapter Twenty-Three

Rilla opened her eyes. Someone had pulled back the curtains and light flooded the room. She blinked and stared at the window and furnishings, trying to orient herself.

Confused thoughts clogged her mind, moving slow as sludge against the bank of a river.

Heloise entered the chamber and leaned over the bed, her round face blocking out the ceiling and the window's brightness.

'What time is it?' Rilla asked, licking her dry lips.

'Just past noon.'

'I must have slept for hours.'

'You've had a nice little rest since his lordship came.' Heloise plumped the pillow. Her breath smelled of mint. 'I'll let Miss Imogene and his lordship know you're awake.'

'Imogene is here?'

'Indeed, arrived yesterday evening.'

With that, Heloise bustled away, her heels striking the floor with an efficient *click-clack*.

Alone, Rilla stared again about her bedchamber, the hearth with the fire set but not lit, the water glass and jug, the medicine bottles juxtaposed with her hairbrush and mirror.

The conversation with Paul came back to her in disjointed scraps like a half-remembered dream. She rubbed her hand across her forehead. A heavy, hopeless feeling lined her stomach.

She'd told him everything.

She'd told him about his mother, little lost Sophie and even the cat that had fallen down the well.

Rilla swallowed. She remembered the change in his expression. She'd seen it before, seen it even in her own mother's face. But she'd had to tell Paul. She could not let him think his mother had been murdered.

A footfall sounded in the hall outside. She jumped, her gaze darting to the door, conscious of a confused mix of anticipation and apprehension.

'Rilla?' Imogene slipped into the room.

'Oh, I thought—but I'm glad it's you. I'm so glad you've come.'

'How are you feeling?'

'Better.'

Imogene sat in the chair by the bed. She looked pale, her face drawn with dark shadows under her eyes. 'I was so worried.' Her voice shook.

'I know. I'm sorry.'

'Father wanted to come, but couldn't. His gout was too bad.'

'I'll visit as soon as I am well.'

'You don't need to. He'll be able to come soon and it is probably best you do not to travel.'

'Imogene, I—actually, I...I want to go. I need to leave here for a while.' Rilla paused, meeting her sister's eyes, and then allowed her gaze to slide away towards the row of medicine bottles on the dressing table.

'Why? Is something wrong?'

'I told him,' Rilla stated flatly.

Imogene gasped. Silence fell between them, broken only by the clock's ticking.

'You mean about your moments?' Imogene said at last.

'Yes.'

'Why? My God, why?' Imogene stood, her hands clasped tight together.

Melodramatic, Rilla thought, in a hopeless detached way.

'I had to. In my delirium, I unearthed a letter written by his mother. The letter made it clear that she was not suicidal, but now he fears that someone killed her. But I know it was an accident.'

'No, you don't, Rilla! You don't *know* anything.'

'I do. That is what you and Mother never understood. I know it just as clearly as if I'd witnessed it.' Rilla spoke calmly. She felt almost relieved to say the words.

'You shouldn't have said anything.' Imogene

paced to the window. Her hands twisted in agitation.

'And let him think that his mother was murdered?'

'But Paul might think you're mad. He could put you away like Great-Aunt Ellie and…and Father would have no power to stop him.'

'I know.'

Imogene turned and came back to the bed. 'How can you be so calm? This was Mother's greatest fear. How can you lie there?'

'What else can I do?'

'Keep your silence in the first place!'

'I could not let Paul think that someone might have killed his mother—I couldn't,' Rilla said.

'But did it do any good? Did he even believe you?'

Rilla paused, dropping her gaze. 'No,' she said at last.

'So you put yourself at risk and it didn't do him the slightest bit of good. In fact, you've added to his worries. Now he thinks his mother was murdered and his wife is crazy.'

'I had to. I had to try. I love him.' She spoke so softly that Imogene bent forward to hear her.

'*Oh.*'

'I know it's dreadfully unfashionable.' Rilla tried to laugh, but the attempt sounded wobbly even to her own ears.

'Does he love you?'

'No, and this will make him like me less.' Rilla felt the prickle of tears—she would not cry.

Imogene took her hand gently. 'Heloise said he was very worried when you were ill.'

'Paul looks after people. It is what he does. I think he hopes it will make up for not keeping his mother safe.'

'But Heloise said—well—he was with you night and day. And if he cares, surely he wouldn't do anything...drastic.'

'He would absolutely put me into an asylum if he thought it for my own protection.'

Imogene's grip tightened. 'Rilla, he went out. You don't...you don't think that he's gone to fetch the doctor...to examine you?'

A cold fear washed through her. Rilla met Imogene's frightened eyes and felt the sweat dampen both their palms. 'In all likelihood he would have sent the footman.' She tried to smile.

'I suppose. But perhaps it would be wise for you to visit Father after all.'

'I do not know if it is wise or cowardly, but I want to go. I can be myself with Father. He's the only person in my life who's really accepted my moments.'

Hurt flickered across Imogene's face. 'How can you say that? You know I love you, despite your moments.'

'I know,' Rilla said with a half-smile. 'Despite my moments.'

\* \* \*

Some hours later, Paul stood in the study, conscious of both leaden exhaustion and a restlessness that prevented him from staying still even for a moment.

He poured a brandy, swallowing the harsh liquid in a gulp before setting the glass on the desk's polished wood. The room felt cool. He had not ordered a fire lit and the hearth stood empty.

He'd bathed, ridden his horse and eaten, but he couldn't stay still. He hadn't even let Giles shave him, much to that gentleman's chagrin.

Lady Wyburn had taken a tray in her chambers and retired, pleading exhaustion from their recent journey. He should, he supposed, provide company for his sister-in-law. He certainly could not spend the evening pacing. It wasn't sensible.

For some moments Paul sat at his desk with unusual indecision. The thought of small talk with Imogene seemed worse than this restless solitude.

And really he should go to Rilla. He rubbed his temples. Part of him wanted to believe her, wanted to believe she'd communicated with his mother's ghost.

Except it went against reason.

And what if this madness grew? What if she became a danger to herself? There must be some kind of treatment. There must be something...

'Excuse me, my lord. There is a visitor.'

Paul turned sharply. Edison stood in the doorway, his face set in lugubrious lines.

'This late? Get rid of him.'

'Unfortunately it is Lord Lockhart. He asked for her ladyship. I told him she was indisposed, but he happened to see Miss Imogene descending the stairs. I'm afraid she agreed to give him audience. In the drawing room, my lord.'

'Damn.'

'Yes, my lord. My sentiments exactly. That's why I thought to inform your lordship.'

Paul crossed the massive entrance hall. As he neared the drawing room he heard Imogene's voice. It sounded high, the cadence clipped, although he could not make out the words.

When he entered, Imogene stood in the centre of the room. Lockhart lolled in a nearby chair, his legs thrust towards the hearth.

'I have no money. You know I don't,' Imogene was saying. Tears shone in her eyes.

'Lockhart!' Paul barked. 'How dare you come here and distress my sister-in-law.'

Both occupants started, their eyes swivelling to meet his. Imogene blanched, and appeared even more upset by his presence.

Lockhart recovered first. 'Good to see you, Wyburn.'

'I cannot say the same.'

'My lord, I—' Imogene started, hands fluttering like nervous moths. He had never seen her so undone.

'Imogene,' he said, gentling his voice as he stepped towards her. 'I do not like to see you distressed, particularly with Rilla ill. Sit for a moment.'

'Edison!' He summoned the butler, who still hovered a little behind. 'Please escort Lockhart to the library. I will be there shortly.'

Lockhart opened his mouth as if to protest, then, catching Paul's look, shrugged. 'Very well.' He stood and followed Edison down the hall.

The door shut and Imogene all but collapsed into an emerald-silk armchair. She looked small—young and unhappy. Paul went to the sideboard lined with crystal decanters. He poured her a sherry.

'Why don't you tell me what Lockhart has said to upset you?' He handed her the glass. 'It sounded as though he wanted money.'

She nodded. Although pale, she appeared more composed.

'If it is about your father's debts,' he continued, 'I will honour them. I will be forwarding those instructions to my man of business.'

'It was not about my father's debts.'

'Then what?'

She sipped her sherry, her expression so distracted that he doubted she even tasted the drink.

At last, straightening, she met his gaze. 'Rilla said that she told you about her moments?'

He frowned, briefly unsure of her meaning, but gaining comprehension with the worried intensity of her gaze.

'What has Lockhart to do with that?' He spoke abruptly. He did not want to discuss Rilla with anyone, even Imogene.

'Jack grew up close to us and heard the village talk.'

'About the child, Sophie, you mean?'

'She really did tell you everything,' Imogene said, in an astonished way. 'Yes, Rilla dreamed of Sophie's location. It could not be explained as a coincidence. Anyhow, now Jack is...'

'Blackmailing you?' Paul said with disgusted understanding.

She looked at him and then away. A flush flooded her cheeks. 'Yes.'

'Damn him.' Anger pulsed through him.

'Rilla has always feared people knowing. Our mother did too. She had an aunt—anyway, Mother told us never to tell anyone. I cannot believe that Rilla told you.'

Paul frowned. 'You did not want her to?'

Imogene shifted uneasily. After a moment she looked up. 'Father always accepted Rilla's eccentricity, but Mother feared that if Rilla married, her husband would think her mad and—and send her to an asylum.'

'You think I'd do that?' His voice was harsh with pain.

'You wouldn't?'

'Does she think that as well?'

He remembered the fear and hurt in Rilla's eyes and knew the answer. He also realised the bravery and trust it had taken for her to have told him her secret. To have even married him in the first place.

'Jack says that if I don't pay him money, he'll tell everyone and people will think that insanity runs in our ancestry,' Imogene said.

Paul stood. 'I will handle Lockhart. Has he blackmailed Rilla too?'

'I…' She hesitated, dropping her gaze. 'Yes, she gave him a brooch, the diamond one.'

His hands tightened into fists. If the man were in front of him now, he'd not resist the urge to strike him, to feel the satisfaction of fist against bone.

'You have my word,' he said between clenched teeth. 'Lockhart will not hurt my wife.'

Paul opened the library door. Lockhart sat in the wing chair and Paul studied him for a moment.

Although the earl leaned back, Paul detected a subtle difference in him. His fingers drummed nervously against his thigh, despite the affectation of ease. His waistcoat, although made of good cloth, was stained and his eyes, always heavy-lidded, were now ringed with dark circles.

Paul sat in a chair set at the other side of the hearth. 'I understand, Lockhart, that you have taken to blackmail,' he said without preamble, his expression impassive and his voice bland.

Lockhart stiffened, but answered easily enough, 'Blackmail—such an unpleasant word.'

'But accurate.'

'Perhaps.' Lockhart shrugged. 'I'm certain the delightful Miss Imogene has enlightened you on the situation.'

'I would appreciate your version.'

'Anything to oblige. You see, I've found myself in straitened circumstances. While reminiscing with my mother about happier times, I recalled several strange episodes in Amaryllis's childhood.'

'The dearth of intelligent discourse at your home is greater than I imagined.' Paul spoke lazily, although the muscles in his shoulders tautened.

''Zactly so. We remembered that Amaryllis literally dreamt up the location of that poor child.' He helped himself to snuff, and closed the box with a metallic *ting.* 'Name of Sophie, distant relative of yours, I believe.'

Despite the self-assured gesture, the earl's hand shook.

Paul levelled his gaze. 'You are blackmailing my wife and sister-in-law because my wife saved a child's life?'

'But in a way so curious that one must consider her either bewitched or mad.' Lockhart took out a linen handkerchief and dabbed his nose.

Calmly Paul stood and pulled on the bell cord, then reseated himself.

'I require two footmen,' he said upon Edison's entry.

'Yes, my lord,' the butler replied, then left.

Paul turned his attention back to Lockhart. 'And what amount were you considering?' he asked in bland, conversational tones.

'A thousand pounds.'

Paul let his gaze drift over the shelves and their many leather volumes. Rilla must have been very frightened to have handed over the brooch. She was too feisty to be easily blackmailed.

And brave.

That last thought hit him with a mix of pride and humility.

Lockhart leaned forward and thrust out his hand. 'Do we have an agreement?'

Paul did not take Lockhart's hand. Instead he withdrew his glance from the books. 'No.'

Lockhart dropped his hand with a *thwack* against his thigh. A sudden wildness entered his eyes. 'You will regret—'

Paul stood. 'You will return my wife's property. If you choose not to do so, I will alert the authorities of the theft. Sir George's gambling debts will be paid, but after that you will receive no further funds from my wife, Sir George, or myself.'

'But I need—I warn you, my conversations may well touch on incidents Amaryllis would prefer unmentioned.' All pretence of nonchalance had gone. He spat out the words and his gaze looked frenetic.

'I advise you to remain silent, Lockhart. If I hear so much as a whisper against my wife or her family, I will use my influence to discredit your name so that no club or decent establishment will grant you entrance.'

The earl barked with harsh laughter. Spittle hung from his lip. 'Good God, man, that is your worst? You think I care? I might lose everything! The London house. Everything!'

'So I have heard. However, I believe the estate at Lockhart is still safe, as it is entailed and you could not gamble it away. Go back to it. Make it profitable while you have the chance.'

'And if I do not?'

'I will ensure that your creditors, near and far, ask for immediate payment of their accounts. Moreover, if I find your mother is also spreading rumours, she will be placed in a similar position.'

Lockhart blanched. 'You'd do this for Amaryllis? She isn't worth it. The woman belongs in an insane asylum.'

'The woman is my wife and my wife is saner than most of England.'

Lockhart shifted, glowered. His shoulders rose in a shrug, then dropped in a sudden, deflated gesture. 'I will say nothing.'

'I'm glad,' Paul said.

At that moment, Edison and the footmen entered.

'The earl was just leaving,' Paul told them. 'Please escort him from the property.'

'I won't forget this, Wyburn,' Lockhart muttered sullenly.

'I hope you do not.'

Paul watched as Lockhart walked away, flanked by the footmen. The door slammed.

Paul sat. It was not a conscious movement, but rather his legs gave way. And, as he sat within the silent room, he smiled and felt a bubble of mirth.

'And it took that ludicrous nincompoop to make me see it!'

# Chapter Twenty-Four

Paul stepped into Rilla's chamber. The curtains had been opened and he blinked in the bright sunlight. Rilla lay in the bed, propped up with pillows. Her skin still looked pale in contrast to the red-gold banner of her hair.

As he neared the bed she glanced at him and smiled—but not in her usual wonderful, too-wide grin. This was restrained, a mere twisting of the lips.

'You were able to sleep and eat something?' he asked.

'Yes, Heloise brought broth.' Her voice was stronger than before.

'That's good.' Paul sat on the chair, pulling it closer to the bed. There was so much he wanted to say, but he didn't know how or where to begin. How could he express his love? How could he explain that although he would never understand her 'moments', he could accept them?

'Paul, I need a favour. I want to go home.' She

spoke quickly, her eyes meeting his, then sliding away.

His heart squeezed, the words he had been trying to form dissipating.

'Home?' he said.

'I mean to Father. Just for a little while. Just to recuperate.'

Her voice dropped so low he leaned forward to hear her and she looked so afraid, so pale, lost within the sheets and blankets of the double bed.

Her father, he realised, was likely the only person who had accepted her. The others, even her mother and Imogene, had loved her, but had also failed her.

As for himself... She had trusted him and he had turned from her.

'Of course you can visit your family,' he said gently. 'I'll talk to the doctor.'

'Thank you.' She did not look at him, but he saw her exhalation and relief.

'Rilla, you need to know.' He looked across the room to the window and the bright blues and greens of the outside world. A fly crawled across the pane. 'I would never limit your freedom. Imogene said that has always worried you. You need to know I would never do that. You have my word as a gentleman.'

She met his gaze. 'Imogene spoke to you?'

'Briefly. I think I understand a little.'

'Good.' She smiled, a small smile, but a real one.

She might not love him, but perhaps she would fear him less.

Heloise knocked and entered in her usual bustling way. Paul stood and took the chance for escape, ludicrously glad to be saved from further conversation with his own wife.

What had he expected? he wondered, as he walked to the cool darkness of the corridor. Had he hoped that Rilla would forget how he'd pushed her away at every opportunity during their brief marriage? How she had shared her secret and he had condemned her? How he had fought and hidden from his own growing love for her?

Because he did love her—heart, mind and soul—with both his rational and his irrational being—with his all.

*'My love for you is everlasting. You need to know this and never doubt it.'*

The words from his mother's letter flashed in his mind, bringing him up short. He had the sensation of falling in space, as though flung from his horse.

*'You need to know.'*

His father hadn't known.

His father had died not knowing.

Rilla did not know.

Right now, Rilla did not know how much he loved her.

She didn't know—

Rilla continued to stare at the ceiling, which was very dull. She wished she could see something dif-

ferent, but it was awkward to look out the window
from this angle. Of course, she could ask Heloise
to prop up her pillows, but Heloise was bent on
rearranging the bottles on her dressing table with
a noisy clatter.

Rilla's thoughts flittered. Yes, *flittered* was the
right word, like moths, nebulous fluttering things,
impossible to grasp.

On one hand she felt relieved. Paul wasn't going
to incarcerate her. She had his word, and he was
a man of honour.

She wished...

But Paul was so rational. He might not imprison
her, but he would never, could never, accept that
which defied logic. He had always fought caring
for her and his fight would be so much easier now.

The door pushed open with such force that it
crashed against the inner wall.

Rilla jumped, jolted into wide-eyed wakeful-
ness.

Paul strode into the room. She stared. He looked
so different than he had moments before, his face
set and eyes fierce.

'Heloise, leave us!' he ordered.

Heloise gave a startled cry. The perfume bottle
she held dropped with a splintering of glass.

'I'm sorry. I'll just—'

'Leave!'

She scuttled from the room.

'What? What is it? What has happened?' Rilla
asked.

'I love you!' The words blasted from him. 'I love you! I love you!'

'No—' She didn't believe him. She couldn't.

'Don't contradict me, woman.'

'Don't call me "woman". I'm not the scullery maid!'

'No, the scullery maid would be silent.' He laughed, a little wildly she thought.

Like he was *not* in control.

'Rilla, I love you,' he said, more gently, his voice low.

Her mouth dropped open. Her mind whirled. She wanted to believe him, but couldn't. He must be drunk, exhausted, or both.

'Paul.' She forced her voice to calm, although she still heard its tremor. 'You're in shock because I was ill. You can't love me. You've always said—'

'I was a fool and an idiot.'

'You're mistaken.'

Uncertainty snaked within her. She could not trust his words. It would hurt too much. Like the trapdoor opening under a hangman's noose.

Paul sat beside her on the bed and carefully took her hand as though it was both precious and fragile.

'Look at me.' He leaned over her so that his intense gaze blocked out all else. He spoke in deep, measured tones that rang with truth. 'One is mistaken in a game of chance or when buying a horse. One is not mistaken in love. I love you. I love the way you smile. I love your spontaneity. I love your kindness. I love that you cover Edison with green slime and that you take butter churns for walks. I love the way you look at me when you think I'm an unfeeling autocrat. I love your flush when you're angry and that wonderful catch in your breath when I make love to you.'

'I—I almost believe you.'

Hope filled her, and elation, a wild, wonderful, joyful, bubbling feeling like fizzy champagne. She wanted to hold him, to shout for joy and make passionate love with him.

'Almost? Almost! What will it take? And what is that vile smell?' He crossed the room and flung open the window.

'Forget the "almost". I believe you,' she said, laughing because he looked so funny as he held the curtains. 'And, Paul—I love you too.'

He froze at her words, one hand still holding the heavy curtains. He let the velvet swish into place and walked back to her. Uncertainty flickered through his darkened gaze.

'Don't say it if you don't mean it, please,' he said, his autocratic voice husky. 'I don't expect your love. I'm willing to wait for it. And earn it.'

She stared up at him, letting her feelings show at last. 'I love you. I've loved you for ever. I fell in love with you when I tumbled out of the tree—although I tried not to.' Tears stung.

'You're crying.' He bent and wiped her eyes with his handkerchief, the cloth soft against her cheek.

She sniffled. 'It's the perfume.'

'Liar.' He sat beside her. The baleen bedsprings creaked.

'And now you take back the first compliment you ever gave me?'

'Which was?

'That I was honest, although lacking in discretion.'

'Utterly, and it is an admirable quality—' His voice broke.

'The honesty or lack of discretion?'

'Both.'

'Oh, Paul,' she said and sneezed.

'Right, we're getting out of here.'

He picked her up and strode with her across the room and through the adjoining door to his dressing room. Then, with great gentleness, he placed her on the daybed.

'I hadn't thought Heloise so careless,' he grumbled. 'Spilling perfume.'

'I believe you scared her witless, my lord. And she doesn't frighten easily.'

'Makes two of you.'

Rilla smiled, but became serious, her teeth worrying her lower lip. 'Paul, what about...my moments?'

He sat beside her, so close that she could feel the warm, muscled strength of his thigh, the comfort of his arm circling her and the warmth of his breath. 'You are saner, braver and more intelligent than any woman I know.'

'But, it is so strange. I can't explain—'

'And people are frightened by things we don't understand. I was too. But Lockhart helped me make sense of everything.' He grinned.

'Lockhart?' She spat out the name, wriggling upright. 'He's never helped anyone in his life. Was he here? No doubt he was spreading more lies.'

'Stay still, you're too distracting, although I've missed that feistiness. Yes, Jack was full of lies. But then I said something to him that made sense of everything.'

'Told him you wished him to go to hell, I would hope.'

'Most unladylike. Pray do not speak so at Al-mack's.'

'I might if I see that particular gentleman.'

'I told him that you were a woman of good sense and character.'

She giggled. 'I sound positively fustian.'

'But absolutely sane.' He shifted, twisting his body so that he could cup her face with his hands. 'Science is not only about what is known. It is about what is unknown and trying to understand things we don't yet comprehend. We don't yet understand about the sun and the moon, but we do not fear them. I may not fully understand, but I absolutely know that you are good, kind, sensible, wonderful and brave. You were so brave to tell me.'

Rilla reached up to run her fingers along his chin and push back that stubborn lock of dark hair. 'I couldn't let you think someone had hurt your mother. Even if you didn't believe me, I had to try. Can you believe now that her death was an accident?'

'Yes. It is not logical or sensible, but I can believe it. I believe it because I believe you.'

'Oh.' She blinked back the blur of her tears.

He leaned forward and pressed his warm lips to her forehead, her nose and her damp cheeks.

Her lips parted. She gasped that soft, joyful gasp she always made when she was happy and his mouth claimed hers.

'No one,' she whispered when she could speak again. 'No one except Father could accept it. And Father would probably think it eminently sensible if Zeus popped out of his morning toast. Even Mother and Imogene couldn't really accept it, although they still loved me.'

'That must have been hard.'

'A little.'

'More important, do *you* accept it?'

She shrugged. 'I've had years of hating it and fearing it.'

'And we'll have years to learn about it and grow from it.' He kissed her again, more deeply. 'A lifetime.'

'But Jack—'

'Was blackmailing you. He will give back the brooch if he has not sold it and will never try it again. You have my word.'

'Thank God,' she whispered. 'Paul?'

'Mmm…'

He eased them both so that they lay in the bed

and he could pull her close. She curled into his warmth. He smelled of soap and leather, and she could hear the steady thump of his heart.

'I love you,' he said.

'I love you too.' Briefly, their movements stilled.

'Never leave me,' he muttered with a ragged breath.

'I promise to infuriate you for years to come.' She pressed a kiss against his bristly cheek and giggled, running her fingers along the strong line of his jaw. 'I can't believe Giles let you out looking like this!'

'Only under extreme duress.'

'Perhaps it is just as well, because I've had a superb idea for an invention. A razor. One able to power itself. Think how much time it would save Giles!'

Paul groaned, trapping her fingers with his own. 'And think how much blood it would cost me. Never. You'd decapitate me and I need a long life. I need to prove my love for you. Besides, your inventions may have to take second place. I have other plans to keep you busy.' He nibbled an earlobe.

'Other plans?'

'Starting with this.' He trailed kisses across her cheek until he reached her mouth and Rilla quite forgot about the butter churn, the bread kneader and even the razor.

# *Epilogue*

$\mathrm{A}$utumn sun filled Sir George's garden. Rilla and Imogene sat in dappled shade under the yellow leaves of the chestnut tree, sipping tea. It was hot and deliciously strong.

Lady Wyburn dozed in a chair, her snores pleasantly intermingled with the crisp rustle of autumn foliage and the splash and grind of the dairy's butter churn.

Rilla glanced over her teacup towards that squat building and grinned. Her churn was at last in operation. In fact, even Kate admitted that the device saved labour, although it still overflowed on occasion. Moreover, Paul had promised to build a second and larger model for the Wyburn Estate.

Paul and Rilla had been visiting Sir George for several days and were enjoying the break from the business of rebuilding the cottages at Wyburn.

'Gracious, I fear I must have dropped off for a brief second,' Lady Wyburn said from beneath her bonnet. 'Has anything transpired?'

'Nothing out of the ordinary,' Rilla answered. 'Father remains indoors with his Greeks and Julie remains outdoors with Lord Alfred.'

Rilla glanced to where she could see Julie St John's pink bonnet, a bright splash of colour bobbing against the garden's muted greens and yellows. Julie and Lord Alfred had been spending considerable time together, as Lord Alfred was currently visiting an acquaintance in the neighbourhood.

'I do wish they'd speed things up. Julie and Lord Alfred, not your father and the Greeks,' Lady Wyburn said. 'I've never known such dallying. We'll be all in our dotage before anything is settled. Ah, here they come now.'

Indeed, the couple was walking towards them. Rilla smiled. Julie's cheeks looked as pink as her beribboned bonnet.

'Tea? It's still hot,' Rilla offered.

'And Mrs Marriot's sponge cake is particularly delicious,' Imogene added.

'Not for me,' Lord Alfred said. 'If you'll excuse me, I must depart on urgent business.' He bent low over Rilla's hand before hurrying away.

'And about time,' Lady Wyburn said with satisfaction.

'He asked me,' Julie whispered, blushing.

Lady Wyburn nodded. 'For your hand, I presume, and not your preference in vegetables. Do sit, my dear.'

'I am so happy. I cannot believe that he asked me.' Julie sat with a rustle of her pink flounces.

'And we cannot believe it took so long, you pea goose.' Rilla poured tea and added sugar, the spoon tinkling against the cup.

At that moment, the house door opened and Paul strolled towards them.

Rilla smiled as she always did whenever she saw her husband and felt that wonderfully familiar bubble of joy.

To a stranger, Paul might appear much the same as the man Rilla had toppled upon months previously. His physique, as always, was impressive—tall, handsome and muscular. His eyes missed little and his face remained hard and angular, except for that single, kissable dimple.

And yet Rilla knew her viscount had changed immeasurably.

Paul bent low and brushed his wife's lips with his own. He smelled of soap and grass and horses.

'Paul, delightful news,' Lady Wyburn announced, waving her bonnet at a fly circling her head. 'Julie is going to be married.'

'My felicitations,' Paul said and sat on a vacant chair.

'Indeed, it suits me very well,' Lady Wyburn said, replacing her headgear. 'I'll be returning to London soon and can help with the trousseau, although I suppose your mother would want to do that and I don't want to tread on her toes. Imogene, we really must find you a husband.'

'I'm in favour,' Imogene said. 'As long as he is at least an earl.'

Paul grinned. 'No mere viscount for you.'

'We'll have to see what we can do for you during the next Season. Indeed, I expect to be unusually busy.'

Paul stiffened, frowning. 'Stepmother, you have a certain glow to your countenance that I suspect may not be entirely due to Julie's nuptials.'

'Indeed, I have a plan.'

'Another plan? No, absolutely not! I will not endorse any more of your schemes,' Paul said firmly.

'Really? But my last one worked out quite splendidly. Quite splendidly indeed.'

Lady Wyburn smiled and helped herself to a second piece of Mrs Marriot's cake.

\* \* \* \* \*

15_ST19

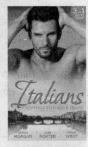